A DARING DISGUISE

Dolly glanced around the busy gymnasium. Though no one had questioned her gender in the week since she'd been working at Creevy's Pugilist Academy, she suffered painfully from episodes of self-doubt. What if one of the other boxers studied her too closely, noticing the lack of whiskers on her chin, or the absence of an Adam's apple?

Worst of all, what if she couldn't hide her attraction to Dick Creevy?

Drawing in a deep breath, Dolly steadied her nerves. If Creevy hadn't guessed she was a woman by now, he never would.

Tongue in cheek, Dick folded his arms across his chest and gave her a critical top-to-bottom appraisal. "You're not ill, are you, boy?"

With a gulp, she shook her head.

"You look a bit peaked, son. Haven't been chasing after roundheels, have you?"

"Roundheels?" Bewildered, Dolly shrugged her shoulders.

With a sigh of impatience, Dick said, "Good lord, you're not that naive are you? You haven't taken up with a floozie, now, have you?"

Dear Romance Reader,

In July, we launched the Ballad line with four new series, and each month we'll present both new and continuing stories set everywhere from medieval England to the American West—the kind of passionate, romantic stories you love best, written by the most gifted authors. At the back of each book, we'll tell you when you can find subsequent books in the series that have captured your heart.

This month talented Cindy Harris introduces the charming new *Dublin Dreams* series. When an anonymous benefactor brings together four penniless women in one stately Dublin square, none of them expect to find love. Yet in the first book, the widow of a dissolute gambler meets her romantic match when she has **A Bright Idea.** Next, rising star Linda Lea Castle presents the second of a trio of spirited *Bogus Brides*. In **Mattie and the Blacksmith,** a schoolteacher who longs to be properly courted discovers that the most unlikely suitor may be the one who steals her heart.

Fabulous new author Lynne Hayworth is also back with the second installment of the *Clan Maclean* series, **Autumn Flame.** Will a spirited pickpocket make a proper wife for the overseer of a Virginia plantation? Finally, Cherie Claire concludes the atmospheric *Acadians* trilogy with the story of **Gabrielle,** a woman who will risk anything to save the bold privateer who has claimed her, body and soul. Enjoy!

Kate Duffy
Editorial Director

Dublin Dreams

A BRIGHT IDEA

Cindy Harris

ZEBRA BOOKS
Kensington Publishing Corp.
http://www.zebrabooks.com

ZEBRA BOOKS are published by

Kensington Publishing Corp.
850 Third Avenue
New York, NY 10022

All Kensington Titles, Imprints, and Distributed Lines are available at special quantity discounts for bulk purchases for sales promotions, premiums, fund-raising, educational, or institutional use.

Special book excerpts or customized printings can also be created to fit specific needs. For details, write or phone the office of the Kensington special sales manager: Kensington Publishing Corp., 850 Third Avenue, New York, NY 10022, attn: Special Sales Department, Phone: 1-800-221-2647

Zebra and the Z logo Reg. U.S. Pat. & TM Off.

First Printing: April, 2001
10 9 8 7 6 5 4 3 2 1

Printed in the United States of America

Prologue

At the end, she was peaceful, her long auburn hair splayed across the pillow, her white linen gown and the counterpanes surrounding her as she wilted from fever.

Her husband sat at her bedside, holding her hand, pressing a damp cloth to her forehead. For a year, Mary had battled to survive her illness. Now she was tired and ready to succumb. But Devon Avondale wasn't prepared to let her go. He couldn't imagine Mary leaving him. It was still inconceivable to him that he would continue living after she had gone.

Stroking the sensitive skin of her forearm, he lowered his head and prayed for a miracle.

Her voice, hoarse and weak, drew him from his silent world.

"Don't be sad, Devon."

He beat back the tears that stung his eyes. Mary was so much braver than he. He didn't want her to know what a coward he was, and how frightened he was to be losing her. "You're going to be all right, Mary. When the fever breaks—"

Her parched lips curved upward. "No, Devon. It won't be long now."

He leaned forward, nestling his head on her breast. She stroked his hair. As Mary's breathing grew more labored, Devon's arms went around her and he held her as tightly as he dared. The heat of her body soaked through him. He needed her. He couldn't let her go.

If she wasn't going to live, he wanted to die.

"Devon, look at me."

He lifted his head.

"My journal—" She pointed a frail finger at the small, brown leather-bound journal on her bedside table. "When I am gone—"

He shook his head. He couldn't bear to hear her talk that way.

Her voice took on a firmness that surprised him. "The journal is for you, love. In it, you will find a reason to live . . . and love again."

With a sob, he pressed her fragile hand to his lips. Then, as she drew her final breath, he covered her mouth with his.

It was a fine spring morning, and Mary O'Roarke Avondale had just died in her bed at Number Two Fontjoy Square.

One

Dublin, 1870

Ferghus the butler—and, of late, the groom, cook, and scullion maid, too—stood in the doorway, wiping his hands on an oily apron front. "There's a man bangin' his fist on the front door, m'lady."

As if she hadn't heard.

Lady Dolly Baltmore's darning needles stilled. Looking up from the woolen stocking she was mending, her green eyes narrowed and watered. The late-afternoon sun streaming through the window of her sitting room added scant illumination to the rapidly deteriorating interior of her northern Dublin town house, much less the tiny threads at her fingertips.

The light seemed to dim even as Dolly blinked her single remaining servant into focus. She could have lit a lamp, but oil was dear, gas was precious, and expensive candles were reserved for entertaining friends, when making a pretense of affluence was as necessary as breathing. Rather, she would darn by the window until her stitches became invisible.

Then, when darkness made knitting with even her largest needles impossible, she would retire to her bed and spend the long, miserable evening plotting her revenge on Dick Creevy, the man who, by murdering her husband, Lord Boyle Baltmore, had dispatched her to this hellish existence.

But if her snobby sister-in-law dropped in for tea tomorrow afternoon, Dolly and Ferghus would lay out an extravagant platter of watercress sandwiches, biscuits, and scones. If she were invited to a country house party, she would sneak to the larder and fill her portmanteau with preserved fruit jams and loaves of soda bread before returning home. And, if she really screwed up her courage and dared a rented carriage ride round St. Stephen's Green, or a stroll down Grafton Street, Dolly would smile at passersby and waggle the carefully rewoven fingers of her lace gloves.

In the year since her husband's death, Dolly's life had evolved to a frightening stage of duplicity.

The crash of the front door's huge brass knocker, shaped like a *claddagh* and polished to brilliance for the sake of appearances, shook the rafters.

Ferghus shifted his weight and cleared his throat. "Like I said, they's someone at the door, m'lady."

Dolly's fingers resumed their nimble movements. Calmly, for she tried her best never to look frightened in front of Ferghus, she asked, "Is it a bill collector?"

"Most likely, mum. He's wearin' a mask."

"Pardon?" Her needles slipped awkwardly in the toe of the stocking. "Did you say he's wearing a *mask?*"

"It's a black one like some fancy nabob might wear to a masquerade party! Dressed awful queer for a bill collector, if you ask me. What with his fine serge trousers, dark blue frock coat, lavender gloves, and top hat, he could pass fer a lord!" Ferghus stroked his chin. "And he's carryin' an envelope, m'lady. A thick, cream-colored, very important-lookin' envelope it is, too, with a big red gob of wax sealing it all up, nice and tidy like. A bill, I suspect."

Or worse, Dolly thought. It was only a matter of time before one of her creditors served her with a summons to appear in court and explain her refusal to pay her bills. "Good heavens, Ferghus, and how could you see all that without opening the door to the man?"

"I been watchin' him for the past half hour, mum, from me upstairs window! I don't know who he thinks he's foolin', but he's got to get up a mite earlier in the morning if he thinks to make a flat of ole Ferghus. Pulled up in a fancy carriage, he did, and left it parked down the street, half a block away, in front of the O'Toole's house. Walked the rest of the way, so's we wouldn't notice his rig, I s'pose. Then, as he made it up the walkway, that's when he donned the mask, of all things! Never did get a good close look at his face, though."

"Why would a bill collector wish to conceal his identity?" Dolly wondered.

"Mebbe he don't want folks knowin' what he does fer a livin'." Ferghus huffed his indignation. "And listen to him now. He's pounding on the door like a madman!"

"Well, he didn't start off so rudely," Dolly said grimly.

Indeed, the masked man's first few knocks were simply too polite to provoke Dolly's interest, or to motivate Ferghus to open the door. As creditors appeared at the front door in increasing numbers, their visits created less of a stir. The mysterious man with the important-looking envelope knocked for twenty minutes before Ferghus abandoned his chores and descended to the drawing room.

"Perhaps he will grow tired soon, Ferghus, and leave us in peace."

As if on cue, the door knocker sounded again, this time violently enough to rattle the porcelain bric-a-brac on the mantelpiece. Setting her sewing aside, Lady Dolly clapped her hands over her ears. Her nerves were as frayed and worn as the heels of her stockings, and she wasn't at all certain whether she could continue to hide her fear from her single remaining servant.

She *was* afraid. Her paper-thin bravado couldn't shield her from the poverty that she battled. Her credit at the butcher's was wrecked. Ferghus couldn't be expected to work for free forever. It was only a matter of time before her bill collectors caught up with her and the bank foreclosed on her house. Already she was lonely and alone. Soon she would have no place to live and no food to eat. Her husband's legacy would be complete.

Damn Dick Creevy!

Something inside Lady Dolly snapped. Leaping up, she crossed the room and stalked past a gaping Ferghus. Fury and fright propelled her down the staircase. If that annoying bill collector wanted to talk to her, well, then, he would get a piece of her mind! She was tired of being victimized. She was tired of feeling helpless.

"Lady Dolly, don't!" Ferghus followed close behind her.

But before her servant could stop her, Dolly threw open the door. And froze in shock at the sight of the masked man staring back at her.

He lowered his lavender-gloved fist. Though his features were concealed by the black mask he wore and the top hat pulled low over his brows, Dolly could see he was a well-built, finely groomed gentleman. The fading sun did not completely obscure the details of his appearance. His coat was immaculate, if not a tad austere. His bearing was dignified. His eyes, pools of pale blue liquid through the slits of his disguise, held a sort of restrained kindness.

"Who are you?" Dolly finally managed.

"I didn't mean to disturb you."

The man's voice disturbed her because it was gentle and refined, and she was so lonely and afraid. But she tamped down her emotions, and lifted her chin. It wouldn't do to look vulnerable. It wouldn't do to appear weak.

"Then why, sir, were you beating on my front door as if it were a bodhran?"

He held out the envelope.

Hesitating, Dolly searched the man's eyes. The smug satisfaction most bill collectors enjoyed seemed absent in this man's attitude. Slowly, she accepted the envelope and turned it over. Her name was neatly printed on the front. The upper left-hand corner of the vellum square was blank.

She broke the wax seal and slipped a heavy cream-colored card from the envelope. A long moment passed as she scanned the words, then read them slowly, then reread them. More shock poured through her veins. Her pulse skittered, and her knees felt weak beneath her threadbare muslin skirts.

"What is it?" Ferghus asked, peering at the missive.

"A miracle," Dolly whispered.

Tears blurred her eyesight as she looked up to thank the mysterious masked man who delivered the envelope. She had a hundred questions she meant to ask him. She thought the letter had been mistakenly delivered to the wrong person. It wasn't likely that something so fortuitous and lucky would be happening in Lady Dolly Baltmore's life.

But the mysterious man was gone.

Vanished.

Halfway down the block, a gleaming carriage rattled away.

Dolly stood in her doorway, the envelope and thick stock card trembling in her hands. A breeze lifted the curls on her neck. For an instant, optimism surged through her. Perhaps, Dolly told herself, life would soon change for the better. Perhaps her troubles were all behind her.

Turning, she said, "Start packing, Ferghus. We're getting out of here."

"Packin', mum?" The old man scratched his chin. "So that's it, is it? We've been evicted by the bankers? Well, don't worry, m'lady; we'll figure somthin' out. We always do, don't we?"

Closing the door softly, Dolly nodded. "We're moving across the river, Ferghus, into a town house near Merrion Street and Ely Place. The address is Number Two Fontjoy Square."

Ferghus's brows shot up. "If yer gotta go broke, yer might as well go in style."

"I don't know how it happened, but my plight has come to the attention of a benefactor who wishes to remain anonymous."

"I s'pose that explains the mask."

"The man in the mask was merely the messenger, according to this letter. At any rate, the gentleman who is my benefactor . . . or I suppose he is a gentleman, anyway, and I shall call him a gentleman until I discover otherwise . . . has kindly offered me a place to live. There is one contingency in this bargain, however, one thing I must agree to do in order to live in the house."

"I won't have ye compromising yer principles, ma'am!"

"No, it's nothing like that, Ferghus." Dolly glanced at the letter before sliding it into the pocket of her skirts. "My benefactor wishes me to live at Fontjoy Square, but I must assist in the renovation of the house and the cultivation of the garden in the center of the square. And I must never tell anyone how I came to live in the house. Oh, everything—supplies and matériel, that is—will be paid for, and in a year, if the gentleman is satisfied with my industry, the house will be mine, free and clear."

Ferghus puffed out his chest. "Not to worry, mum. By the time I get through with it, Fontjoy Square will make Mansion House look like a peasant's hovel!"

"You don't have to come, you know, Ferghus. I cannot afford to pay you."

"I wouldn't think of runnin' out on ye, ma'am. You'll pay me when ye can."

Dolly squeezed the man's arm. "Of course I will." She moved toward the stairs. "Now, let's start packing. The letter says we are to come immediately. And I'm eager to see what sort of bargain I have made."

Ferghus tugged his forelock and smiled. "There ain't much to pack, m'lady. We've sold everything 'cept what's in the drawing room, dining room, and yer bed-chamber. I'll have ye ready to go by the morning."

With butterflies swarming in her stomach, Dolly forced a smile. How foolhardy and capricious a notion was it to accept this stranger's offer? How dangerous was it for a widowed woman to abandon her home and move across the river, into a rundown town house she'd never seen before?

It was an utterly preposterous and irresponsible thing to do, and she knew it. This mysterious benefactor could be a murderous rogue, for all she knew. This offer of sanctuary in exchange for some home decorating could be a nefarious scheme to defraud her.

But defraud her of what? She had nothing left to lose except her pride, and if she lived another day in an unheated house half emptied of furniture, she would surely forfeit that, too.

Pausing at the steps, Dolly looked at Ferghus. "You must think I'm terribly naive and foolish."

Unaccustomed to such familiar talk with his employer, the man blushed furiously. "You've had some hard knocks, m'lady. I don't suppose there's many ladies who could hold up their heads through the hardships you've endured. You're as brave as any soldier I've ever met, Lady Dolly. And I'm proud to be yer servant."

"Thank you, Ferghus." She'd heard that sort of talk before. Even as a young girl in boarding school in Switzerland, Dolly was described by her peers as "fearless." But in her heart, she lacked true courage. She'd always been afraid to lower her mask of bravado. She'd always known that people wouldn't like her if they knew the truth about her. Her stiff upper lip was very often an act worthy of the stage.

But she wasn't incapable of making a decision. "I realize it must seem insane to accept an offer of sanctuary from a man I've never met. And I have no assurance he'll live up to his word. But I don't have many choices right now, and the ones I've got are all fairly bad."

Ferghus, clearly discomfitted by Lady Dolly's unexpected confidence, nodded.

"Fontjoy Square, at least for now, is a hedge against starvation. . . . And if we leave quickly, without much fanfare, well, then, the bill collectors—"

"They won't find us, mum, not if we leave tomorrow."

"We shall leave tonight, Ferghus." With a sigh, Dolly started up the steps. At the first landing, she said over her shoulder, "Have we enough shillings to hail a hackney cab, Ferghus?"

"Just enough, ma'am."

"Go and fetch one, then. Forget the furniture. We'll leave it behind. My portmanteau will be packed within the half hour. I want to go now. I cannot stand to spend another night in this house, Ferghus. Can you understand that?"

In reply, the servant slipped out the door to hail a carriage, while Lady Dolly Baltmore picked up her skirts, ran the rest of the way up the stairs, and flew into her bedchamber. Tossing her gowns, shoes, and undergarments into a worn leather valise, she wondered again if she were crazy.

Perhaps she was. But she was tired of being victimized. Moving to Fontjoy Square might turn out to be the worst mistake of her life. She wouldn't know until she got there.

Dick Creevy never left her thoughts.

Even as her rented carriage rumbled across the Ha'Penny Bridge, Dolly was preoccupied. The man who killed her husband was constantly on her mind—an object of endless speculation, a seemingly bottomless source of pain and bitterness.

She knew little about him, other than what she read in the daily papers. Creevy was famous, yet reclusive. His incongruous refinement, erudition, and elegance were widely known. Most boxers were spurned by high society, yet Creevy could have had the upper crust of Dublin eating out of his gloved hand. In point of fact, it was Creevy who rebuffed the aristocrats. A ruthless fighter in the boxing ring, he was an enigmatic iconoclast in the civilized world.

It was a dangerous obsession, and she knew it. But she could not rid herself of the idea that one day she would meet the famed pugilist who had delivered the mortal blow that felled Lord Boyle Baltmore. She had to understand why her husband had been killed. She had to confront the man whose brutal act of violence had robbed her of her comfortable life, thrusting her into poverty.

Dolly's rented cab rumbled to a halt. A chilly mist blurred Fontjoy Square, lending it a watercolor fuzziness. As Ferghus paid the driver, Dolly stood on the cobbled street, peering curiously at the silhouettes of five town houses, all of them facing a central garden.

Not that she could make out the details of the houses, or the garden, for that matter. In the gloaming, the houses swam in violet-tinted shadows, appearing rather ghostly and serene.

A ticklish excitement moved through her as she wondered just who her new neighbors were. On the street opposite hers, two redbrick houses shared a single terrace. The northern side of the square was occupied by a very grand house, built in the Palladian style. At the southern end stood a fine example of Georgian architecture, a mushroom-colored stucco house with gleaming white balconies and columns.

The cab departed, and Ferghus, laden with baggage, pushed open the gate that fenced the small yard in front of Number Two. A protesting squawk of rusty iron jolted Dolly from her pensive mood.

"Got a key, mum?"

"The letter said the door was unlocked." Without even looking at him, Dolly felt her servant's incredulity. She stood beneath the portico, shoulders thrown back, cheeks burning. She didn't begrudge Ferghus his doubts; she was simply embarrassed that anyone should witness her desperate impulsiveness. After all, the whole concept of a mysterious benefactor, a masked messenger, and an unlocked Georgian town house in the fashionable part of Dublin sounded like a fairy tale. Was she insane to believe that her luck had changed for the better?

Gaslights fizzled on either side of the plaster entablature, and for the first time, Dolly saw evidence of the house's ill repair. The front door, once coated in glossy black lacquer, was shedding. The semicircular fanlight above it contained more broken panes than not, reminding Dolly of an upside-down jack-o-lantern's grin. The brass knocker was dull. A shutter on the second floor looked askance at its window, and the brick facade was overgrown with ivy.

As Ferghus pushed open the door, the house exhaled a dank and moldy sigh. "Not exactly the cheeriest home I've ever seen, mum," he said, lighting a lamp in the foyer.

Crossing the threshold, Dolly gaped at her surroundings. Scuff marks marred the black-and-white checkered floor. Staleness hung about the house like faded curtains. Yellowed calling cards littered the top of a half-moon pedestal table. There was an unsettling dreamlike ambience in the house, a presence that Dolly couldn't identify, a pervasive feeling that unfinished business had occurred here. "This house has been neglected, Ferghus, that's all. Perhaps it needs a little tender loving care. That's why we are here. That's why I've been chosen."

"By the rood! Ye sound as if you expect to see a ghost!" With a snort, the old man shut the front door.

"I have no hopes of such a thing," Dolly replied, her heart racing, her senses digesting this sudden change in circumstances. It was too much to take in all at once. She needed her privacy and a night of quiet contemplation. She needed time to absorb the meaning of this mysterious bequest. She needed a plan.

She needed to be alone with her new house.

Starting up the steps, she said, "Bring my valise, Ferghus. The hour is late, and I'm exhausted. As soon as I find my bedchamber, I will be turning in for the night. There's plenty of time to explore the rest of the house and the grounds tomorrow."

"And the garden," the man grumbled, following behind. "Mustn't forget about that."

"And the garden."

The master suite smelled faintly as if it had been closed up for the season. But it wasn't nearly as musty or depressing as Dolly had expected. The dampness that she'd smelled below stairs was happily absent, and the thick Axminster carpets were dry and fresh.

Cautiously, Dolly moved around the room. A woman's touch was evident in the heavily flounced bedcovers, ormolu writing desk, and Chinese wallpaper. A sterling silver hairbrush, perfume atomizer, and ivory-framed hand mirror lay neatly atop a vanity. Rows of books, most of them travelogues and poetry, lined the upper shelves of a Queen Ann secretary. Whoever had previously resided here was a person of elegance and expansive interests. Whoever had created this decor, chose that tole screen, purchased that Waterford vase, or crocheted that lace doily, was a woman whom Dolly probably would have liked very much.

Tossing her bonnet on a tufted chaise longue, Dolly shivered off the sensation that she was occupying another woman's private quarters. This home was hers now. For whatever reason, perhaps just because he had learned of her poverty and pitied her, Dolly's benefactor had chosen *her* to live here. She wouldn't let an isolated moment of squeamishness eclipse her survival instinct. She wouldn't allow superstition to obscure her logic.

"Is ever' thin' awright, mum?" Having unburdened himself of Dolly's luggage, Ferghus backed out of her room. "If so, I'll find the servant's quarters, and go about makin' me own nest, so to speak. If there's tea to be found, I'll brew a pot and bring it up before you retire."

Nodding, Dolly set about acquainting herself with the house's accoutrements. Gaslighting and modern plumbing were welcome amendments to the house's Georgian origins. A spacious closet adjacent to the bedchamber boasted dark wood dados, tile floors, a circular window fitted with stained glass, and a claw-footed tub deep enough to swim in. After an initial spurt of rusty water, a hot, clear stream flowed through the pipes.

With a growing sense of relief, Dolly tossed in a packet of lavender sachet, *borrowed* the week before from the ladies' room in the Shelbourne Hotel. While the tub filled, she peeled off her clothes, and thought how vastly superior her new house was to her old one north of the Liffey. Even in its dilapidated state, Number Two Fontjoy Square was more than a collection of whitewashed bricks and mortar. It was a home that yearned to please. It was a house with a need, the need to have someone live in it.

Easing her body into the bathwater, she realized how out of place she'd always felt in Boyle Baltmore's house. She'd never admitted that during her marriage; perhaps, she hadn't known until he was gone. But Boyle's death and the subsequent confusion surrounding his affairs, brought the kaleidoscope of her marriage into sharp focus.

Her marriage was a house of cards, and its collapse, while impossible to ignore, had been doubly difficult to conceal. The strain of pretending everything was all right, when in reality, nothing was, had penetrated Dolly's bones and soul so deeply, she wondered if she would ever understand the truth of her relationship with Lord Boyle Baltmore.

Had her life with him been nothing more than a sham? Had Boyle's oft-professed need for her been nothing more than a magic trick, a sleight of the heart, an optical illusion?

She needed to know. Had to know.

Would know.

But for now she would content herself with this house's welcoming embrace. For now, the woman who had never accepted charity would accept the alms that this house, its previous occupant, and her mysterious benefactor offered her.

Warmth crept through her veins, dispelling the chill of her fears, her hunger and her desperation. She was safe in this house, this house that was as bereft as she. Whoever had bathed in this tub before her, whoever had tread the carpet of that bedchamber, and read the poetry that filled that bookshelf, had gone and left a vacuum in this house's heart. The house needed to fill its emptiness; the house needed Dolly.

Closing her eyes, she smiled. Her muscles relaxed and her fears slipped away.

Ferghus was right. She did sound as if she expected to see a ghost. But if a ghost appeared, Dolly sensed it would be a friendly one, an ally.

In the meantime, Dolly's thoughts turned once again to Dick Creevy. Grateful as she was for them, the creature comforts of Fontjoy Square did nothing to soften her resolve. She had no intention of abandoning her plan to meet the man who had killed her husband.

Two

The riverside pub across from Creevy's Pugilist Academy was nearly empty at three o'clock in the afternoon. The working men of Western Dublin labored at their factory jobs, or hadn't yet come off the fishing boats, while the ladies of the night had hours earlier melted into the sanctuary of a well-earned sleep.

In a short time, the pub would come to life, pulsing with laughter and music. But for now, it was the perfect spot for Dermott O'Callahan, longtime boxing manager and agent, to confront his client on a thorny subject.

"We don't need to fight the Viking, Dick! Heaven knows, we don't need the blunt!"

"It's not the money I'm interested in, Cal. It never was money that motivated me to box."

"Don't do it, then!"

The cords in Dick Creevy's neck tightened. Imagining the Viking's potato-shaped face, his superior bulk and height, not to mention his boulder-sized muscles, made Dick's heart thud. He needed to fight that giant. He wasn't certain why, but he couldn't resist the temptation to meet Dublin's most vicious fighter in the ring.

Though he preferred to drink fine Bordeaux, Dick suddenly found the taste of his Guinness enormously pleasing. "It's the chance of a lifetime, Cal. Tell his agent we'll do it."

"I shouldna' ever told ye that Goliath challenged ye. I'm a fool. That's what I am!"

"You're the best agent and trainer a fighter could have," Dick replied. "Why else would I have kept you on now for fifteen years?"

" 'Cause I've kept ye from gettin' killed, that's why. Up till now, that is. Don't do it, Dick! Eric the Viking is nought but a bloodthirsty brute with a taste for killin'! Fer him, boxin' ain't no gentleman's sport; it's legalized murder!"

Dick Creevy swallowed another long draft. "There's nothing more to discuss, Cal. I've made up my mind. Anyway, I should think you would be happy. The purse is big enough for both of us to retire."

"If ye win, me boy. If ye win. But if Eric gets his weight behind a punch to the side of yer head, you'll be leaving the ring in a funeral cart, just like Lord Baltmore."

Dick pinched the bridge of his nose, attempting to stave off the blinding pain that accompanied his memories of Lord Baltmore's death.

O'Callahan looked contrite. "Sorry. Didna' mean to stir up old mem—"

"It's all right. It's been on my mind ever since that Lloyd's of London's fellow showed up, asking all those questions. Queer episode, if you ask me. . . . I barely tapped Lord Baltmore on the side of his head, and he went down like a ton of stone. Besides, I don't intend to let the Viking kill me, Cal. I intend to win."

"The thing is, you don't have to fight no more. You could retire and live a life of leisure, if ye wanted to."

"True enough." Dick chuckled. "But I don't think I could do that."

"Why not? Find a nice lady; settle down. Maybe even have a baby or two."

"Little too late for that now, I'm afraid."

O'Callahan's shoulders sagged and his rheumy eyes scanned the room. For a moment, he fell silent, his fingers drumming a nervous tattoo on the side of his beer mug. Then he took a deep breath and leveled his watery gaze at Dick.

"Awright, I'm gonna tell it to ye straight. Word on the street is the Viking has it in fer ye. You've been ridin' high too long, Dick. The other boxers resent your toplofty manners and arrogance. Especially the ones like Eric who wouldn't know a soup spoon from a shovel. Gettin' in the ring with him is like signin' yer own death warrant! It's insanity; that's what it is! I won't be responsible—"

"Want to quit me, Cal?"

"Of course not!"

"Then I'll relieve you of the responsibility. From now on, your job is to count the beans. Leave the boxing to me, Cal, and don't worry your pretty little head about it."

"I do worry! You're too old!"

"Thirty-six is hardly ancient!"

"But Eric's twenty-three!"

Dick's irritation bubbled over. His mug hit the table with a thud, sloshing beer. "I've never been in finer shape, Cal. You know that!"

"Oh, you're a devil, you are!" With his face puckered, the agent looked as if he'd been caught downwind of a charnel house on a hot day. "You and I both know that thirty-six is nearly over the hill for a boxer these days."

"My right hook's never been more deadly," Dick said quietly.

O'Callahan lowered his head, and peered at Dick from beneath shaggy brows. "You like it too much, man. Fightin' that is. It's like you want someone to hurt ye. 'Tis not a healthy obsession."

Dick drank his beer. He didn't dare voice the truth of the matter. It wasn't that he liked to fight; it was that he had to. His body needed the release. His mind needed the numbness that only a good pounding could produce.

"You'll never be the same, Dick. Mark my words. If the Viking doesn't kill you, he'll maim you. Or blind you. Or damn near break every bone in yer body!"

"He won't hurt me, Cal."

Not any worse than I've been hurt in the past—by Kitty Desmond, by Rafe O'Shea, by myself.

Dick drained the rest of his beer, slammed the glass on the table, and stood. "I'll win the fight; you'll see. We'd better get back now. I've got a new student arriving this afternoon. Don't want to be late."

The older man stood wearily, his face a picture of defeat. With a sigh, he said, "New student? I don't recall scheduling a training session fer today."

"That's because you didn't. This one came in through a rather unusual channel." The two men tossed several coins onto the table, nodding at the tap girl as they exited. They crossed Lower Bridge Street, heading toward the river, then entered a half-timbered Tudor-style facade situated between another pub and a chophouse with greasy windows.

"Name's Dahl Mohr," Dick continued. "Sent me a note by messenger just this morning, requesting an immediate interview. Says he wants to learn the ins and outs of boxing. Claims to be somewhat of a weakling—underdeveloped, formerly a sickly child."

Passing through the entrance area of Creevy's Pugilist Academy, ticket booth on one side, long mahogany bar on the other, medieval pretense gave way to utilitarianism. Having been gutted and redesigned years earlier, the building was centered around a gymnasium, or arena, where fighters trained and sparred.

On occasions when matches were held at Creevy's, wooden benches were brought from the storeroom and arranged around the ring. Printed broadsheets advertising famous fights were tacked to the walls. The smell of male exertion and leather was strong and biting. The afternoon sun, slanting through long rectangular windows cut high in the walls, was powdered with specks of floating dust.

"Some thug gave him a bruisin', eh? Took his girl from him, I'll wager. Well, if anyone can turn him into a man, you can, Dick." Skirting the edge of the gymnasium floor, O'Callahan eyed a single athlete, his taped fists pounding a red punching bag that hung suspended from the ceiling. "See that feller? Looks like he's tappin' his granny on the shoulder, don't he? Think I'll go and give the boy a wee talk; see if I can set him straight."

O'Callahan crossed the wooden floor, leaving Dick to enter the dark corridor that led to the men's changing rooms and saunas. His office, a tiny closet with poor ventilation, was the first door on his right, just before the communal shower area where most of the men who frequented Creevy's Pugilist Academy washed the perspiration and dirt off their bodies, usually no more than twice a week.

Turning into his private quarters, Dick's thoughts were focused on the Viking. Was he really making a mistake as O'Callahan had so vigorously argued? Had he finally overestimated his ability to withstand pain?

He had to win; that was true enough. Besting Eric the Viking was no sure thing. But Dick was older and, technically speaking, a better fighter, even if he lacked the bulk and ferocity of the bloodthirsty Viking. If he kept his wits about him, and avoided a fatal blow to his head, he could win the match.

He had to try. He couldn't turn down the challenge. Couldn't walk away from a fight. Couldn't allow himself to escape the pain.

A young man, no more than eighteen years old, sat in the chair beside his desk, staring up at a faded Sadler's Wells poster on the wall. The lad's head turned as Dick entered, and the boy's impossibly green eyes widened. Good Irish stock, he was blond and generously freckled. With one quick glance, Dick noted the boy's thin legs, delicate hands, and slender shoulders. A heavy tweed jacket and blowsy plus fours did little to disguise an almost-girlish frame.

Squelching a chuckle, Dick thought O'Callahan's prediction was amazingly accurate. This young man had undoubtedly been bullied around a bit, and now wished to prove to his tormentors that he wasn't a weakling.

"Dahl Mohr, I presume?" Dick extended his hand.

And was shocked to feel the soft, uncallused palm that seemed to nestle in his grasp.

Dolly had arrived at Creevy's Pugilist Academy in a rented cab she'd hailed three blocks from Fontjoy Square. Even Ferghus hadn't seen her slip from the house, her bobbed curls tucked beneath a woolen cap, her long skirts replaced by a pair of men's plus fours. For the first time in her life, Dolly was grateful that her breasts were small. Impish features and slender hips aided in her transformation from dowager baroness to acolyte boxer.

Her alter ego had been carefully concocted the night before, after she'd climbed from her bath and settled into bed. It was there, beneath her pillow, that she found the second envelope, sealed with a glob of red wax, just like the first one. A gift from her benefactor, this one contained enough money to buy a new, luxurious wardrobe, hire a housekeeper, even begin the necessary refurbishment of her house.

The money felt like silk in Dolly's fingers, full of promise—downright seductive. She'd forgotten how powerless she felt beneath Boyle's financial tyranny, always wondering whether he would spend their household budget at the racetrack, never patronizing a single dressmaker because of the embarrassment of unpaid bills.

Visions of bonnets and fripperies had danced in her head. Ferghus needed new boots. A Brighton holiday would be lovely. She would like to buy a small carriage and two matching grays. Dolly knew, even without inspecting the stables in the rear of the house, that they would need to be updated. There were a thousand things Dolly needed or wanted. But in the end, after a sleepless night spent marveling at her sudden good luck and plotting her revenge against Dick Creevy, there was only one thing she wished to spend her money on.

Boxing lessons—with Dick Creevy himself.

The idea came to her in the dead of night. Her pulse had skittered at the thought of it, the perfect ruse, the plan—so simple it smacked of genius—to impersonate an aspiring boxer and insinuate herself into Creevy's life and environment. Only then could Dolly discover what sort of man Creevy truly was. Only then could she learn why he had murdered her husband. Only then could she exact her revenge.

Of course, she didn't know what form her revenge would take. Not yet, anyway. She had to get to know Creevy first, find his Achilles' heel, the chink in his armor. She had to get beneath his skin and ingratiate herself to him. She had to observe him in his most private unguarded moments. In order to betray him, she had to first befriend him.

And so it was with trembling fingers that Dolly laced up her oldest pair of brogans, normally reserved for doing chores in the garden. She bound her tiny breasts, flattening them even closer to her chest, and scissored her riotous blond hair until it was no more than half an inch long on the crown and curled around her ears like a boy's.

Staring at her reflection in the vanity mirror, she gasped.

The image of a freckle-faced young man stared back at her. A reckless thrill ran through her. Cutting her hair had been as impulsive an act as asking Lord Boyle Baltmore to marry her some ten years previous, as dangerous as accepting a mysterious man's offer to live in a house she'd never set foot in.

Yet even as she tested the new sensation of a bare neck, she couldn't resist a surge of self-satisfaction. She might be impulsive, but she was not one to look backward or wallow in regret. Running her hand down the back of her neck, she shivered. The image in the mirror—the shape of her jawline, the gentle curving of her ears—pleased her.

She thought she should choose a name as close to her real one as possible. "Dahl Mohr," she'd said out loud. "Principally from Ulster, but me mum was an Englishwoman." She announced herself to the mirror, paying close attention to the sound of her voice. With any luck, the tone of it would be perceived as a boy's adolescent falsetto. She tried not to sound too girlish.

Still, all the preparation in the world couldn't have prevented her voice from cracking when she introduced herself to Dick Creevy, and felt his big, strong fingers close around her hand.

Not because his fame intimidated her. Not because her courage buckled, or her because her determination flagged. But because of the tremor of shock that went through her body when his gaze met hers.

His eyes were dark brown flecked with gold, long lashes, and deep set. Riveted to her chair, Dolly stared up at those eyes, her hand seemingly glued to the inside of Dick's.

An awkward beat passed. She'd done something wrong; she could see it in Creevy's eyes.

Her mind spun, reliving her introduction to Creevy. Hadn't she complied with the dictates of etiquette? Didn't a lady extend her hand first, inviting a gentleman to shake it? *Yes!* her silent thoughts screamed. A lady did not rise, but remained seated when a gentleman entered the room.

Except she was no lady. She was Dahl Mohr, Creevy's newest boxing student—if he accepted her into his academy. Belatedly mindful of her newly fabricated persona, Dolly snatched back her hand, yanked off her cap, and leaped to her feet, stammering, "Pleased to make your acquaintance, Mr. Creevy."

The man's lips, surprisingly full, parted in a smile that revealed his overlapping front teeth. "Relax, lad. This isn't your first day at Trinity." With casual ease, he half sat, half leaned on the edge of his cluttered desk, one booted foot on the floor.

Resuming her seat, Dolly found it impossible to ignore the appeal of Dick's broad shoulders and corded neck. His legs were compact and muscular, draped in soft wool trousers. Even his cap-toed boots were beautifully formed. Truly, there was not a thing about him she didn't find attractive. His magnetism had not been overstated by the newspaper accounts she'd read.

He radiated strength, yet there was nothing uncontrolled or potentially savage about him. His long fingers, laced elegantly across his thighs, were perfectly manicured. His brow was intelligent, his jaw solid. With his thinning hair and conservative English tie, he could have been a bank president; with his twinkling eyes, an actor on the stage. But he was a fighter—a man who made his living taking punches and giving them. No wonder Dublin society didn't know what to make of Dick Creevy. The incongruities in his affect were myriad.

Creevy's office, already small, shrunk further. The air was suffocatingly humid, laden with masculine aromas that were suddenly wildly erotic. This was not a place for ladies. But, with each passing moment, Dolly felt less and less a lady.

"You're not the right type," Dick said abruptly. His eyes raked her body. "You're too . . . little, for one thing."

She rallied quickly, pushing to the edge of her chair. "I'm strong for my size, Mr. Creevy, you'll see. And

I'm tougher than I look. Take me on, and I'll be the best boxing student you ever had. I swear it!"

His eyes narrowed. "You should be at choir practice, Mr. Mohr, not here."

"Excuse me?"

"You sound like a girl—a girl with a rather pretty voice, I might add."

Her cheeks suffused with heat.

Chuckling, Dick leaned forward and picked up her hand. He turned it over, quickly brushing his fingers across her palm. Fire prickled beneath her skin. Then, almost as if he realized what he'd done, as if he wondered why in the devil he had done such a thing, he dropped her hand.

His Adam's apple bobbed. "Just as I suspected. Your skin's as soft as a kid glove. What have you been doing all of your life? Collecting coins? Playing the piano?"

"Piano playing would have given me calluses on my fingertips, wouldn't it have?" Dolly lifted her chin a notch. *Dear God, he's not going to refuse to teach me, is he?*

"Yes, I suppose it would. But the fact remains that you're too soft for the ring. I don't think you're right for my academy, not right at all."

"But, I *am* right, Mr. Creevy. With the proper instruction, I can be the best featherweight boxer in Dublin, all of Ireland, perhaps!"

A moment of silence ticked by, while the heat of Dick's gaze ignited more brushfires on Dolly's cheeks. He studied her too closely, frowning, his suspicion palpable. He was right to be suspicious, Dolly thought. After all, his instincts were those of a killer's. Surely, he recognized a con artist when he saw one.

"Haven't you ever heard the expression, don't scam

a scammer, Mr. Mohr?" Dick's voice was velvety and seductive, weighted heavily with an undertone of menace.

Can he see straight through me? "I'm not scamming you, Mr. Creevy. I want to learn to box."

"Why?"

"I-I like the sport. Boxing is a real man's sport, not some prissy game like cricket or golf, not some controlled riot like rugby or football. Boxing requires skill and coordination, dexterity and quickness. Oh, I know most people think boxing's all about brute strength, but I—but *we*—know better. Don't we, Mr. Creevy?"

He smiled crookedly, almost sadly. "You're lying."

"Lying?" Dolly stood, her fists clenched at her sides. It felt odd to act out her emotions, to show the anger she normally kept hidden inside, but her disguise emboldened her. Perhaps it was she who deserved to be on the stage, for suddenly she felt at ease with the part she'd chosen to play. She was a feisty young man whose integrity had been insulted. She was an eager pupil who wanted to learn. She was anybody and everybody who had ever wanted something so badly he could taste it, but was being denied the opportunity to reach for it because of looks, size, or gender.

Indignation poured through her veins. "Take it back, Mister! Dahl Mohr ain't no liar!"

Creevy patted the air with his hands. "All right. Sit down. Don't get overset. I'm sorry. It's just that I don't believe you're here to learn the fine art of pugilism. I think you're here to learn to *fight*. And there's a big difference between fighting and boxing."

Dolly lowered herself to the chair, her muscles quivering. She'd passed the initial test, then, that of convincing Dick Creevy she was a boy. And she'd shown him she was a lad with spunk, too. That was good, she thought, her breathing returning to normal. That was very good.

"Maybe I want to learn how to fight *and* how to box. Why don't you let me decide that for myself?"

"You're going to have to, if you stay here," Dick replied. "By the way, what made you decide you wanted boxing lessons in the first place? Did some bully beat the daylights out of you for flirting with his girl?"

Though Dolly had anticipated this line of questioning, she could never have guessed how easily the lie would come to her lips. Ducking her head, she nodded. "Happened in Ulster, sir. That's why I moved south; couldn't live with the shame."

"Want to tell me about it?"

She worked the brim of her cap with her fingers. "Not really. Had to do with me sister and a gang of thugs. I tried to protect her, truly, I did. But she wound up dead and I wound up wishin' I was. 'Cept I'm not, and one of these days, I have to go back to Ulster—"

"All right, all right. That's enough. I think I understand." Dick sighed. "Your nose might get broken. Your lips will be split more than once; that's a promise. That perfect skin of yours will be pounded, beaten, and smashed. And that doll face of yours will no longer be so pretty. That's *if* you're serious about being a fighter, Mohr. If you merely want to build up muscles—"

"No, no, I want to fight. I want to box, too. If I can earn me livin' with me fists, that's what I want to do." She looked up and met his gaze, her heart fluttering, her blood pulsing with need. She'd begun a dangerous deception, and there was no turning back. She was that lad from Ulster who watched helplessly while a bunch of ruffians murdered his sister. She was young and hungry and full of pain. She needed the strength and guidance of an older, wiser, stronger man. She need to learn the things that only Dick Creevy could teach her.

His head tilted. He was studying her again, staring at her as if he couldn't quite figure out whether she was a total fraud or a harmless boy who needed a lesson in courage. At length, he said, "All right, Doll Face, you're in."

The quirking of his lips unleashed a flood of lava in her bloodstream. The crooked smile he flashed nearly undid her composure. When Creevy stood, reaching for her hand, Dolly's stomach twisted. Allowing him to slowly pull her to her feet, she stared into his deep brown eyes. His gaze held hers, and for a moment, they stood in his office, holding hands, silently appraising one another.

Then, in a flash, Dick remembered where he was, who this freckle-faced lad was, and why he had agreed to teach such a fragile-looking boy.

It was because of the story the child told.

A youngster unable to protect his family was no different than a man unable to protect his wife. Dahl Mohr's pain was Dick Creevy's pain. It was a pain that would not abate. And it was why Dick fought even when he didn't have to. It was why he couldn't stop fighting. It was why he agreed to fight Eric the Viking, a man with fifteen-stone more *muscle* than Dick.

Releasing Doll Face's tender hand, Dick suppressed a shudder. Good God, but this lad was a peculiar creature, with his girlish eyes and uncallused skin! And what was wrong with Dick that he felt such a tenderness toward the boy? Was he going daft in his middle age? Had he taken too many blows to the side of the head?

A strange sensation overtook him. His fingers itched to tousle the boy's hair. He didn't do it, of course. He kept his distance, even stepped back an inch. Perhaps he needed a woman. It had been too long, Dick told himself. When a man started looking at teenage boys the way he was looking at Doll Face, something was wrong.

Something was very wrong, indeed, he reminded himself, and had been wrong for years.

Suddenly, that old familiar need to get in a boxing ring and pound his fists into another man's body closed in on him. Anger licked the back of Dick's neck, arousing and inciting him. He needed an outlet for his rage. He needed a channel for the gushing emotion that welled up inside him, threatening to explode.

"You'll start tomorrow at ten o'clock in the morning," he said tersely, embarrassed that he'd shown so much of himself to this wet-behind-the-ears greenie. "By the way, I hope you don't think I'm going to teach you for free."

"Of course not," Doll Face replied. "Here." The boy pulled a wad of pound notes from his pocket and thrust them at Dick.

Wanting nothing more than to escape the lad's presence, Dick jerked his chin in the direction of his desk. "Put it over there," he said. "I'm late for my sparring session."

Then he dashed out the door and down the corridor, hurrying to the safety of the dressing room. After he'd shifted from his street clothes to his boxing shorts and undershirt, he found refuge in the boxing ring and cold comfort from the brutal punches he endured. When he finished a grueling workout, his head was numb and his limbs tingling with exertion.

"You're not ready for Eric the Viking," O'Callahan told him as he left the ring, climbed through the ropes, and dropped to the floor.

Grunting his response, Dick slung a damp towel around his neck and headed for his private office. He'd be ready for the Viking long before the clang of the first-round bell. He wasn't worried about that. Another broken nose, another fractured jaw, another bruised kidney—injuries such as those wouldn't kill him.

No, Eric the Viking wasn't his concern. But Dahl Mohr was. Even before his first lesson with the kid from Ulster, Dick regretted that he hadn't turned the boy away and refused to teach him. There was something about Dahl Mohr that unnerved Dick, something he liked, but didn't want to. Perhaps it was because the boy was too pretty to be a fighter. Or perhaps it was because the boy was depending on Dick to make him into a man.

In the dressing room, Dick stared into the mirror above the sink. How in the hell was he going to teach Dahl Mohr what it meant to be a man—when he didn't know himself?

Three

Dolly walked the three blocks home from the place where she disembarked her rented carriage, then—miraculously—made it to her private quarters without encountering Ferghus. Less than twenty-four hours after arriving in Fontjoy Square, Dolly considered her new address *home*. And after her morning at Creevy's Pugilist Academy, it represented sanctuary, too.

Perhaps she eased so comfortably into life at Fontjoy Square because of the discomfort she'd felt at Creevy's gymnasium. Dressed like a boy, feigning the manners of a man, and lying about her identity, gender and raison d'être had been, at first, an adventurous lark. But the stakes were raised considerably when Dick Creevy stared into her eyes and told her she was too "little" to be a boxer. The game she played suddenly deepened to dangerous measures.

Creevy honed in on her feminine qualities like a hawk focused on a chicken. And in doing so, he'd revealed a very powerful element of his personality, an uncanny insight, a keen nose for the counterfeit.

He sensed immediately that Dolly wasn't what she purported to be. Luckily for her, he didn't intuit the entirety of her deception. The absurdity of her fraud, she surmised, the unlikelihood that a woman would want to take boxing lessons in the first place, was all that saved her from exposure.

The midday sun brightened her bedchamber. The bath she enjoyed on her return home rinsed away a thin layer of her worries. But a glance in the mirror and a quick survey of her damp curls reclaimed a portion of that uneasiness. What would Ferghus say when he saw her shorn hair? How would she explain her repeated morning absences to the one servant who for the past year had conspired with her to conceal the true state of her finances?

"They's someone here to see you, mum." Lately, it seemed that Ferghus was always hovering in the doorway, fidgeting with unwelcome news.

"It isn't another bill collector, is it?" Dolly blurted. Old habits were hard to break. "Though I can't imagine how one would have found us."

"No, mum. Not a bill collector. Not unless they've started dressin' up like ladies."

"If a fairy godmother can appear in the guise of a man wearing a mask, I suppose a creditor can don a morning gown," Dolly replied. "Does our visitor have a name?"

"Lady Claire Kilgarren, m'lady. Says she lives next door at Number Three Fontjoy Square."

That information lifted Dolly's eyebrows. Tossing aside a book of Lord Byron's poetry, she stood and smoothed down her dark blue muslin skirts. It was a relief to be out of her plus fours and boots. Trying to walk, talk, and act like a man had put a bit of a strain on her nerves.

Ignoring Ferghus's gaping stare, she considered the

hug of her girdle and the bulk of her small bustle a welcome accoutrement of her femininity. She knew how to maneuver in her womanly garb. She didn't fear that her natural mannerisms were egregiously out of character with her own sex.

Dolly paused in the doorway, facing Ferghus. "You needn't think I've gone insane, Ferghus, simply because I've cut my hair. It is a symbol of my new beginning."

"You've never been afraid to start anew," the old man observed.

"I hear the style is all the rage in London . . . or is it Boston? Well, it doesn't matter. Perhaps it isn't the fashion at all. But I like it, and that's all it signifies."

"And you never were a slave to fashion." Ferghus was conspicuously noncommittal as to whether he approved or even liked her new coiffure.

"Thank you." Dolly chose to treat her servant's comment as a compliment, nonetheless. "I will be in the parlor with our guest."

Thankfully, that was the one room Ferghus had straightened up that morning. While Dolly was at Creevy's Pugilist Academy, Ferghus had dusted, swept, and freshened the foyer and guest parlors—the areas of the house most likely to be seen by visitors. He'd worked for Dolly long enough to know how important it was to have a suitably impressive room in which to receive acquaintances. Even to Ferghus, the value of appearances was not lost.

Stepping into the parlor, Dolly couldn't resist a quick scan of the room. After all, she'd never seen it before. Now, acutely aware of the woman ensconced on the camel-back sofa, she could only afford a glance. Handsome furniture, heavy and dark, thick oriental carpets, significant paintings, and walls of shelves crammed with books, imprinted themselves on her mind's eye as she crossed the room.

Her visitor replaced a cup and saucer on the table beside the sofa. With a mild surge of pleasure, Dolly noted that the china was more than satisfactory, another example of her predecessor's fine taste and discretion. The image her household projected, even if it was, technically, another woman's household, reflected Dolly's self-image. She'd struggled for years to project the proper image, in spite of, and sometimes because of, Boyle's inadequacies as a husband. In some dim corner of her mind, she found it odd that in this new house, where she should have felt a stranger, she felt so at ease.

Would this play-acting come to an end at some point? Would this house absorb her completely, erasing the old Lady Dolly? Or would she simply melt into the shadow of the woman who had lived here before her?

Standing before her guest, Dolly felt a flash of dizziness. She'd spent the morning masquerading as a boy, and here she was pretending to be the mistress of this fine, slightly rundown house on the fashionable side of Dublin. How long could she sustain this fraud? She didn't know anymore where the real Lady Dolly Baltmore ended and the pretend one began. She was a paper doll with a different disguise for every occasion.

Steeling her nerves, she extended her hand.

A handsome kid glove slid into Dolly's palm. From beneath a puffy bouffant of blond hair, a pair of Sevres-blue eyes peered up. Rose-tinted lips, shaped like a bow, tentatively curved upward. The voice that emerged from those lips was birdlike and girlish, cultivated not so much in the classroom as in the rarified confines of haute European society.

"I am Claire—Lady Kilgarren—your neighbor. I've come to welcome you to Fontjoy Square."

Suppressing the urge to curtsy, Dolly smiled and sat on the chair opposite the sofa. "How kind of you to pay a visit so soon after my arrival. Please forgive the cluttered state of my surroundings. Ah, I'm afraid the rest of my staff hasn't arrived yet from the country."

Lady Kilgarren nodded in apparent sympathy. "Yes, I understand how difficult it is to make do without servants. Mine have all but abandoned me. A young married couple has stayed with me, but I can barely afford to pay them a penny."

Trying not to show her surprise, Dolly poured herself a cup of tea. Over the rim of her cup, she eyed Lady Kilgarren. The woman's suit was immaculate and expensive, but hardly new. When the lady sipped her tea, shiny patches showed on the elbows of her pale blue serge jacket. It was evident that she shared the same state of genteel poverty that Dolly did.

"It is so difficult to find good help," Dolly remarked.

"Particularly when one cannot pay them," the woman said baldly.

The tea scalded Dolly's throat, causing her to cough. When she'd caught her breath, she said, "Excuse me, am I to understand that you are . . . that you are . . ."

"Broke." Those wide blue eyes never wavered.

For a moment, Dolly simply stared, taken aback completely by this lady's honesty. A part of her wished she could be equally candid and admit that she was broke, too. It would have been such a relief to have someone to commiserate with.

But the part of Dolly that believed appearances were everything, wouldn't allow her to confess her true state of affairs. "I am sorry for your misfortune, Lady Kilgarren. Knock on wood, that should never happen to me. I'm a widow, you know. This house was, er, my husband's town home before we married. He rented it out when we moved to the country. That was many years ago. Had I know what rundown condition this little house was in, I would never have moved here so precipitously."

"Did your husband die very recently?"

"A year ago, but I had a difficult mourning period. When it was over, *poof!* I decided I wanted to return to the city. Packed up my suitcases and drove here with one servant as quickly as I could. That's why the house looks so shabby, you understand."

"I think it looks fine. I'm becoming accustomed to shabby, myself. When will the rest of your staff be arriving?"

"Soon."

"Well, until then, please let me know if there is anything I can do for you. Not that my little staff can be of much help. But it's nice to know there is someone next door you can depend upon."

"Thank you, Lady Kilgarren." Dolly's chest ached with gratitude and remorse at her duplicity.

"Call me Claire, please. After all, I hope we will be seeing much more of each other. I was so happy to see some sign of life around here! I've been in Number Three for two weeks, and I haven't seen a soul in any of the other houses. Well, except for the big house on the opposite end of the square."

"Who lives there?"

"I don't know. A gentleman, I believe. I've seen him in his carriage passing by, and I've seen him walking the perimeter of the garden once or twice, but I've never seen him up close. I daresay, I don't know a thing about him."

"And you've only lived here three weeks?"

"Before that, I was supporting myself as a governess. Living with distant relatives, actually, and being treated as if I were the scullery wench!"

Dolly gasped. "How dreadful!"

The pretty blond leaned forward. "It was horrible! Like something out of a romance novel! 'Struth, I thought I would spend the rest of my days there, and die a bitter woman with no friends and not a penny to my name! Imagine my surprise when—"

At last, Lady Kilgarren reined herself in. Inhaling through her nose, she pursed her lips.

"When what?" Warming to Lady Kilgarren's openness, Dolly reached for a lemon biscuit on the plate beside the teapot. Where Ferghus had obtained those little treasures, she couldn't imagine, but they were as deliciously tart as Lady Kilgarren's *on-dits*.

"Imagine my surprise when *another* distant relative died and left me a tidy little inheritance and a house on Fontjoy Square."

"You must have a very big family," Dolly observed.

"Well, it isn't as if Fontjoy Square is the most sought-after property in Dublin, is it? Gracious, I don't mean to insult you; you've just moved in yourself. But there's not a house on the square that doesn't need major renovations. And the garden in the center of the square is a tangle of weeds; haven't you noticed?"

Dolly shook her head. "I've only been here since yesterday. I'm afraid I haven't had the opportunity to look around." Recalling that part of her bargain with her mysterious benefactor was to refurbish the garden,

Dolly added, "But I do so love a beautiful garden, don't you?"

"Yes. Do you suppose we could combine our efforts in that respect? Try to clear the jungle and create a really wonderful garden, like the one at St. Stephen's Green?"

"I think that would be delightful." Despite the fact that there had not been a wee bit of honesty in the gammon she'd thrust upon the woman, Dolly genuinely liked Lady Kilgarren. She actually looked forward to getting into that garden and mucking about in the peaty black earth.

"We mustn't waste any time," Lady Kilgarren said. "Spring is for planting in this clime. If we get our tulip seeds down now, we might have a batch of Holland beauties before July!"

"I'll send Ferghus to the nursery tomorrow morning." Dolly smiled. "And I'll meet you in the garden tomorrow after nuncheon. Do you have an old apron and a pair of trousers?"

"Of course! I may be a duke's daughter, Lady Dolly—"

"Call me Dolly!"

"But a year spent patting babies' bottoms and wiping runny noses brought me down a peg or two, I'm afraid." She stood, her pretty face radiating with good humor. "I can't say I'm bitter, Dolly. I never knew what it was like to have to earn one's way. I always thought a woman needed a man to define her life, but I've learned otherwise. I don't need a man, and I don't want one. How about you? Would you like to have another husband?"

Rising more slowly, Dolly hesitated. The question took her by surprise, and she suddenly realized she hadn't even given a thought to remarrying in the year since Boyle died. It was almost as if she still expected him to walk through the door, toss his hat and cane on the sofa, and proceed to regale her with some outlandish story about how he'd been *taken* at the track, or fleeced by a sharpster at a card table, or rooked out of this month's mortgage payment.

But he wasn't going to return, and there wasn't going to be a final opportunity to confront the man and ask him the questions Dolly was craving to ask him. Questions like, *Why weren't you honest with me? Why didn't you tell me we were on the brink of bankruptcy when you died? Why did you die and leave me nearly destitute, to fend for myself, when all I ever did was love you and obey you and treasure you like a dutiful wife should?*

"Oh, dear, I've been too bold, haven't I?" Lady Kilgarren reached for Dolly's hands and gave them a squeeze. "I'm afraid it is always my mouth that gets me in trouble. Story of my life, actually. If I could only button my lips—"

"No, it's all right. I suppose a year of mourning wasn't quite enough. I still cannot believe he's gone."

"There, there. Don't cry."

Dolly sniffed once and touched the corner of her eye. Then, meeting Lady Kilgarren's clear blue gaze, she forced a smile. After a moment, the smile slid more comfortably into place, and she walked with her arm linked in her neighbor's to the drawing-room door. "Do come and visit often. I enjoyed our chat."

"I predict, Lady Dolly Baltmore, that you and I will get on famously, and become best friends."

"You sound like a schoolgirl. I haven't had a best friend since I was in boarding school in Switzerland. I do hope you and I don't get into as much trouble as Mary and I did!"

Gently shrugging, Lady Kilgarren let loose a girlish chuckle. "We can't get in trouble planting tulips, can we?"

"For a duke's daughter, you're refreshingly earthy!"

"I've never shied away from my duties, Dolly. That's what *breeding* is all about; isn't it?"

"Is it? I thought it was about manners."

"It would be bad manners on my part to leave the responsibility of that garden solely to you. We'll tend it together, you and I. I'm looking forward to getting started."

"See you tomorrow, then."

Later that night, Dolly retired to her bedchamber, wistful, hopeful, and sad, all at the same time. She would make a friend of Lady Claire Kilgarren and that was something to be happy about. She'd encountered a man who heated her blood, and that gave her a great measure of relief, since she'd long feared she would never experience physical desire again.

Yet her triumphs were mitigated by the falsities on which they were based. She wasn't the prosperous widow Lady Kilgarren thought she was. And she certainly wasn't the eager young lad Dick Creevy saw her as.

As sleep overcame her, she envied Lady Kilgarren her ability to be candid about her poverty. She didn't relish masquerading as a boy.

But the deception she would yet perpetrate on Dick Creevy was unavoidable. Because he was the man whose murderous actions created the necessity for her duplicity.

Dolly's ability to rationalize her actions was nearly as great as her acting skills.

She told Ferghus that she had joined a small political group composed entirely of women who gathered twice a week to discuss the issue of Home Rule and the chances of getting a female elected to the Irish Parliament.

"You shouldna' be goin' out alone, m'lady," he'd responded. "At least allow me to accompany—"

"No, Ferghus. Someone might recognize us, and that simply wouldn't do. The group meets clandestinely. That is why I must dress in these ridiculous clothes."

"If I'd a'seen you on the street, I'd a'thought you was a boy!"

Gratified, Dolly said, "Just so. All of the women in my club disguise themselves. Some of the members have husbands who would strenuously object to their being involved in reform politics. I know dressing like a man sounds tawdry, Ferghus, but for the first time in years, I feel as if I am doing something important."

"I understand," the man replied skeptically.

"Thank you. Now, if anyone questions my whereabouts while I am out, you must say that I am visiting a sick relative. Do you understand?"

He nodded as she pulled her cap low over her eyes and left the house. Of course, he didn't understand, and Dolly knew she ran a certain risk of discovery by allowing him to see her in her boyish garb. But there was no alternative, really, because Ferghus was an omnipresent character in her life, and not likely to turn a blind eye to her frequent disappearances. She only hoped her fabricated political activities would be sufficient to appease his curiosity and dissuade him from following her.

Stepping inside the gymnasium, she was assailed by a din of gloved fists punching stuffed leather bags, the slap of jumping ropes on the wooden floor, and the shouts of trainers barking instructions at their protégés.

Her heart thudded as she made her way to the dressing room. Though few heads turned to look at her, and hardly a curious stare was aimed in her direction, Dolly felt conspicuously foreign. The clubby atmosphere of the locker area and dressing room only intensified her nervousness. She hadn't prepared herself for the sight of men parading about completely nude.

Proceeding quickly to the nearest bench, she attempted to avert her eyes. But she couldn't stare at the floor constantly. The most casual observer would single her out for a fraud, or worse. And every time she lifted her gaze, she saw a sea of muscular male bodies, broad naked backs, hairy chests, rippling bellies, taut haunches, smooth white buttocks, and flaccid penises.

She sat on the bench, frantic for some place to cast her eyes. Bending over, Dolly picked at her bootlaces. A pair of naked feet walked past, mere inches from her fingers.

A male voice, clearly that of a native Scotsman, said, "Hello, kid. You wouldn't happen to be Creevy's new pupil, would you?"

Reluctantly raising her chin, Dolly came eye to eye with the man's manhood. Her breath caught in her throat. In a flash, her gaze skittered up, past a flat stomach and amazingly well-formed biceps, to the twinkling blue eyes of a very handsome, middle-aged man.

He grasped Dolly's hand and shook it so hard her teeth rattled. "Name's Sean Conway. Creevy said you were a bit wet behind the ears. Well, you'll soon get over that. Good luck, laddie. Your instructor's waitin' for you in the gym, now."

"Thank you," Dolly managed, talking to the man's naked hips as he sauntered away.

Hurriedly, she pulled off her clothes. She'd already donned her loose fitting drawstring short pants; she wore them beneath her plus fours. Her chest was flattened by thick strips of muslin, and her delicately shaped arms were covered by a gray athletic shirt borrowed from Ferghus. She had only to change into her newly purchased leather-soled boxing shoes to be ready for her first lesson. Then, with a deep inhale and a sense that as soon as she stepped into that gymnasium, there was no retreating from her plan, she exited to the locker room.

"Aye, there, boy!" The booming male voice, combined with the hearty slap on her back, gave Dolly a double jolt.

Which tripled when she turned and drank in Dick Creevy's physique.

Four

Dolly's smile trembled on her lips as her gaze met his. Nerves jangling, she prayed for strength to hide her bewilderment. Why Dick Creevy's presence upset her equilibrium, she couldn't comprehend. He was just a man, a man who'd killed her husband. She shouldn't even notice the fact that his jaw was unshaven. She certainly shouldn't speculate as to what those coarse whiskers would feel like scraped along the length of her neck.

But she couldn't suppress the tiny eruptions of warmth beneath her skin. Dick's approach, every step he took toward her, heightened her awareness of his physical prowess. With his gaze fixed on her, and his head tilted in her direction, it suddenly seemed as if there were no one in that huge gymnasium except Dolly and Dick. As he closed the distance between them, a smile slowly spread across his face. Unable to look away, Dolly puzzled over her own reaction. His overlapping front teeth appealed to her. His too-large, oft-broken nose was a museum-quality objet d'art.

What was wrong with her? She did not like Dick Creevy. She hated him, in fact. She had already made up her mind to loathe him! He had killed her husband,

and she was here to wreak her revenge, in whatever form she ultimately deemed appropriate!

With a shudder, Dolly reminded herself where she was, and why. By the time Dick Creevy stuck out his hand to shake hers, she had stilled her quirking lips and regained at least a semblance of mental competency.

"Not good to be late, kid. From now on, I want you out on the floor five minutes before our lesson begins." The smile faded, but the heat in his eyes remained.

"Sorry, sir." Dolly fidgeted, acutely aware of the paleness of her skin, the softness of her scant curves. Could she possibly fool Dick Creevy into believing she was a young man?

Perspiration plastered his cotton undershirt to his thickly muscled chest. His shoulders were broad, his burnished skin flawless. His baggy short pants revealed legs so classically shaped and perfectly muscled, she felt she was staring at the sun; if she didn't look away, her eyes would surely scorch.

When Dick Creevy good-naturedly punched the side of her arm, Dolly nearly fell over.

His brows arched. Clearly, he hadn't expected her to be so light in her boxing shoes. Jutting his chin toward the far corner of the gymnasium, he said, "Come on, then. If I'm going to teach you the art of defending yourself and your loved ones, first I've got to know what you're made of."

"Flesh and blood, same as you." Dolly's voice, even to her own ears, sounded pathetically feminine.

"How old did you say you were?" Dick's scrutiny as they walked side by side gave her goose bumps.

"Twenty, sir." Anticipating Dick's question, Dolly had given some thought to her answer. Her skin was blessedly unlined and clear, her body lithe and thin.

Without the trappings of womanly garb, her features were a bit bland and straightforward. Her calves were well formed and taut. She thought she cut a rather fine figure in her boxing attire; somewhat ruefully, she realized that her masquerade didn't require much effort.

But the one thing she couldn't change was her voice. She'd always had a firm melodic voice, a pleasant contralto that Boyle had once described as angelic. Disguising it completely was not only impossible, but imprudent, as well, since she would no doubt revert to her normal tone in periods of stress. Best not to attempt a disguise she couldn't pull off. So she spoke naturally, hoping Dick Creevy would simply attribute her feminine tones to a late adolescence.

"I don't believe you." He drew to a halt, challenging her with his stormy eyes.

Dolly's gut twisted. "I am not lying, sir."

"You can't possibly be twenty years of age. Not with that squeaky voice."

Squeaky? She wanted to ball up her fist and plant a fiver in his nose.

Hands on hips, he said, "Why don't you just tell me the truth now. You're not a day over sixteen, are you?"

She brazened it out. "I am twenty years old, Mr. Creevy, not that it signifies a whit. I'm plenty old enough to be here, if not according to my years, then certainly based upon my experience. I wasn't exactly leading a charmed life in Ulster, if you please."

Dick seemed to consider that a moment. After a length, Dick sighed. "Can you jump rope?"

She nodded. Jumping rope as a young girl with Mary O'Roarke was one of her most cherished memories. Mary and Dolly had jumped for hours, at boarding school in Switzerland, then, during the summer, at

Dolly's parents' home in Waterford. Images, most of them pleasant, some of them painful, flooded Dolly's brain. Could she jump rope? Well, she hadn't developed her diamond-shaped calves sitting at a desk studying Latin.

Not waiting for her answer, he handed her a length of braided hemp. "Show me what you can do."

Not because she feared failure, but she because she rankled at Dick's authoritarian tone, Dolly hesitated. A blink passed. Swallowing her protest, she took the ends of the rope and stepped away. If she was going to continue this farce, she had to do as Dick Creevy told her. Refusal would mean her dismissal from the pugilist academy and would sound the death knell to her scheme.

A flick of her wrists put the rope in motion. Slowly, Dolly began to jump, her feet skipping lightly on the floor, her rate of breathing steadily increasing. The exercise felt good; a warm glow soon prickled at her skin. A light sheen of perspiration dampened her neck and shoulders.

He watched her, his arms folded across his chest, expression guarded. He watched her feet and her legs, and as her movements quickened, he watched her hips. Her breasts, compressed against her chest, were nonetheless sensitive to the impact of her jumping and—had her imagination totally consumed her?—the masculine scrutiny of Dick Creevy's stare.

That was impossible! He was looking at a boy, she reminded herself, jumping faster. Her year of mourning, and sexual abstinence, must have affected her. Her chest tightened and her muscles burned. Creevy's appraisal of her physical form and movement was disturbing both because Dolly feared exposure as a fraud, and because everywhere he looked at her a candle burst of heat ignited.

She told herself she was crazy. The heat welling up inside her was the result of her animation, nothing else. She'd been sedentary too long, and this sudden activity elevated her heart rate and aggravated her senses. Her body had no control over the sensations roiling through her. The excitement she was feeling had nothing to do with Dick Creevy. Or the way he tilted his head. Or the way his eyes went black as his gaze lit on her lips and thighs. Or the obvious hardening of his manhood, evident beneath the thin cotton of his short pants.

Dolly's heart squeezed painfully. The rope went slack in the air, then fell to the floor with a slap. Gasping for breath, she leaned forward, hands on knees, chest heaving.

"Are you all right, lad?"

Creevy's fingers closed around the scruff of her neck. His grasp slipped on her sweat-drenched skin, and for an instant, in a gesture that seemed as natural as it was dangerously erotic, he grappled the tangled curls on her nape. Then he snatched back his hand as if he'd accidentally touched a hot poker.

Bent at the waist, Dolly lowered her head, grateful that Creevy couldn't see her features. Shock and confusion coursed through her veins. The exertion of her exercise made her light-headed. Dick Creevy's touch had left her weak-kneed and slightly nauseated.

Finally, she straightened. "I'm a little out of shape, sir," she puffed. "Perhaps my lungs are not what they should be. But with the proper training, I'll get stronger, sir. You'll see. Just give me time."

Creevy's frown deepened. "You're not cut out to be a fighter, boy. Why, you barely jumped for five min-

utes, and look at you! You're as out of breath as a
virgin on her honeymoon! Why don't you just forget
about it, eh, kid? Whatever grudge you're nursing isn't
worth killing yourself over."

Dolly's jaw clenched. Defiance sizzled at her nerve
endings. She'd come here to meet Dick Creevy, to get
to know him, and to discover why he'd killed her husband. She would not be turned away or run off. She
would not be intimidated.

Between labored breaths and gritted teeth, she said,
"I . . . will . . . fight!" She propped her hands on her
hips and stared back at Dick's hard, menacing gaze.

"Little fool," he muttered. "You're nothing but a . . .
doll face." He tossed her a towel and jerked his thumb
toward the dressing room. "Be back on Thursday morning. Same time. Take the rope with you. You'll need it
to practice."

Nodding, she wiped her face with the cotton rag.
Exhilaration leaped through her body. She'd gotten
through her first training session with Dick Creevy,
without being discovered. She'd fooled him. She was
"in." Now, all she had to do was stay in.

"I'll expect you to be able to jump rope for ten minutes on Thursday morning, no resting, no stopping. If
you work hard between now and then, I believe you
can do it. If you can't, don't bother to return."

Her optimism faded. Of course, staying in was not
going to be easy.

The knock at the door and the succeeding patter of
footsteps on the stairwell were inaudible above the
steady slap of the rope on the exposed-wood floor. Only
when her bedchamber door flew open and Lady Claire

Kilgarren stood gaping on the threshold, did Dolly quit jumping.

Ferghus hovered behind the interloper, his grizzled face puckered. "Sorry, m'lady, I told Lady Kil—"

A rustle of crinoline drowned his indignation. "I could not believe my ears," Lady Kilgarren said. She wore the same pale blue morning suit, the same bone-colored half boots buttoned up her ankles, as she had the day before. A flutter of lace and a cameo broach accentuated her swanlike neck. Tapping a parasol on the floor, she stared wide-eyed at Dolly's dishabille. " 'Struth, I cannot believe my eyes, either! What in Erin's name are you doing?"

"It is called exercise," Dolly said, between pants.

"I told her—" Ferghus started.

Holding up her hand, Dolly interrupted. "Would you fetch us some tea, please?" When Ferghus was gone, she tossed the rope on the bed, and toed the edge of the carpet back into place. Grabbing a large towel, she directed her guest to the small sitting area in the corner of the bedchamber.

"Are you ill?" Lady Kilgarren asked, perched on the edge of the French provincial chintz-covered settee.

Dolly threw her aching body onto a chaise longue. Stretching out her bare legs, she inhaled deeply. "If I were, I wouldn't be able to jump rope for ten minutes at a stretch, now, would I?"

Lade Kilgarren touched her temples. "Perhaps your affliction is not, ah, *physical,* dear."

"You think I am insane because I have taken up exercise?" Dolly chuckled. "Why, my lady, it is the latest thing. I assure you. There is even a famous doctor in Battle Creek, Michigan, who claims to have proven that diet and exercise are the major factors in influencing a person's health and happiness."

"If I am not mistaken, that same doctor advocates total sexual abstinence, even between married couples."

"Then, I should be a very healthy lady, indeed," Dolly replied, running her fingers through drenched curls.

As Ferghus fussed with the tea tray, Lady Kilgarren studied her neighbor with a keen eye. The young woman looked remarkably boyish in her short cotton pantaloons and sleeveless undershirt. Her breasts were practically nonexistent, her slim legs taut and muscular. With her close-cropped hair, inquisitive green eyes, and freckled nose, she could easily pass for a teenage boy.

Was she . . .

With a shiver, Claire dismissed that ridiculous notion. Of course, Dolly wasn't a young man masquerading as a woman! It was a foolish, malicious thought, and Claire was disgusted with herself for even wondering such a thing. Besides, Dolly's voice was distinctly feminine. And she'd shown real emotion when she talked about her deceased husband, hadn't she?

Having dismissed her overprotective servant, Dolly said, "Was there something you wanted to see me about, Lady Kilgarren?"

"Call me Claire, *please.*" She accepted the cup her hostess offered. "I apologize for my rudeness. I have never entered anyone's home, much less rushed up their stairs and barged into their bedchamber, without invitation. It's just that . . . well—"

"When Ferghus told you I was in my room, jumping up and down, you thought—"

"I thought you were sick, or—"

"Crazy."

Claire gave a reluctant nod.

"And now?" Dolly probed.

"Well, now . . ." Claire half smiled. "Now, I'm certain of it."

The women locked gazes. Color rushed to Claire's cheeks. Dolly's eyes twinkled, and her lips twitched. Then, without warning, the ladies burst out laughing. For a full minute, neither could articulate a sentence. Tears actually rolled down Dolly's cheeks, and Claire daintily covered her lips with her gloved hand to keep from showing every tooth in her mouth.

When she'd caught her breath, Claire said, "It felt good to laugh, didn't it? I can't remember when I did last."

Unlacing her shoes, Dolly agreed. "I'm afraid I haven't had much to laugh about lately." She threw the leather trainers on the floor, pulled her knees to her chest, and tucked her feet beneath her.

"I suppose you haven't, had you? Is your ailing relative any better?"

For an instant, Dolly appeared not to comprehend Claire's inquiry.

"Ferghus told me all about it," Claire explained. "I don't mean to pry."

"No. It's just that, well, I have a tendency to keep things to myself. Perhaps, I am too guarded. I find it difficult to speak about unpleasant things."

"We're just the opposite, you and I. I've been told I am too bold for some people's tastes. Lord knows, I have never learned when to keep my mouth shut."

But Claire could not figure out how inquiring as to the health of Dolly's relative was a breach of etiquette. Had her social gyroscope slipped so far off its axis that she couldn't have a friendly conversation with her neighbor without offending the poor woman?

After a blink, Dolly said, "Oh, yes. Aunt Esther's condition has worsened considerably, I fear."

"I am sorry. But I did not come here to depress you, Lady Dolly. I came to deliver a bit of good news."

"I could use some."

"We have two new neighbors . . . ladies . . . unmarried ones at that!"

"Four unmarried ladies living in one square city block?" Dolly rolled her gaze toward the ceiling. "What are the odds of that, I wonder?"

"Pretty slim, I should wager. But that's not all." Claire sat a little straighter, fairly bristling with excitement. She wasn't sure why, but she liked her curly haired neighbor and wanted to see her smile. The diminutive woman reminded her of a scrappy kitten, easily wounded but never dispirited. There was a toughness about her that Claire envied, even though she sensed that beneath that guarded facade, Dolly hid a fragile spot.

"What else?" Dolly prompted.

"There's to be a party, dear. A grand ball at Mr. Avondale's house. Not till next month, and by then, we will have met our two new neighbors. But it's never too early to begin thinking about what we shall wear, is it? Though I cannot afford to order a new gown."

"Who is Mr. Avondale?"

"The gentleman who lives at the opposite end of the square, of course. I told you, didn't I? I've seen him passing by in his carriage. Always tips his hat, smiles a little as if he isn't quite sure whether he wants to, and never stops to pass the time or chat."

"Apparently, he is not as unsociable as you thought,

Claire. Then again, perhaps he has spied his pretty blond neighbor at the opposite end of the square, and now has contrived an excuse to meet her."

A silly instant of panic fluttered in Claire's chest. She had thought the man rather handsome, from a distance. Sipping her tea, she allowed her mind to imagine what it would mean if he did take a fancy to her. But the thought only fueled her panic. Closing her eyes, Claire shook the notion out of her head.

She hadn't realized a moment of silence had ticked by until Lady Dolly set down her cup with a clatter. "I did not mean to tease you. 'Twas improper of me. Please forgive—"

"Don't mind me, Dolly. I was simply woolgathering. A terrible habit, I'm afraid."

After a beat, Dolly said, "Tell me something. What would you do if this Mr. Avondale *were* interested in courting you? I mean, how would you go about it? How would you manage such a thing at this stage of life? Without chaperones. Without a father to watch over every step of the gentleman's overture?"

"Why, dear, you make it sound as if we are ancient."

"More tea?"

"If I drink another cup, I shall have to retire to the water closet, dear, an endeavor that, considering this whalebone corset, requires entirely too much time and effort."

"My point exactly," Dolly said, smiling wryly. "We may not be ancient, but we are not children, either. My muscles are cramping something awful even as I sit here. Sometimes I think this exercise is merely aging me."

With a sigh, Claire admitted, "Yes, I don't have the energy I once did. But I am only twenty-five years old." When Dolly didn't volunteer her own age, Claire added, "My, you *are* a guarded woman, aren't you?"

"You're not much older than I," Dolly replied cryptically. "It's just that I feel so old, as if my life is over, as if, somehow I have thrown it away. And I was wondering if you ever have felt the same thing."

Sighing, Claire thought, *Yes, I know that feeling all too well.* But to her already-saddened new friend, she answered softly, "And why do you feel that life has passed you by, dear?"

A freckled knuckle flew to Dolly's lips. Her voice caught in her throat as she spoke. "I don't suppose it is any of your concern."

"I would like to know." Claire leaned forward, drawn to Dolly's suffering. Despite the prevailing mores that dictated the suppression of one's emotions, Claire held to the theory that talking was good for the soul. There was only one thing she wouldn't talk about, and that was a blot on her past, never very far from her conscious thoughts. But for now, she focused on Lady Dolly's anguish. The younger woman was so obviously unhappy.

"I suppose it is because of Boyle's death, God rest his soul," Dolly eked out.

"Do you miss him that much?"

Dolly closed her eyes, summoning the image of her deceased husband. Did she miss him? At that moment, she could barely even remember what he looked like. Yet the thought of living the rest of her life without him was still a frightening and unreal proposition. Even after a year, she could hardly accept the fact that he was dead. He was simply too ingrained in her life to be dead. Boyle was too deeply embedded in her own identity to be extinct. If he was dead, then she was, too.

Clenching her fists, Dolly drew in a deep breath.

Composing herself, she forced the calm back into her voice. "I miss the life I had with Lord Baltmore, yes."

What she didn't confide was that life with Lord Boyle Baltmore had never been a bed of roses. But it was all she knew, and as long as he was alive, she'd been secure in the thought that the bills would eventually get paid, and that there would be food on the table, even if Boyle was fretting over a racing form while they ate. It wasn't an ideal existence, but it was far preferable to the one she led now.

Who will take care of me now? she wondered.

Dolly's ears rang as she gulped back her tears, and for a minute, she was deafened by the sound of blood rushing through her veins.

At length, however, Lady Kilgarren's voice, pearl-like in its refinement, filtered through Dolly's jumbled thoughts. "If you liked being married so much, dear, why don't you do it again?"

"Pardon me?" Dolly blinked away her tears and stared at her wide-eyed guest. "Did you suggest I should remarry?"

"You asked me how I would feel if Mr. Avondale turned his attentions toward me. The real question is, how would *you* feel if a man took a fancy to you? Would you welcome such an overture, or would you run away?"

"I-I do not know," Dolly said, bewildered.

" 'Twouldn't be a betrayal to your husband, you know. He is dead, dear."

Something in Claire's tone of voice brought a bubble of guilty laughter to Dolly's throat. Swallowing it, she said, "Yes, I know. But he's the only man I have ever known. It would be so strange. . . ."

"I wager you would grow accustomed to another man more quickly than you might expect."

The thought was a sobering one. Over the rim of her teacup, Dolly met Claire's gaze and wondered. Was it possible that the feelings she'd experienced in Dick Creevy's presence had nothing to do with her physical exertion and everything to do with her attraction to him? Was it possible that the quickening of her pulse each time he was near had nothing to do with the nervousness associated with her fraud? Was it possible her need for a man hadn't expired with the death of Lord Boyle Baltmore?

And finally, was it possible that Dick Creevy was attracted to her as well?

"Impossible," she said aloud.

"Nothing's impossible, dear," Claire replied.

But Lady Kilgarren didn't understand. Dick Creevy thought Doll Face was an eager young boxing acolyte, a gangly teenage boy with an infatuation with pugilism. There was no way on God's Emerald Isle that Creevy was going to be physically or emotionally attracted to Doll Face. He wasn't a pervert; he was a red-blooded Irish male brimming with masculine arrogance and sexuality. Dolly had gotten close to him by posing as a boy. And in doing so, she'd cut herself off from ever knowing him as a woman knows a man.

Five

Dolly's pulse quickened at the sight of Dick Creevy striding across the gymnasium floor. His shoulders and hips rolled as elegantly as a man-of-war at sea. His legs, long and lean, were impossible to ignore. His dark gaze impaled her. When he smiled in her direction, a wave of unease swept through her.

The clap he gave to her shoulder nearly knocked her down.

Frowning, Dick said, "Sorry. Didn't mean to hit you so hard. Did I hurt you?"

"N-no." Suddenly nervous, Dolly braced her knees.

"You look *different,* Doll Face." Dick Creevy studied her through narrowed eyes. "Is there something the matter with you?"

Other than the fact I am not who I am pretending to be? Other than the fact that your physical presence is damn near intolerable?

"I'm fine, sir. Thank you."

She wasn't fine, of course. Dolly glanced around the busy gymnasium. Though no one had questioned her gender in the week since she'd been working at at Creevy's Pugilist Academy, she suffered painfully from episodes of self-doubt. What if one of the other boxers studied her too closely, noticing the lack of whiskers on her chin, or the absence of an Adam's apple? What if the call of nature arrived while she was in the dressing room? What would she do then? How would she conceal her anatomical plumbing?

Worst of all, what if she couldn't hide her attraction to Dick Creevy? What would she do when the urge to rise on her tiptoes and offer her lips to his became unbearable?

Drawing in a deep breath, Dolly steadied her nerves. She had nothing to worry about, really. She could control herself; she was a rational, analytical, pragmatic woman. And if Creevy hadn't guessed she was a woman by now, he never would.

Tongue in cheek, Dick folded his arms across his chest and gave her a critical top-to-bottom appraisal. "You're not ill; are you, boy?"

With a gulp, she shook her head.

"You look a bit peaked, son. Haven't been chasing after round heels, have you?"

"Round heels?" Bewildered, Dolly shrugged her shoulders.

With a sigh of impatience, Dick said, "Good lord, you're not that naive, are you? It's loose women I'm talking about, or in your case, overgrown street urchins! You haven't taken up with a floozie, now, have you?"

Heat suffused Dolly's face. Was this the way men talked to one another? Words of indignation flew to the tip of her tongue, and she barely managed to bite them back. It wouldn't do to lecture Dick Creevy on manners or morals. Instead, she stammered out a negative response, half-amazed that Dick Creevy thought anyone as clumsy and coltish as she was capable of bedding a woman.

But her awkwardness irritated her, and her near misstep frightened her. She might have fooled Creevy temporarily, but if she didn't soon conquer her nervousness, and play her character far more convincingly than she had up till now, she'd never wheedle her way into the man's confidence.

She had to forget who she was and abandon her old habits and mannerisms. She had to *be* Dahl Mohr, Dick Creevy's new pupil, the lad he'd taken to calling Doll Face. She had to train herself, not only to box, but to slip into the role of Doll Face as easily as she slipped into her drawstring exercise pants.

"No, sir, I haven't been chasing loose women."

"Not that there's anything wrong with *looking* at a pretty girl, mind you. I believe it is healthy for a grown man to indulge in a little bed sport now and again. But you're too young for the likes of that. Best you wait a few years before sampling the pleasures the opposite sex has to offer. Understand?"

"Yes, sir."

"Not that it's any of my business," muttered Dick, tousling her curls. "Forgive me if I've been too nosy. It's just that I don't want you to throw away your chances at being a good boxer by catching some dread social disease. There are some bad ones out there, you know. Some of them you can't get rid of."

Dolly's scalp tingled and her insides twisted. Even the man's most meaningless touch—a quick swipe at her unruly hair, a completely innocuous gesture meant to reassure a young man—wreaked havoc on her nervous system. How was she going to stand a long-term regimen of exercise and sparring lessons? How was she going to school herself to react like Doll Face, the teenage protégé, instead of Lady Dolly Baltmore, the love-starved widow?

Dick, his expression suddenly serious, reached for a braided length of hemp that hung from a peg on the wall. "Did you do as I told you? Did you practice jumping rope?"

"You told me to train at home, didn't you?" She caught the rope Dick tossed her. "Of course I did."

"Ten minutes, lad. Or you'll not be darkening my doorstep again."

Dolly started jumping, her feet tapping lightly on the wooden floor. After a few minutes, her breathing grew more shallow and her skin slicked with perspiration. After a few *more* minutes, her chest ached and her leg muscles burned. But she continued to jump for as long as she could. And she didn't quit until black spots were leaping before her eyes.

The rope slipped from her hands and her knees buckled. Dolly tried to stay upright, but nausea and dizziness challenged her resolve.

The floor tipped beneath her, and the walls swayed violently. Dimly, Dolly heard Dick's voice calling out, "Doll Face, Doll Face," but she couldn't form an answer. A swirling blackness sucked her down, swallowing her, enveloping her in senselessness. The last thing she remembered was a pair of strong arms hooked behind her knees and back.

When she awoke, she was in Dick Creevy's tiny office, stretched out on a cracked leather sofa, a damp cloth draped over her forehead, a woolen blanket tucked beneath her arms.

* * *

O'Callahan drew to a halt at the threshold of Dick's office. First he stared in openmouthed curiosity at the academy's newest and youngest student, lying prostrate on the sofa and looking for all the world as if he'd gotten the wind knocked out of him. Then he turned an equally puzzled look on Dick. "What the devil 'appened to the little beggar? Get his bell rung, did he?"

Dick sat behind his desk, fingers steepled beneath his chin. Motioning for O'Callahan to take a seat, he shook his head. "Hardly. Hasn't even been in the sparring ring yet, as a matter of fact. No, I'd say the lad is suffering from exhaustion. As a result of overtraining."

"Overtraining?" The older man's face wrinkled in a knowing grin. "Are you certain that's what he's been doin'? Lads like him start early, you know. If he's been on his own for a while, without a mama to watch over him, there's no telling what kind of trouble he's gotten himself into. I thought he looked a trifle pale meself when I saw him earlier."

"So did I. But I gave him the mildest warning possible about the dangers of cavorting with unclean women, and he actually *blushed*. No, Cal, he's an innocent thing, too young to dally with women and too stupid to know what he's missing."

"Bless his wee heart." O'Callahan's voice dripped with sarcasm.

"Keep your voice down, will you? He obviously needs some rest."

"Am I supposed to whisper the news to you, then?"

"What news?"

"The Viking's agent has suggested a certain date, one month from now. The letter came in this morning's post."

Dick didn't hesitate. "Write back. I accept."

O'Callahan's lips thinned. The old man had already yelled and argued, and done everything he could to dissuade Dick from accepting the Viking's invitation to box. Dick's decision was intractable, however. Recognizing defeat, O'Callahan sighed. "You're a fool, you know that, don't you?"

"I can do without your recriminations, Cal. It's bad enough that every boxer in town wants to beat me to a pulp. I don't need you to pound on me, too."

"It ain't Eric the Viking who is beating you, son. You're beating yourself up, if you ask me, and you're doin' a pretty damn good job of it, too."

Resentment sluiced through Dick's veins. He didn't like being forced to confront his demons. Balling his hands into fists on the arms of his chair, he shot his longtime friend a look of warning. "I'm in no mood for sermons today, Cal."

"Do you think that fighting Eric the Viking is going to make up for what happened to Lord Baltmore last year? Will gettin' your face pummeled to mincemeat make you feel better about what Kitty Desmond did to you?"

"I don't mind the pain," Dick ground out. "At least it makes me forget everything else. And at times it's the only thing that makes me feel alive."

"I've know you a long time, Dick. Before Kitty Desmond came along and broke your heart. Before that scoundrel you called a best friend betrayed you and nearly got you killed. You've been angry at every woman in the world since Kitty ran off with that rapscallion, and I can't say I blame you."

"That's enough, Cal."

"I'm not finished! Been holding my tongue for years, now, as if I was wearin' some sort of scold's bridle. But it's time I tell you what I think, Dick. And it's time you listen."

"I'm not listening, Cal." Dick turned his head, effectively dismissing O'Callahan by refusing to look at him.

"To the devil with you, then. I just hope that if Eric the Viking lands a lethal blow to your head, you die a quick, merciful death."

"Like the one Lord Baltmore died?"

" 'Twasn't your fault," replied O'Callahan, his voice weary with resignation. He stood, and after a brief hesitation, left the room.

Dick remained seated, his heart galloping, his eyes burning with unshed tears. O'Callahan was right, of course, about many things. Dick was angry, all right, and he had been ever since Kitty Desmond had run off with Rafe O'Shea. But Cal was dead wrong about one thing. Dick wasn't angry at every woman in the world. Dick was angry at himself.

Were he not such a fool, Kitty would still be alive today, and so would her child, *their* child.

But he *was* a fool, and it was his reckless act of jealousy that had resulted in her death. Kitty's death, her *murder,* really, destroyed the man Dick Creevy had once been. It turned him into a fighting machine, an unfeeling creature with a limitless endurance for pain, a *monster.*

Dropping his face in his hands, he exhaled a sigh of despair. Had he any doubts about his own wretched character, the death of Lord Boyle Baltmore a year earlier erased them. The unsuspecting man climbed into the ring with Dick Creevy on a bet. Twenty minutes later, he was dead. And though no one—not the police, not the aristocracy, not even the sporting set—blamed him for Baltmore's death, Dick couldn't think of the man's lifeless body without feeling ill.

Standing, he rolled his shoulders, trying to unknot the kinks in his muscles. He needed to get inside the ring; he needed to don his gloves and go a few rounds with one of the bruisers in the gymnasium. He needed to hit something, someone. He needed an outlet for his anger.

Most of all, Dick Creevy needed to feel something other than the pain that had been clawing at his heart for years.

Dolly listened quietly, afraid to move a finger or turn her head, lest Dick and O'Callahan take notice of her. But they hadn't bothered to check on her state of consciousness, and so she laid very still and held her breath and heard the entire conversation.

As Dick moved around his desk, Dolly removed the damp cloth from her forehead, and looked at him.

He drew up short beside the sofa. "How long have you been awake?"

"Long enough to hear you say you're going to fight Eric the Viking."

"Eavesdropping on a man's conversation with his trainer isn't wise, lad. Next time you find yourself in that position, I strongly suggest you announce yourself."

"You knew I was here." Prostrate beneath Dick Creevy's stare, Dolly felt vulnerable and exposed.

Thankfully, he was too annoyed with her to take notice of her mottled neck. "Yes, but you were as senseless as a doornail when I laid you out on that sofa."

She swung her feet over the side of the sofa and sat up. "Here. Thanks for the rag."

His voice softened. "You're welcome. Feeling better?"

"You shouldn't fight the Viking, you know." Once she'd blurted out those first words, Dolly couldn't stop. Not even when Dick's eyes snapped and his lips pressed together in a straight line. "O'Callahan's right! You'll get yourself killed, and for what? It's not worth it, Mr. Creevy. Please reconsider!"

"Why the devil are you so concerned about my welfare?" Creevy growled.

"Why wouldn't I be? You promised to teach me boxing, didn't you? You took me as a pupil against your better judgment. I'm grateful for that, Mr. Creevy, truly I am."

"You're paying your way. I haven't done you any favors."

"You don't need my money. You're teaching me because you know I want to learn, and because you were too kind to turn me away. You don't know it, Mr. Creevy, or perhaps you don't want to admit it, but you're a generous man. A kind man. You needn't fight the Viking to prove your mettle. You needn't subject yourself to pain in order to atone for your—"

"That's enough!" Dick slammed one fist into the palm of his open hand. "In the military, that sort of nonsense is called insubordination. I'd have you dancing in the wind if I were your commanding officer and you spoke to me that way."

Cold fear gripped Dolly's bones. "I-I'm sorry, sir."

"I don't give a damn if you're sorry," the big man seethed, leaning forward, his neck muscles taut. "Just don't ever let it happen again."

Gripping the edge of the sofa, Dolly nodded. Friction

hung in the air of Dick Creevy's office long after he'd left. Sitting alone, fearful even to stand and exit, Dolly at length gave in to a sob. In a flash, her pretense crumbled. She'd barely worked her way into Dick's inner sanctum and already she'd committed a grave error in judgment. She'd dropped her mask, and reacted to the man as a woman. She'd spoken her mind and revealed what was in her heart.

But in doing so, she'd angered him and pushed him farther away from her. Instead of nearing her goal—that of learning what led up to Lord Baltmore's death— she'd distanced herself from the one man who could answer her questions. She'd be lucky if Mr. Creevy didn't summarily dismiss Doll Face Mohr from the pugilist academy without further discussion. She—or rather, he—deserved to be banished from Dick Creevy's sight.

Creevy was right; eavesdropping on the man's conversation with O'Callahan was dreadfully rude.

As she made her way to the men's dressing rooms, boldly meeting the gazes of a half-dozen totally naked men, Dolly realized her day hadn't been a total loss. She'd learned one thing about the death of her husband: Dick Creevy felt enormously guilty about it.

The boy got stronger. After two weeks, he jumped rope for thirty minutes without rest. He did one hundred sit-ups without stopping. He caught the weighted leather ball that Dick threw to him without stumbling. He was the most determined, dedicated pupil that the pugilist academy had ever seen.

The other students, as well as the professional boxers who trained at Creevy's gym, noticed the slender blond lad. Following Creevy's lead, they called him Doll Face. Given the boy's pluck and toughness, the nickname was not an insult but rather a term of masculine endearment.

The same thickly muscled men who pounded one another's faces in the sparring ring had lifted their brows when they first spied the boy panting through his exercise regimen. But after a few weeks of watching the boy, they nudged one another's sides and said, "Aye, and that little Doll Face is a feisty one, ain't he? If he keeps it up, he could be the featherweight champion of Dublin, maybe all of Ireland!"

All this, and Dahl Mohr had yet to set foot in the ring.

Arms crossed over his chest, Dick watched the boy drop to the gym floor, his nose to the well-worn wood. Without complaint, the boy pushed his body off the floor, then lowered it, his arms working like pistons in one of those newfangled steam engines.

He did push-ups for ten minutes, until sweat plastered his thin cotton shirt to his back.

"That's enough, Doll Face."

The boy did two more before he stopped. For an instant, his body collapsed to the floor. Then he shoved off and leaped to his feet, his face aglow, his skin slick and rosy.

Beads of perspiration dotted the boy's lip.

An amazingly feminine upper lip.

With a shiver, Creevy tore his gaze off Doll Face. He stared, instead, at the dust motes dancing in the sunlight that streamed through the upper windows of the gymnasium. And he wondered if he'd lost his mind. Or if too many weeks without the comfort of a woman had affected his sexual yearnings.

There was something *different* about that boy, that

was certain. Dick couldn't put his finger on it, but there was something about Doll Face that wasn't quite *normal*. Perhaps it was the kid's enthusiasm for the sport of boxing, or his willingness to punish his body with a brutal regimen of exercise. Perhaps it was the boy's infectious grin or easy laugh. Perhaps it was the kindness so evident in Dahl Mohr's pleasant, almost girlish voice.

"Care to join me for a beer?" Dick asked him one evening after they'd finished a particularly grueling session.

They crossed the nearly deserted gymnasium and headed toward the men's dressing room. Dahl wiped his freckled face with a towel and shrugged. The boy's eyelashes flickered—an amazingly girlish affectation, it seemed to Dick. Not for the first time, a vague suspicion concerning Dahl's gender entered his mind. But he quickly dismissed it; no woman could withstand the physical abuse Dahl Mohr had put himself through during the last week.

"Don't think I should, really."

Was that a blush that spread across the boy's face?

"Come now, you've got yourself overheated," Dick said. "A strong mug of lager will fortify you, put some wind back into your sails. We won't be long, just an hour or so. Got somewhere you need to be? I can hire a cab to take you home."

His suggestion had an unsettling effect on Dahl. But the boy acquiesced, agreeing to meet Dick outside the gymnasium on the street in ten minutes.

In the dressing room, Dahl disappeared behind a row of lockers and benches. Was there a reason the boy hid his body so effectively? Rinsing his sweaty body in the large communal basin, Dick wondered how the lad managed to shift from street clothes to training gear without showing his nakedness. Was the boy so backward that the sight of big, sweaty male bodies unnerved him?

Amused by his protégé's shyness, Dick took extra care in slicking back his thinning hair. Staring at his reflection in the small foggy mirror above the sink, he noticed the lately acquired wrinkles that bracketed his eyes. He was getting older, a fact much emphasized by Dahl Mohr's youthfulness. Perhaps that was why he enjoyed the boy's presence, he mused. Perhaps there was a paternal instinct at work here, a desire to teach someone younger everything he knew, to pass on the legacy of his knowledge, to be something more than just a lonely old man.

Poppycock! He knew he was deluding himself. He had no paternal instincts. He'd proven as much when he recklessly gave chase to Kitty Desmond, causing the carriage accident that took her life—and that of his child's.

Rolling his shoulders beneath an elegantly cut black serge jacket, Dick strode the length of the gymnasium floor. Outside, he found his favorite pupil nervously pacing the edge of the street, cap pulled low over his eyes, hands stuffed in pockets.

Gripping the boy's shoulder, Dick guided him across the street. Inside the darkened pub, they sat at Dick's favorite table. A wave and a wink to the redheaded tap girl produced an instant round of beer. "They've got a decent lamb stew here, Dahl."

Hesitating, the boy looked out from beneath the brim of his cap.

"Go ahead, it'll put some meat on your bones."

"All right, then." Dahl smiled bashfully at the bosomy serving girl.

"Don't you want to take off your cap?" Dick asked, when the girl had placed two bowls of thick, fragrant stew in front of them.

Reluctantly, the boy bared his golden curls. Then he dipped his spoon into his bowl and drew it to his lips. Puckering, he gently blew the steaming lamb and potatoes.

"Too hot?" Dick's table manners were hardly uncivilized. He was as comfortable dining on smoked salmon and caviar with aristocrats as he was supping on Dublin coddle and ale with his fellow boxers. But he couldn't help noticing Dahl's extended pinkie finger. Suddenly, the young boy resembled a dowager countess sipping tea.

Dahl's eyes rounded. He met Dick's gaze, and looking embarrassed, quickly dispensed with the ritual of blowing on his food. Instead, he tucked into his food and ate greedily, as if he hadn't filled his stomach in a fortnight.

Savoring his stew while carefully watching his companion, Dick concluded the boy suffered from a lack of male influence. At length, he said, "Tell me, Doll Face, was your father around much when you were growing up in Dublin?"

The question seemed to take the boy by surprise. "No, sir. Not really. As a matter of fact, I didn't really know my father."

"I suspected as much." Ignoring the boy's questioning look, Dick probed a bit further. "Have any brothers, do you?"

"None, sir. Just my sister. The one I told you about."

"Ah, yes. Well, I'm sorry about her."

"That's why I came to Dublin, sir. That's why I'm here."

"Looking for revenge, are you?"

Dahl's lashes flickered. "I suppose you could say so."

"There's no comfort in revenge, Dahl. Though I suppose you'll have to learn that lesson on your own. I can teach you what to do with your fists. You alone must choose your battles."

"You're not really going to fight Eric the Viking, are you?"

Tension shot through Dick's gut. "You're not too young to understand the value of knowing when to speak and when to keep quiet, Dahl. Whatever you heard in my office is none of your business. Forget it."

"If O'Callahan thinks it's too dangerous, why would you?"

"We were discussing your education as a fighter, not mine."

"The Viking's nearly twice your size. He's younger and bigger, and if what I've heard the fellows in the gym say is true, he's a killer. He fights dirty. You'll never win."

Dick's fingers tightened around his beer mug. "Don't worry about it."

"But I do." The boy's expression was earnest, his tone pitiful. "You could get hurt."

"So what?" Dick threw back his head and drained the rest of his beer. Thunking the glass on the table, he growled, "What difference would it make to anyone if I did get my head knocked off? Don't you understand anything, kid? I've got no family, no children, no wife! And no hope of ever having any! The Viking can put me out of my misery, for all I care! Outside the ring, my life is—"

He stopped, clamping his lips shut, staring in horror

at the bewildered look on Dahl's face. The boy had provoked him with his caring, meddlesome attitude. Dick didn't want to be mollycoddled; he didn't need it. The child's nagging was a nuisance. But Dick hadn't any cause to snarl. His outburst was completely out of line.

Ordinarily, Dick would have clamped a lid on his feelings and allowed them to simmer. His emotions came to a boil only when he was in the ring, hammering another man's body or being pounded by some murderous bruiser. That was the only time Dick felt alive. Fighting was the only thing that made Dick's life palatable—and even then, it was *barely* so.

"I just wouldn't want you to get hurt," the boy said softly.

"You'd find another teacher."

"I want *you* to teach me how to fight. Another teacher won't do, I'm afraid."

A lump formed in Dick's throat. He couldn't remember the last time anyone had depended upon him for anything other than a salary or a handout. His own daughter hadn't grown old enough to stare at him so adoringly, much less ask for riding lessons or advice regarding the opposite sex. And Kitty Desmond certainly never sought his counsel.

So why did this young freckle-faced lad need his tutorship so badly? Why did it matter to Doll Face Mohr whether Dick Creevy lived or died?

"Well"—Dick cleared his throat—"enough of that."

"Well"—Doll Face hoisted his tankard—"if you're determined to fight the Viking, you'd best start training now. I mean, really training. I'll help you."

A bark of laughter escaped Dick's lips. "Oh, you will, will you?"

"I don't mean I'll train you; you've got O'Callahan for that. But I'll work with you. Jump rope with you. Watch you work in the ring. When you get tired, I'll urge you on. When your muscles hurt, I'll rub that evil-smelling ointment on them."

"Thanks, but I've got Cal for that."

"Cal's getting old. You need someone younger. You need me."

"I don't need anyone," Dick replied, a bit more tartly than he'd intended.

"You're an island, are you? Well, we'll see about that."

Dick ducked his head and ate the rest of his stew, wiping the bottom of his soup plate with a piece of soda bread to get the last drop of broth. When he was finished, he laid his spoon beside his plate and sat back, squaring his aching shoulders, stretching his biceps. A massage would feel good, now that Doll Face mentioned it. But why did the boy's suggestion seem so provocative?

Because he is staring at me the way a woman stares at a man.

Shock registered in Dick's body, clutching at his heart and twisting his gut. His suspicions could be ignored no longer. Doll Face Mohr was infatuated with him.

Well, he thought, suppressing his phobic reaction, that sort of thing wasn't entirely unheard of, even in the hyperbolically masculine world of boxing.

But it certainly wasn't something Dick wished to encourage. His own inclinations leaned strongly in the direction of the female gender. He thought he should make that clear, lest there be any misunderstanding between himself and this impressionable youth. The boy would undoubtedly grow out of this silly, ill-fated crush. In a few weeks' time, he'd meet a pretty girl and lose his heart, and Dick Creevy would be nothing more to him than a middle-aged drill sergeant with a death wish.

"Look, Doll Face, er, I mean Dahl. I don't mean to be rude, but I'm perfectly capable of taking care of myself. And Cal is perfectly capable of training me, regardless of his feelings concerning this fight. The Viking isn't the first man I've ever squared off with, you know."

"This fight is different. You know it, and Cal knows it. And I feel it"—the boy tapped his chest—"in here."

"You *feel* it." Dick's gaze lit on Dahl's flat chest. Was it his imagination, or did there appear to be two gentle mounds . . . *No!* He truly was losing his mind. "Well, then, you're free to hang around the gymnasium as much as you like. But don't expect me to spend every waking minute of my day with you. I've got other responsibilities, understand."

Dahl's face lit. "It's settled, then."

"What's that?"

"We'll train together."

Dick nearly groaned. "Did you hear what I just said?"

But the boy didn't stay to listen. Cramming his cap atop his head, he stood. Awkwardly, he thrust his hand at Dick, as if the two were solemnly sealing a deal.

Gripping the lad's hand, Dick was struck by the delicacy of his fingers. "Fish bones," he said, giving his student an extra squeeze.

Dahl yanked back his hand, but his smile never wavered. "Tomorrow, then. I'll see you bright and early."

"Tomorrow," Dick replied, signaling for another beer.
Tomorrow.

He couldn't remember when he'd last looked forward
to there being another tomorrow.

Six

Nor could he cease thinking about Doll Face Mohr. In the two weeks that followed, Dick developed what could only be described as a mild obsession with his pupil. He attributed it to the fact that he'd never before tutored such a determined, if not talented, pupil.

Doll Face was indefatigable, training tirelessly, ignoring sore muscles and eschewing the comforting massages offered in the men's dressing room. The lad soaked up knowledge like a sponge, staying long after his lessons were over to watch the other fighters, or to discuss the finer points of boxing strategy, such as whether a man succumbed more quickly to head or body blows.

As a result of the boy's enthusiasm, Dick trained harder, too. His training sessions with Doll Face started earlier and ended later every day. Their conversations grew more intimate. They talked about everything from boxing to politics to beer. They laughed, mostly at themselves, sometimes at the politicians of the day, and they pushed their bodies to the physical limit. Dick found himself missing Doll Face when the lad was gone, and ignoring everyone else, especially O'Callahan, when he was near.

He truly was crazy. He told himself that often during

this period. Doll Face was just a kid, a punk, a scamp who'd been bullied by thugs and didn't want to feel powerless ever again. His adolescent infatuation with his boxing coach was innocuous, and perhaps, if Dick were forced to admit it, even a little flattering. As a matter of honor, Dick pointedly ignored the boy's adoring looks and flickering lashes.

What he couldn't ignore was the fact that Dahl's pale limbs grew more taut by the day. The boy's biceps grew firmer and his shoulders broader. His endurance increased exponentially. He had the heart of a lion.

Nevertheless, Dahl's overall figure retained an oddly feminine shape. To his great relief, Dick wasn't the only one who thought so. The men who had dubbed the lad Doll Face developed a collective affection for him. Their opinions about his slender waist and girlish voice evolved into open, good-natured teasing. Doll Face became something of a mascot at the academy. His ready smile and puckish attitude won many friends, chief among them, the gruff O'Callahan.

One night, after the two men had shared an exceptionally brutal workout, Dick slapped the back of his own neck and kneaded the thick cord of muscles beneath his fingers.

"Sore muscles, eh?" the boy asked. "Is your neck stiff, Mr. Creevy? Would you like me to rub it?"

Averting his eyes, Dick could almost believe he'd heard the voice of a young woman. But when he looked at Dahl Mohr, he saw a nearly flat chest and thin hips, a face unadorned by lip rouge or powder, close-cropped hair . . . and the guarded expression of a youthful boy.

"Did I say something wrong?"

Stunned by the thoughts whirling in his head, Dick shook his head. "I'm sorry. What *did* you say?"

"I said, would you like for me to rub your neck? It's late, sir, and the man who does it in the dressing room has gone home."

Dick considered the invitation.

Then quickly and curtly declined. "No."

"Ready to go some more, then? Ready to let me in the ring with you?"

Dick stared at him. *Ready to let me in the ring with you?* Did the question have a double meaning? Or was Dick reading far too much into the boy's words?

He stared full into the boy's guileless face.

Nothing in Dahl's unblinking stare suggested weakness. Nothing in his behavior connoted foppery. In fact, there was nothing frilly, feminine, or effete about the young man. Doll Face Mohr was itching to get into the ring to spar, something that Dick had not yet permitted, something only a man would want to do.

Yet there was something so faintly alluring about the lad that Dick couldn't help wondering what was beneath the boy's knickers. At the same time, Dick wondered if he had fallen prey to some vile form of sexual illness. His imaginings were far-fetched and dangerous. He should loathe himself for what he was thinking. He should be disgusted with himself.

But at that precise moment, as the shadows lengthened on the gymnasium floor, he wasn't. He was merely disturbed and—

"Mr. Creevy? Are you all right?"

Curious. His body's needs were manifest. A heaviness settled in Dick's loins.

"A fighter must get accustomed to sore muscles," he replied at length, eager to rid his mind of his unhealthy thoughts.

With a shudder, he suddenly thought of Mrs. Bunratty, Dublin's premier madam. He'd do well to visit Mrs. Bunratty's establishment as soon as it was practical. Surely a romp in the sack with a warm, willing woman would cure this restlessness that had overcome him in these last few weeks. It was worth a try. He'd do anything to rid himself of the deviant speculations that were plaguing him.

The boy's voice interrupted his musings. "Are you ready to go a round with me, then, Mr. Creevy?"

Startled, Dick let go a chuckle. *Get in the ring with this porcelain-skinned child? Take a punch at Doll Face?* Was the lad as crazy as he?

"What's so funny?" Dahl asked.

Stifling his amusement, Dick said, "Sure, I'm ready, laddie. But you aren't."

Doll Face propped his hands on his hips. "That's not true! I'm stronger than I've ever been! I've done everything you've told me, and you haven't heard a peep out of me about it. I don't see the other men working this hard. Look at that man! He is in far worse shape than I am, and he's in the sparring ring!"

"Getting his face trampled, too," Dick said, glancing at the overweight man in the boxing arena. It wasn't unusual for bored aristocrats to fancy they'd like to take up the sport of pugilism. A round or two of sparring with a professional, however, usually dampened their ardor.

"If he gets his nose broken, that's his business, isn't it?" the boy pressed.

Reluctantly, Dick nodded.

"That's what he's paying for, isn't it—to get in the ring and learn to fight?"

"That man's not—" Dick stopped short of saying what he felt. *That man is not you, Doll Face. That man doesn't have the features of a China doll.* "That's old Mr. Sullivan, a banker who sits behind a desk all day. He'd pay a fortune for the privilege of having another man swing a fist at him."

"Maybe I haven't paid as much as Mr. Sullivan, but I've paid what you asked. And I have just as much right to get in the sparring ring as he does, Mr. Creevy. You can't deny me!"

"It's too early. You haven't trained long enough. Maybe next week."

Green eyes flashed. Doll Face's bottom lip swelled in a decidedly unmasculine fashion. It was a pout more appropriate to a sullen, manipulative little minx than an angry young man. An unbidden heat swept over Dick's body. Damn, but he needed a woman—as soon as possible!

"I want to fight, sir! That's why I'm here!"

"All right, then. Hit me," Dick offered, holding his arms away from his body.

Not surprisingly, Doll Face's eyes widened and his jaw fell slack. "Did you say—"

"You heard me. I said, hit me!"

Glancing at the sparring ring, Doll Face stammered, "Bare-knuckled? Without gloves to soften the blow?"

"I can take it." The kid didn't have enough strength in his entire body to injure Dick Creevy. Suppressing a smile, he patted his stomach. "Come on, Doll Face. If you want to get in the sparring ring with me, then show me what you've got. Hit me. As hard as you can!"

The boy's mouth formed a little *O*. His cinnamon-dusted cheeks darkened. His shoulders rose and fell with the rhythm of his breathing. His hands balled into fists.

Retreating a step, Dahl looked for a moment as if

he were going to back off Dick's challenge. But, then, his eyes glowed with ferocity, and as Dick watched, his expression turned to stone.

They held each other's gaze. A current of awareness passed between them, a shared sensation of physical tension. Friction, as palpable as the thudding in Dick's chest, weighted the air.

Holding his breath, standing as still as a statue, Dick silently urged the boy to lash out. He wanted to feel the youth's weight crushing into him. He wanted to absorb the brunt of that seething, pent-up anger. He stretched out his arms and gave a nod, inviting Doll Face to strike.

Head lowered, the boy stepped into the punch. His arm shot out and his fist drove like a battering ram into the wall of Dick's abdominal muscles. Then he reared back, eyes blinking wider than ever, bottom lip trembling.

"Oh, God," the boy breathed. "I didn't mean to hurt—"

"You didn't." Dick smiled. Exhaling, he lowered his arms. "Though I must admit I am surprised at the strength of that blow. That's a good arm you've got there. Maybe you will be a boxer after all. Someday."

"You mean I didn't hurt you at all? My punch was nothing more to you than an annoying swat on your belly?"

"I wouldn't say that. I'll be feeling a bruised tummy before the day is over."

"But I hit you as hard as I could!"

"Gave it your all, did you?"

"Yes!" The boy looked as if he were about to cry.

Dick reach out and cuffed Dahl's neck. "That's all anyone can ask of himself, then, isn't it? Eh? Don't feel bad, Doll Face. Not every man is a born athlete. You'll get stronger. You've just got to work harder."

Emotion pinched Dahl's features. "I will work harder," he said through gritted teeth. "And I'll show you! I'll show you how tough I really am!"

Dick knew exactly how the boy felt. Dahl had screwed up the courage to hit another man as hard as he could, and now he was flooded with relief, regret, exhilaration, and exhaustion. That blow, for Doll Face, at least, had been a release of tension and anger. But the ineffectiveness of his strike was an equally devastating attack on his manhood, his sense of power. Now, he struggled with the knowledge that his power was limited, that there would always be someone stronger than he, someone who could fell him with one punch, someone unbeatable.

The boy's frustration was barely contained. His jaw clenched, and his limbs went as stiff and rigid as boards.

"Lesson's over for today." Dick pivoted. He had to get away from Doll Face, not just to escape the boy's overwhelming emotions, but also to hide the grimace that clawed at his lips.

Walking toward his office, arms swinging easily at his sides, he hoped and prayed the afternoon's meal would not make a reappearance. His gut felt like a runaway buggy had slammed into it. Streaks of pain shot through his chest and wrapped around his ribs. He'd never admit it to Doll Face, or to anyone else for that matter, but the boy's blow had been amazingly well placed and painfully hard. For a lightweight, Dahl Mohr packed a powerful punch.

Turning into his private quarters, Dick released a sigh of anguish. If a boy named Doll Face could hurt him that badly, what sort of devastation would Eric the Viking wreak on his middle-aged, out-of-shape body?

Mrs. Bunratty had taken an inordinate amount of time in dressing. So few of her gowns were suitable for daytime; most of them boasted deeply low-cut bodices, impractical bustles, and enough crinoline for a man to swim in.

At first she'd felt a twinge of irritation when she opened the vellum envelope and read Creevy's request. Why could he not attend her establishment like other men? Why was it so important that he not be seen frequenting a house of ill repute?

But in the end, after considering the generosity he'd shown her and several of her girls over the years, she penned a quick note accepting his invitation. She liked and respected Dick Creevy. The fact that she had to call upon him at his boxing studio should have been a minor inconvenience.

And it would have been—minor, that is—were it not for the dearth of decent, conservatively cut gowns in Mrs. Bunratty's wardrobe.

It took her maids three hours to get her dressed. The carriage ride to the wrong side of Dublin, and the river stench that greeted her when she got there, was unpleasant. The sight of all those sweaty half-nude male bodies filling an equally sweaty-smelling gymnasium had nearly sickened her. Mrs. Bunratty, for all her sexual worldliness, didn't like to see naked men. And she didn't like to set foot outside her house. House calls were for doctors, she told herself, entering Creevy's office. Not for true professionals, such as herself.

Clad in a green-and-white striped morning gown, a

cap with ostrich feathers looming above her head, and a bustle the size of a small poodle, Mrs. Bunratty stood on the opposite side of Dick Creevy's desk. Despite her immunity to masculine admiration, which she supposed was a hazard of her occupation, Creevy's crooked smile sent a faint wave of heat through her body.

He stood and reached across his desk, taking her gloved hands in his. "Would you care to sit?"

"I cannot," she replied honestly. "If I do, my underskirts will flip me head over heels."

"Never have understood the need for all that crinoline." Dick skirted the edge of his desk and stood beside her. "Thank you for coming."

"I wouldn't venture to these parts for anyone else, I can assure you."

The gentleman boxer didn't mince words. "I would like to retain your services, Mrs. Bunratty. I am very keen on meeting a woman, a certain kind of woman."

"I'll do whatever I can, Mr. Creevy." Mrs. Bunratty's curiosity was piqued. Tilting her head, she studied Dick Creevy, recalling the first time he had visited her establishment, not many months after the tragic death of his young wife and child. Few people knew the details of that sordid affair, but during the past five years, Mrs. Bunratty had learned much about Dick Creevy. The odd thing was, the more she got to know him, the more enigmatic he became.

This sudden request for a certain kind of woman, for example, was totally out of character. "It isn't like you, Dick. Is there something you would like to tell me?"

He actually blushed. "It sounds so foolish, I can hardly bring myself to explain. I met someone—"

"Then why trouble with one of my girls? I had always hoped you would meet a nice woman, Dick. You need to get on with your life. It's been five years now, after all."

"You don't understand," he said, twisting his fingers. "This, ah, person, is unavailable to me."

"Married, eh?"

With a shrug, Dick said, "Let's leave it at that, shall we? Suffice it to say, I can't get this person off my mind. It's become somewhat of an obsession, an unhealthy one, I'm afraid."

"Dear boy, you haven't gone and fallen in love with some actress, have you?"

"No."

"The mistress of a politician?"

"God, no."

"A politician?"

His chuckle did nothing to conceal his unease. Mrs. Bunratty, by the same token, could barely disguise her curiosity. She'd never known Dick to harbor any deviant sexual desires; indeed, the women he slept with clamored to sleep with him again. There was never any need to coax or cajole one of her girls into accepting an invitation to Dick Creevy's bed. From what Mrs. Bunratty had been told, the man was as much a gentleman in bed as out. And as much an athlete, too.

Dipping his head, he averted his eyes. "I'll understand if my request disgusts you."

"Darling, I've heard everything. No need to be so harsh on yourself. Come on, now. Tell me what it is you want."

A moment flowed by like syrup, while Dick Creevy rubbed his hands and turned red. At length, he took a deep breath and looked up. "I want a small woman, about this tall." Standing, he held his hand at shoulder level.

"Easily done."

"With blond hair."

Mrs. Bunratty rolled her gaze to the ceiling. "Dear boy, try to find me one without blond hair."

"Short, curly blond hair, cropped like . . . well, like a lad's."

Mrs. Bunratty fell silent, considering.

Dick, his expression slightly feverish, continued. "Green eyes, freckles, and small breasts."

Why not ask for a boy? Mrs. Bunratty started to say. Instead, she clamped her lips shut. It didn't take a genius to see that Dick's desires were at odds with his own notions of what was proper or normal. But *normal* was not something Mrs. Bunratty concerned herself with, much less aspired to. *Normal,* according to her, was a concept as divisive as religion. If Dick Creevy wanted a woman who looked like a blond boy, she would do everything she could to furnish him one.

"This is an extremely tall order."

"If it is impossible—"

"Nothing is impossible, Dick." She'd scourge the city of Dublin if she had to. "But it will require a few days. Can you wait until Saturday?"

"Yes, yes." He squeezed her hands and kissed her cheek. "If anyone were to know about this—"

She held her finger to his lips. "I am offended that you would voice even a doubt as to my discretion. No one shall ever know, dear, except you and me and the girl I choose for you. Where would you like me to send her, by the way?"

"To my home," Dick said. "Have her there at midnight, if you please. And thank you."

"No. Thank you." Mrs. Bunratty deftly palmed the bills that Dick pressed into her hands. Then she turned

Cindy Harris

and swept from the office, striding through the gymnasium and out onto the street where her carriage awaited. Climbing in, she was relieved to be departing Dick Creevy's neighborhood. But her brow was furrowed as she mentally flashed on the faces of the girls who worked for her. Not a single one of them was suitable to satisfy Dick Creevy's fantasy. She really would have to search the crevices of Dublin to find the sort of woman he wanted in his bed.

Pushing back against the plush leather squabs, she smiled. Some clients were more challenging than others. That was what made her occupation so interesting. And the fact that Mrs. Bunratty had never disappointed any of the men who depended on her, or betrayed a single one of their confidences, was what made her the best purveyor of prostitution in all of Ireland, perhaps in the entire British Kingdom.

Dolly pushed off the cold brick wall just as Mrs. Bunratty and Dick Creevy ended their conversation. Flying down the hallway, she made it into the gymnasium just seconds ahead of the woman dressed in green-and-white stripes. Lazily throwing her jump rope over her head, she skipped the width of the gymnasium, her heart pounding a tattoo that was violently out of proportion to the actual work her muscles were performing.

Had she heard correctly? Was her mind playing tricks on her, or had Dick Creevy just asked this brisk, businesslike woman to procure him a woman who looked just like Doll Face?

It was impossible! Dick Creevy thought she was a

boy. Yet, he wanted to make love to a woman who . . . who looked like a boy.

Bewildered, Dolly finished her workout, dressed hurriedly, then hustled home as quickly as she could. She couldn't bear to be around Dick another moment. Aware now of his unusual predilection, she couldn't face him. His craving embarrassed her. She couldn't risk running into him, couldn't afford to attempt a conversation with him. If she did, her alter ego would vanish like a puff of smoke. If she had to look into his eyes, she'd melt with emotion.

An emotion she couldn't identify.

Rushing up the stairs to her bedchamber, she thought perhaps Lady Kilgarren had been right to question her sanity. Dolly hated Dick Creevy. He had killed her husband and robbed her of the scant security she'd had in life. He was the source of her anger and unhappiness.

Why, then, had she wandered toward his office in the first place? Her lesson had been over a half hour before. There was no reason for her to be loitering about the gymnasium other than to chance another casual meeting with him. In all honesty, that was precisely why she hadn't left immediately after he'd dismissed her. She hadn't wanted to part company with him, truth be known. It was as if some invisible force drew her to him, compelled her to seek him out.

Stripping off her damp sweater and pants, she stood in front of the mirror. Slowly, she unwound the muslin strips that bound her breasts. Stark naked, she stared at her reflection, wondering if Dick Creevy would find pleasure in her tiny breasts, her flat belly, the golden down at the juncture of her legs.

A shiver rippled across her skin. She was what the gentleman boxer wanted. She inspired his fantasy.

And unless her instincts had gone completely amok, Mrs. Bunratty would soon be searching high and low for a girl who looked precisely like Doll Face Mohr's twin sister.

A slow, wicked smile curved on Dolly's lips as she ran her hands down her stomach, caressed the gentle curves of her hips, and sinuously planed her own well-muscled thighs.

What better way to wreak absolute revenge on Dick Creevy than to give him what he wanted?

Seven

The women sat in Lady Dolly's sitting room, sipping tea, talking, and appraising one another with wary eyes. They were four unmarried ladies with nothing in common except their recent moves to Fontjoy Square. Had Dolly not been so preoccupied with thoughts of Dick Creevy and the conundrum associated with Mrs. Bunratty's establishment, she might have been more curious as to her neighbors' backgrounds. As it was, she left it to Lady Kilgarren, with her forward ways and probing questions, to ferret out the truth of the situation.

"Tell me, Mrs. Sinclair, how long have you been in mourning?" Lady Kilgarren asked.

Mrs. Rose Sinclair was a raven-haired woman with violet-colored eyes that could only be described as exotic. Sooty lashes fanned her cheeks as she smiled inscrutably at Lady Kilgarren. "Nine months, my lady. I must admit, I am terribly eager to rid myself of these widow's weeds."

"But black suits you, Mrs. Sinclair," chimed in Miss Millicent Hyde. The young lady, barely old enough to be out of the schoolroom, laughed nervously. Her hands trembled as she sipped her tea, and her gaze shot about the room like a frightened bat.

Lady Kilgarren turned her guileless blue gaze on Miss Hyde. "I hope you won't think me too brazen, dear, but why on earth is such a young, innocent thing such as yourself living alone? Why, it's hardly proper! Do tell me you are much older than you appear!"

A violent pinkening of Miss Hyde's cheeks accompanied her obvious discomfort. Large hazel eyes, as vulnerable as a doe's, blinked rapidly, while chestnut curls bobbed nervously at the sides of her head. "A little perhaps. But I'll have you know, Lady Kilgarren, that I am no green girl. I've more than a wee bit of experience beneath my belt, if you understand my meaning."

"I think I do." Lady Kilgarren cast a meaningful glance in Dolly's direction.

Mrs. Sinclair laid a maternal hand on Miss Hyde's knee. "No need to get overset, Millicent. Nor is there any need to confess your sins. We're all of us in the same boat, or so it seems."

"How so?" questioned Lady Kilgarren, not unkindly.

"We're all alone, without a man to protect us."

"I, for one, do not need a man," replied Lady Kilgarren. "A man is nothing more than a nuisance, an overlord who cares for nothing but his own happiness and the satisfaction of his needs."

Lady Sinclair's smile was somewhat sympathetic, or sad, Dolly wasn't certain. "Men are necessary creatures, though, are they not? Without men, there would be no children. Not that I have been blessed with any myself. But I do so adore the little angels."

"You do not like men, Lady Kilgarren?" Miss Millicent Hyde gaped, apparently astonished by the older woman's admission.

"I can only say that I have never met one who I believed I was capable of falling in love with."

"How sad," Dolly murmured.

But her words were drowned by Millicent's reedlike voice. "Sad? Why, I think that is tragic! Men are such strange and wonderful creatures! I wouldn't give a fig for a child."

Mrs. Sinclair smirked. "You are young, dear."

"You'll learn," inserted Lady Kilgarren. "Some man will come along and you'll fall head over heels in love with him, and he with you. Then you'll get married and discover you've been sold into slavery and that wonderful husband of yours, who owns you now, thanks to the dictates of God and Queen Victoria, will grow bored with you, or tired of your vapid patter.

"Perhaps he'll take a mistress—all the better for you, since he's never shown an ounce of interest in pleasing you in bed anyway—or perhaps he'll abandon you to your gilded cage, a summer home in Kent, full of servants and retainers and other distractions, like the sniveling children who ruined your figure and who will one day break your heart by marrying someone totally unsuitable and forgetting all about you. Maybe your wonderful husband will fritter his money away at the track or the gambling hells or at the boxing—"

"Enough!" Dolly's body tensed like a tightly coiled spring. Spilling hot tea on her lap, she pushed to the edge of her chair and met Lady Kilgarren's startled gaze. "Enough, Claire! I cannot tolerate any more of this unpleasant talk!"

"They can't all be that bad," said Miss Hyde.

No one spoke as Claire and Dolly stared at each other. Teacups rattled onto saucers, throats were cleared, and crinoline underskirts rustled with agitation.

Mrs. Sinclair's loud sigh was subject to interpretation. After a moment, she stood, drawing Miss Millicent to her feet, as well. "Thank you so much for your hospitality," she said to Dolly. "I do look forward to seeing you at Mr. Avondale's party next month."

Miss Millicent Hyde offered an embarrassed smile. "Yes. Thank you. And I am looking forward to Mr. Avondale's party, too. Do you suppose there will be an orchestra?"

"Undoubtedly," Mrs. Sinclair said, pulling the younger lady toward the parlor doors.

"Lovely! And do you think there will be very many eligible gentleman—" Miss Hyde's voice, fading down the hallway, cut off abruptly as if someone had clamped a hand over her lips.

At length, Lady Kilgarren stood and smoothed her pale blue skirts. "I do get carried away," she said softly.

"I overreacted," Dolly said, but she was unable to look her friend in the eye. A gust of emotion blew through her like a north wind, threatening to strip her of the self-reliant guise she hid behind. If Lady Kilgarren didn't leave soon, Dolly's weakness and fear would be exposed.

The floor creaked beneath Lady Kilgarren's departing footsteps. When she paused in the doorway, Dolly was tempted to call her back, to spill out her story, confide her deepest dreams and nightmares, explain why the lady's outburst had upset her so.

Instead, Dolly bit her lower lip and gulped back the sob burbling in her chest. She'd come this far without showing the world how frightened she was. She'd beaten the odds and survived a year of mournful destitution without asking anyone for charity, sympathy, or understanding. The only person she'd relied on was Ferghus, and for that she felt guilty. But she figured what little compensation he received from her was better than life as a mudlark, beggar, or criminal.

She wasn't the sort to whine or admit defeat. She wasn't going to do it now—despite the abject terror that clutched her heart each time she pictured herself in Dick Creevy's bed.

"Bring in the next one." Suppressing a yawn, Mrs. Bunratty looked down at her list and drew a heavy black line through the name of another girl. If she didn't find a prostitute willing to capitalize on her blond hair and slender hips in the next hour, Mrs. Bunratty was going to have to send Dick Creevy a post telling him his request could not be fulfilled.

She'd been at it for three mornings straight, and she was sick of the parade flouncing through her office. Not one of them fit the bill—which disgusted Mrs. Bunratty and made her wish she'd never agreed to furnish the woman Creevy had described. She'd taken a huge and troublesome risk by sending word through the underworld that she was looking for a certain type of girl. Nevertheless, she'd been as clear as Waterford crystal in defining her requirements; indeed, if Mrs. Bunratty had advertised her need any more exuberantly, the police would soon be knocking on her door.

She'd interviewed every prostitute in Dublin. If there was a woman who matched Creevy's description, surely she'd have shown up at Mrs. Bunratty's before now. With a glance at the big brass-encased clock on the mantel, Mrs. Bunratty wondered for the hundredth time why Dick Creevy wanted to make love to a woman who looked like a boy.

Footsteps padded lightly across the thick Axminster carpet. A servant pulled the office door shut, leaving Mrs. Bunratty alone with her prospect. The clock ticked loudly as the madam reviewed her paperwork. The tedium of her task had taken its toll on her manners. When she finally did look up, she nearly gasped.

On the opposite side of her desk stood a woman—or was it a girl?—with short golden curls and sparkling green eyes. Her muslin gown was dark blue, conservatively cut with white cuffs and a high, starched collar. Her freckled features were small and boyish. There was only one mystery surrounding the girl's appearance, and that was her figure. Tightly fitted at the waist, her skirt billowed out on layers of crinoline and whalebone hoops, obscuring the outline of her hips and legs.

Mrs. Bunratty, careful not to reveal her surprise and delight, schooled her features. "Turn around."

The girl slowly pivoted.

"Pull up your skirts," Mrs. Bunratty ordered.

Facing her, the girl arched her brows. Then, after the briefest of hesitations, she bent forward, grabbed the hem of her skirts and underskirts, and lifted them.

Her pantaloons, ruffled at the ankles, were thin and gauzy, barely skimming the lines of her hips and thighs. *Very slender hips and thighs,* Mrs. Bunratty noticed. Just the sort of boyish figure Mr. Creevy was looking for.

"How did you hear I was looking for someone like you?"

The girl dropped her skirts. "Heard it on the streets. Lor', everybody is talkin' about it."

"Are you working for anyone else at the present?"

"I'm on me own," the girl said, her melodious voice clipped by a lower-class brogue.

"For how long, if you don't mind me asking?"

"Since I was fourteen, and I'm eighteen now."

"That's a mighty fine gown for a girl working the streets. Hardly the sort of outfit most of my girls wear. What sort of men do you attract dressing like a school-teacher?"

"The sort who likes to sleep with schoolteachers. Anyway, it was given to me by one of them political reformers. A goody-two-shoes suffragist, if you know what I mean."

"Sure you didn't steal it?"

"I'm a prostitute, madam, not a thief."

Pondering that remark, Mrs. Bunratty met the girl's unstinting gaze. It wasn't often that she saw such defiance flashing in a working woman's eyes. When a girl had been on the street long enough, the fire behind her gaze often dwindled. Either this young scamp was lying about her age and experience, or she was an unusually resilient female.

"Any diseases?" Mrs. Bunratty asked.

"None."

"You'll have to undergo a doctor's examination anyway. I can't be too careful."

"I understand." The girl's hands hung loosely at her sides. Apparently unflustered by Mrs. Bunratty's inter-rogation, she seemed equally unthreatened by the prospect of a medical examination.

Now for the big question. "Ever hear of Dick Creevy?"

"He's a boxer, isn't he?"

"A very famous one. Handsome, too, so there shouldn't be any problem, there."

"Why did he want a blond?" the girl asked.

"Dear, it wasn't just a blond that he wanted." But

the girl knew that. She was fishing, trying to find out all she could about the man who'd commissioned *her*. Well, Mrs. Bunratty could hardly fault the girl for asking questions. A good prostitute was one who kept her wits about her, relying on her suspicions as much as her physical prowess. "He wanted a girl with cropped hair, boyish features, and slender hips."

"He wanted a boy, in other words."

"Make of it what you will. You don't have to do it, you know. You can always say no."

"I've made up my mind, I'm afraid. I'll do it."

"Don't you want to know how much he's willing to pay?"

Oddly, the girl's expression registered confusion. To a hardened prostitute, the issue of money shouldn't have been a delicate one. Panic fluttered in Mrs. Bunratty's ample chest. Was this girl truly an experienced prostitute, or a child playacting in a dangerous role?

But the words that next tumbled from the girl's lips removed all trace of doubt from Mrs. Bunratty's mind.

"He'll pay whatever you ask him to, madam, I'm sure. The only real question is, what will *you* pay me for my services?"

"The usual split, dear. Eighty-five percent for the house, the rest for you."

"The usual split is fine, Mrs. Bunratty—just as long as we reverse the percentages. I'll take eighty-five percent, and you take fifteen."

"That's robbery!"

"No, madam. That's prostitution."

"Why, you little—"

"Some of us just know our worth."

* * *

The night crier called the hour of midnight just as Lady Dolly Baltmore emerged from the hackney cab. Standing on the steps of Dick Creevy's town home, she paused, attempting to steady her nerves. Her pulse raced like a thoroughbred horse. Her knees were wobbly beneath her voluminous skirts. Whatever bravado she'd possessed in Mrs. Bunratty's establishment the day before had long since deserted her. Fear and self-loathing twisted her gut like an iron fist.

She raised her hand, then lowered it. The instant she knocked, there would be no going back, no escape from this ridiculous and ill-fated scheme. She ought to turn around and run back to the hackney cab before it pulled away from the edge of the street. She should abandon this silly masquerade before it was too late. . . .

Footsteps sounded on the opposite side of the door. Panic seized Dolly's heart. It *was* too late. What had she been thinking when she undertook to pose as a prostitute? Wasn't it enough that she'd perpetrated one fraud upon Dick Creevy? Did she have to don another disguise to insinuate herself into his life and exact her revenge? Was it even remotely possible that he would fail to recognize the protégé he'd taken to calling Doll Face?

The door swung open to reveal the dour expression of a butler dressed in black trousers and dove-gray waistcoat. "Come in, then," he said, after a quick head-to-toe appraisal. "Can't have you standing out there all night."

Heart thudding, cheeks burning, she stepped across the threshold. So Mr. Creevy's staff knew who she was, and why she was there. How humiliating! Trembling, she handed the man her lace-edged shawl.

A chill swept over Dolly. Suddenly aware of the

depth of her neckline, she shivered. Mrs. Bunratty had insisted she wear this particular gown. "He'll like it, lovie," the older woman had said as Dolly stared at her reflection in a cheval glass. Dolly had swooned at the sight of her tiny breasts perched on the ledge of a padded bustier, practically spilling out. But she'd worn the dress anyway, determined to do whatever it took to transform herself from boxer-in-training to blond siren.

Having received her hat and shawl, the butler scuffled away, leaving Dolly standing in the foyer. An eerie presentiment enveloped her as she looked around, her eyes adjusting to the shadows. Mr. Creevy's entrance hall was mannish and foreboding, with dark wood-paneled walls, marble-topped tables, and several big brass planters boasting overgrown plants with green fronds the size of elephant ears. A single lamp glowed in the corner, failing to penetrate the recesses of the vestibule, adding mystery to the house's ambience. Again, she thought of whirling and bolting out the door. Perhaps it wasn't too late. . . .

"Good evening, miss." Dick's voice, warm and mellow, floated down the staircase.

Startled, Dolly gasped. Her gaze flew up the steps. She froze, hands clasped at her middle, and for a moment, the two stared at each other in thickening silence.

He stood on the first landing, a glass of amber liquid in his hand. His legs, long and lean, were draped in fine black trousers. A gauzy white shirt, open at the throat, showed tufts of dark chest hair. Sleeves rolled to his elbow accentuated burnished forearms, corded with muscle, dusted with hair. Everything about him, his dress, his posture, his stillness, even the way his eyes lit as he appraised her, bespoke a man who seethed with pent-up desire.

Clean-shaven and immaculately groomed, he looked

as dashing as any aristocrat in Dublin—or in London, for that matter. Tentatively, unable to resist the pull of his magnetism, Dolly stepped forward. A closer inspection of the man revealed a less civilized picture. Dick's neck was too thick for a proper collar and necktie. His hands were too large for the glass he held. The twitch of a muscle in his jaw put the lie to his apparent civility.

"You are perfect." His voice was deep and velvety. Chunks of ice, a rare extravagance in Dolly's household, clinked in his glass as he shifted his weight. His hip jutted provocatively, revealing the outlines of his muscled haunches. "Come on. That's it; don't be shy. We'll have a drink in the parlor first, if you like."

Dolly drifted up the steps, as if on a floating carpet of mist. This man who was so familiar to her was also a stranger. She knew one aspect of his personality; now, she was about to learn another. Fear mingled with excitement as she stood on the landing next to him.

She nodded. *I could use a drink.*

He held her hand, caressing the delicate skin of her wrist. He stared at her so intently, so curiously, she wondered if he saw straight through her eyes and into her soul. Then he touched her elbow and gently guided her up the stairs.

In the parlor, never taking his gaze off her, he led her to an oversized leather sofa. She sat stiffly, watching him as he stood at the sideboard, pouring drinks.

"Scotch, miss? Or port?" At the sideboard, he stared at her over his shoulder.

Her heart leaped. Would he recognize her voice? "Scotch," she replied, nervousness twisting her gut.

From across the room, his scrutiny intensified. Sensing his suspicion, Dolly clamped shut her lips, praying that the earth would open up and swallow her.

He returned, boots silent on the thick carpet, lips curled in a knowing half smile. Accepting the drink, Dolly's fingers brushed his, and a wave of heat fanned through her body. She sipped the scotch, grateful for the sting that burned down her throat; it eased her anxiety and bolstered her courage. Then she settled back, daring at last to return Dick Creevy's smile.

Standing before her, he patiently drank his scotch, seemingly unruffled by the rising tide of silence that threatened to engulf the room. He studied her face, his gaze igniting patches of heat on her lips and throat. He made no pretense of ignoring her décolletage; when he looked at her there, her tiny bosom tingled with erotic apprehension.

"Where in the hell did Mrs. Bunratty find you?" he asked, at length.

"An honest answer might destroy your illusion, Mr. Creevy. Let's just say I happened to be in the right place at the right time."

"Your voice—" He shook his head. "You wouldn't happen to be from Ulster, would you?"

"Hardly." Chuckling, she lifted her shoulder in a self-deprecating shrug. "Born and raised in Dublin, I'm afraid, sir. What's the matter? You don't like my voice? Would you rather me not speak at all?"

"No, no. It's just that your voice is so . . . familiar. Hauntingly so, I should say."

"I hope it doesn't disturb you."

His smile turned slightly wistful. "I rather like it." After a pause, he said, "What's your name?"

"Call me whatever you like, sir. This is your fantasy, not mine."

"Would you mind terribly if I called you . . . Doll Face?"

Her heart lurched. "I'm sorry, but it reminds me of something in my childhood, something rather unpleasant. Would you mind calling me Dolly instead?"

"Yes, that's good, too." He drained his glass and set it on a table beside the sofa. "Have you been working in this, er, *line of business* for very long, Dolly?"

"What has my history to do with our arrangement, sir?"

"Nothing. I didn't mean to offend you." His cheeks colored. "Do you know who I am?"

"You're Dick Creevy, the famous boxer. Mrs. Bunratty told me." She scanned his figure from head to toe, precisely as he had done hers. "I'd have recognized you, of course. I've seen your picture in the newspaper, and on the marquee in front of your gymnasium."

"Frequent the riverfront area, do you?"

She pressed her lips together firmly. Ignoring his question, she asked another. "Mind telling me why you wanted a girl who looks like me?"

"Now you're the one asking uncomfortable questions."

"It's all right, then. I suppose it doesn't matter. You're the customer. You can have whatever you like—within reason, of course."

"I don't believe you'll find my tastes, ah, *unusual.*"

A fluttering broke out beneath Dolly's corset. Good God, she truly was going to have sex with this man. *Sex.* Her mind screamed its indignation while her body reacted with shock and pleasure. Could she go through with this masquerade?

"Would you like something else to drink?" he asked.

She realized she'd drained her glass. Dick took it from her, setting it aside, then reached for her hand.

The buckling of her knees made it difficult to stand.

But Dolly managed to face him, chin up, shoulders squared. She held his hand tightly, fearful she would collapse if he let go of her.

Suddenly, he looked uncertain how to proceed, which surprised Dolly, because it was he, after all, who'd conjured this fantasy. It was he who'd ordered up a woman the way some men commissioned a bespoke suit. It was he who'd instigated this charade.

Dolly was merely playing the role of the woman he'd dreamed up.

A dizzying sensation of unreality washed over her. Her duplicity, indeed, her *triple* fraud, was heinously immoral. First she'd disguised herself as a boy in order to get close to the man who'd killed her husband. Then she disguised herself as a prostitute in order to seduce him. Now she was pretending that the act of having sex with a stranger didn't terrify her. If she didn't quit assuming the identities of other people, she would soon forget who she was.

Or had she forgotten who she was a long time ago?

Half turning, Dick offered her his arm. They walked out of the parlor and up another flight of stairs. The silence between them deepened as they turned down a corridor. Dick pushed open a door and stood aside, gesturing for her to enter. Dolly crossed the threshold of his bedchamber, her gaze instantly fixing on the side of his huge four-poster bed.

The door clicked shut behind her. Her breath caught in her throat. Closing her eyes, she stood still as a stone, completely unprepared for the role she'd opted to play.

Was it Dick Creevy who'd invented this role? Or had she?

He stood behind her, his arms around her waist, his

head nestled in the crook of her neck. Warmth spread through Dolly's body as he pressed himself to her, his hands measuring her rib cage, cupping her tiny breasts, caressing her stomach. Cursing the fool who'd invented bustles, Dolly leaned back, clutching Dick's arms for balance. Her head lolled on his shoulder. Her breathing grew shallow and quick.

His beard scraped her flesh, arousing her. A tiny sigh of pleasure escaped her lips.

Turning in his arms, Dolly lifted her face to his, waiting for the kiss she thought would never come.

Eight

"Dolly." He loved saying her name. Just voicing the word aroused him.

She whispered a strangled, "Mr. Creevy."

His pulse thundered. A streak of desperation shot through him. Dick wanted *this* woman more than he'd ever wanted anyone before. But why? Because she looked like someone who cared about him, worried about him, and, when it was all said and done, thought he was a better man than he truly was?

Or was he simply starving for the physical comfort that making love to a woman always gave a man?

Dick's worst fear reared its ugly head. Perhaps he was attracted to this little minx because she looked more like a boy than a fully mature woman. If that were true, then he was indeed a sick and perverted man.

Physical excitement overrode Dick's internal dialogue. He'd sort out his feelings later, when his body wasn't aching and his blood wasn't roaring in his veins. For now, nothing was more important than the woman he held in his arms.

She *was* a woman, despite her short cap of curls and boyish features. She was *all* woman, no matter how threatening her boyish characteristics were to Dick's masculinity. He might have fantasized about a slight figure with slender hips and freckled skin, but the creature whose breasts rose and fell beneath his fingertips was pure female—as were her physical responses. When Dick pressed his lips against her bare neck, gooseflesh appeared. When his fingers tightened on her arms, she clung to him like ivy.

He buried his nose in her blond curls. The scent of her hair, freshly washed and lightly perfumed, thrilled his senses. Her body leaned back, her head falling on his shoulder. Emboldened, Dick tasted the delicate skin of her nape, nipping at her flesh with his teeth.

She shivered beneath his kisses, and a tiny mewling sound escaped her lips. Nimbly, Dick unfastened the long row of cloth-covered buttons that traced her spine. Then he smoothed her gown off her shoulders and massaged her neck. With his thumbs, he kneaded the knots of muscles on either side of her spine, hard and deeply, the way he liked his own sore muscles to be rubbed.

She gasped.

His fingers stilled. "Too hard?"

"Intense," she replied in a small voice.

He rubbed her more gently for a moment, then caressed her back with his palms. She slid her arms out of her sleeves, so that her gown hung at her waist.

"You have a beautiful back." Dick ran his hands along the curves of her shoulders, then gently cuffed her surprisingly taut upper arms. "You're strong for such a small-boned woman."

"I have recently discovered the benefits of exercise."

A niggling seed of caution planted itself in Dick's mind. Few ladies in Dublin had yet added athletic conditioning to their beauty regimens. That a lady of the night would be so scrupulous about her health and strength was slightly stunning. But it was not impossible. This woman was, after all, quite a unique female.

Dick loosened the ties of her satin corset, but stopped short of removing it. Wicked desire fueled his imagination. He wanted to see Dolly undress herself . . . slowly.

He sat on the edge of the bed, one leg crossed over the other. "Come over here." He beckoned with a curl of his fingers.

Her hesitation, the drop of her chin, the flutter of her eyelashes . . . Everything she did excited him. The air in his bedchamber thickened as she slowly crossed the floor. Standing in front of him, Dolly stood for a moment, her gaze direct, her lips slightly parted. Blackness flooded the color in her eyes, pupils eclipsing irises. Her stare was powerfully hypnotic, drawing Dick in, as if she were luring him to a trap. As if she were capturing her captor.

Deliberately, she reached behind herself and unfastened her bustle. Petticoats and crinoline slips came undone. Never taking her gaze off Dick, she slid everything down her hips. Then she stepped out of the tumble of clothing at her ankles and kicked it aside.

His mouth went dry, for she wore no drawers beneath her petticoats, but rather stood before him naked except for corset, garter, stockings, and shoes. His eyes were instantly riveted to the blush of darkness between her legs. In the gas lamplight, her curls glinted like polished gold. She shifted her weight, jutting one hip, unself-consciously showing herself to him. Dick's restraint in not reaching for her then and pulling her onto him was herculean.

"Good God, but you are beautiful." With a wistful

sigh, he tore his gaze off the triangle between her legs, and scanned her figure, toe to head.

Black satin shoes with pointed toes, buttons on the inside vamp, and two-inch heels accentuated slender ankles and well-formed calves. Her legs, encased in black silk stockings, were curvaceous but lean. The bands of flesh between the tops of her hose and the clasps of her garters were erotically pale, dusted with freckles.

His mouth watered to kiss that white flesh. He wanted to bury his nose between her legs and kiss her there, too—an urge he'd never experienced with a prostitute. But he tamped down his eagerness because he wanted his pleasure to last, and because he wanted her to experience pleasure, too. In the back of his mind, Dick realized he'd already spent more time with this woman than he'd spent with any other woman he'd ever paid for. And he hadn't even begun making love to her. If she stayed all night, it wouldn't be long enough. He wouldn't be finished exploring that luscious body of hers before the sun rose.

He'd already loosened the ties of her corset. Now she slowly pulled the satin garment free from her body and tossed it on the floor. Dick's chest tightened and his heart squeezed painfully. "Your breasts are lovely," he whispered, aching to feel those small soft mounds of pale flesh beneath his fingers.

Her nipples hardened beneath his gaze. Her chest rose and fell with shallow breaths, betraying her excitement, stoking the flames of Dick's lust. He looked her in the eye, nodded, and opened his arms. She stepped inside his embrace and placed her hands on his shoulders to steady herself.

With a groan, Dick knelt and laid his cheek against her naked stomach. For a long moment, he remained that way, his flesh against hers, steeping in her heat, breathing in her scent. Then he turned his face into her body and pressed his lips to her soft belly, kissing her, licking her, tasting every inch of skin his mouth could find.

Her grip tightened on his shoulders, and her back arched as she leaned into him. Dolly gasped as he pulled her tighter into his embrace, and when he lifted his head, she looked down, her lips curving in a half smile, her eyes drugged and dazed with desire.

He'd never been so thirsty, so needy, for a woman. He suckled at her breast as she cradled his head. Harsh breaths, sighs, gasps, suckling sounds, and exclamations of surprise filled the room. Dick's kisses became more fervent, his need for her more desperate. Leaning back, he pulled her on top of him and drew her mouth to his.

Her breath was sweet, her kisses full of unexpected passion. Dick hadn't thought a woman getting paid to fulfill a fantasy could so enjoy it. But Dolly wasn't acting, he was quite nearly sure. When he reached between her legs, tangling his fingers in that patch of golden curls that so delighted and intrigued him, he discovered with a certainty that she wasn't acting. Dampness coated his fingers, exciting him further still.

They pushed back on the bed and lay side by side, Dick's head propped on one hand. With his other, he caressed Dolly's inner thighs until her head lolled languidly and her eyes closed. Then he slipped his finger inside her, amazed at the slick wetness he found there, and perhaps a bit flattered by it, as well. He'd never pleasured a prostitute so completely; indeed, he'd never met one that he cared to pleasure.

But this girl was different somehow, and not just because she fit the fantasy he'd described to Mrs. Bunratty to a tee. This girl seemed to crave him, to need him, to instinctively yearn for what only he could furnish her.

A voice in the back of his head whispered, *Poppycock.*

Even in his heightened state of physical excitement, Dick knew he was deluding himself. He knew that in telling himself Dolly desired him, he was merely fueling his fantasy. He didn't care. All that mattered to him now was the wetness on his fingers and the gasp of the woman beneath his touch.

Her body responded as if she were starving for him. Dick was amazed, gratified, and aroused by her labored breathing and her involuntary little cries.

"God, woman," he growled, plunging his finger as deeply inside her as he could.

She moved her hips, redirecting the angle of his fingers toward her belly button. Her voice was deep and throaty. "There."

Then she stiffened, and for a moment—one exquisite, unbelievable moment—Dick felt her inner muscles grip his fingers, pulling at them, sucking them inside her.

He was too concerned with her arousal to think of his own. He'd never seen a woman react so voraciously, so greedily.

And without warning, her excitement escalated again, taking her to yet another plateau. She rolled atop Dick, straddling him, staring down at him with a startling expression of cockiness and control.

Her fingers moved at his waist, deftly unbuttoning his pants. She reached inside his trousers, then his unmentionables, and before Dick could assimilate what was happening, she grasped his throbbing penis.

Instinctively, he clasped her wrists and held her still. "No!"

Her eyes flashed. "Why not?"

He didn't know *why not*. He only knew that no woman he'd ever slept with had been this bold, this aggressive, or this *eager*. He didn't know why he wanted Dolly to stop touching him, or why he was so hesitant to allow her the freedom to do as she pleased. He only knew that as a man, he was supposed to direct the act of lovemaking. He was supposed to be on top, and Dolly was supposed to lie beneath him, quietly and patiently. He was supposed to be in control.

In his entire adult life, the most Dick had ever hoped for in a bed partner was willing indulgence. An occasional display of warmth and affection was nice, but not to be expected. Unabashed enthusiasm was unheard of.

"Why not?" Her frantic scrabbling at his clothes ceased. As her breathing normalized, her tone took on a calm, almost arrogant, tone. "I came here to pleasure you. Why don't you permit me to do just that?"

Dick swallowed hard, searching for words. " 'Tis not . . . proper for you to be so . . . bold."

Dolly returned a chuckle. "Dear, cavorting with a prostitute is not *proper*. Fantasizing about a woman who looks like a lad is not *proper*."

"The devil with you! I don't want a lad!" Dick's anger swelled up in an instant. "And you're daft if you think so! Do I look as if I'm not enjoying this? Do I feel as if I am not aroused?"

Though he cuffed her forearms, her fingers remained coiled around his shaft. A slow smile curved her lips as she tightened her hold on him. "On the contrary, sir, you exhibit every indication of wanting me as badly as I want you. You did, however, tell Mrs. Bunratty you wanted a certain *sort* of girl."

It was difficult to talk above the desire rising in his

belly. " 'Twas an impulse. The description I gave Mrs. Bunratty was of someone I know."

"Someone you wish to do *this* with?" Dolly, her gaze burning, her expression coy, looked down at his naked body.

"Of course not," he croaked. "Someone pleasant to be around, that's all. Someone . . . kind."

"Ah. Kindness is an aphrodisiac, is it not?"

"It can be." He pulled her hands off his body and pressed her palms flat on his chest.

Her tiny breasts squeezed together, the little nipples prominent. As she took a deep breath, she drew up her knees, so that she was hunkered over Dick's body, her naked bottom resting on his thighs, her glistening triangle parted, her womanly folds exposed.

Her brazenness stunned him, alarmed him, unleashed a flood of lava in his loins. "What sort of saucy minx are you? No woman I have ever known was so openly wanton, so easy with her body, so . . ."

"So outrageously sexual?"

Nodding, he released her.

She pushed his arms up over his head, as if she were a wrestler pinning him to the mat.

Yielding, he watched her free his penis from his pants and wrap her fingers around it.

"Do you have any oil, sir?"

His ears popped. Somehow he managed to point a finger toward the nightstand where a small tube of ointment, intended to be rubbed into muscles sore from overexertion, was hidden.

Well, he'd never had a *more* sore muscle, he concluded, as Dolly reached across the bed, found the tube, and squirted a dab of it into the palm of her hand.

The sensation of her fingers, warm and strong and

slippery, moving up and down his engorged shaft was unlike anything he'd ever felt before. Every nerve ending in Dick's body tingled. A thousand points of pleasure pooled in his groin, weighting his legs and loins, drawing his arousal to a climax.

"You had best stop—" His voice caught in his throat.

"I think it is too late, sir."

"If you don't stop, I will—"

"Come on, then. Don't hold back," she urged him, not unkindly.

"But, I want to—" He lifted his head to look at her, but a wave of excitement knocked him flat again. Unable to resist touching her, he grasped her thighs and lifted her hips.

She shifted her weight away from him, refusing to relinquish control.

Dick's need to be inside her, to sheathe himself in her body, was unbearably intense. But so was his need for release. Just when he thought he couldn't stand the ache of his desire an instant longer, Dolly reached beneath him and lovingly cupped the most sensitive part of his manhood. Dick's excitement soared past human restraint, and with a groan, he climaxed.

Spasms of pleasure wracked his body, robbing him of breath. A sense of great relief washed over him. Throwing back his head, Dick sighed and moaned his contentment. Then, after a pause, he stared unblinkingly into the eyes of the woman perched atop his body. Holding her gaze, he felt an overwhelming sense of shared intimacy.

Eyes closed, she rubbed her oil-slicked palms on her belly, then drew her hands up her middle. Massaging her own breasts, she sucked in a ragged breath.

Within minutes, he was hard again. *Just like a teenage boy,* he thought wryly.

Dolly looked down. "Good Lord."

"I should think it has more to do with your good deeds than with the Lord's."

"I wouldn't call this God's work, sir, but it's an honest living."

"Is it now?" He'd have to explore that remark in depth with her . . . later. "What would you say, Dolly, if I asked you to stay the night?"

"You mean, sleep here? With you?"

"I wasn't thinking of consigning you to the servant's quarters."

"I don't know." Hugging herself, she suddenly appeared very naked and vulnerable.

Dick ran his hand up her thigh, unhooking one garter, smoothing her stocking down her legs, testing the silkiness of her skin. "Have another appointment, do you?"

"No, sir. But I don't think it's customary . . . What I mean to say, is, you don't know me—"

"I know enough. I know what I want."

"Do you? I wonder."

"And you are what I want, love. For now."

"Yes, I am precisely who you want. What's more, I am precisely who you think I am. But you don't know me, Mr. Creevy, because you can't see me. You only see what you want to see."

He smiled and frowned at the same time. "You're as clear as a bog."

"As a practical matter, I shouldn't stay because you haven't paid—"

"Don't worry. Mrs. Bunratty knows where I live. I've never stiffed an honest working woman before."

She bit her lower lip. "I've got to be out of here before the sun comes up."

Nodding, he thought it ironic that he'd *paid* this woman to have sex with him. He smiled, happy beyond reason that she'd agreed to spend the night. Then he reached for her feet and unbuttoned her shoes. He yanked off her stockings, pausing to hold one of the sheer ribbons to his nose. The scent of her was as intoxicating as the fumes of aged brandy. With a chuckle, Dick fit his hands to Dolly's waist, pulling her down to kiss him.

"Do you like that?"

"Yes." She pulled back, sat up straight, and stared at him.

His hands moved up her flat, surprisingly muscular stomach to easily cover her modest breasts. Lightly, he pinched her nipples.

She gasped.

Unexpected joy flooded his heart. He loved the notion that he pleased this woman. Previous experiences had left him wondering if he was a good lover. Seeing Dolly enjoy herself was indescribably exciting.

"Why are you smiling?" she whispered.

He shook his head. She wouldn't understand. In all the years he had spent with Kitty Desmond, when he'd made love to her, he'd never felt she loved him back, or wanted him as badly as this little blond sprite did. He'd always been grateful when she condescended to sleep with him. She behaved as if she'd done him a great favor by allowing him to touch her. When he moved atop her, he felt obliged to hurry his lovemaking, to get it over with, so that she wouldn't have to long endure the unpleasantness of his body penetrating hers. He felt as if he imposed on Kitty every time he made a romantic overture.

But this woman smiled when he touched her, and moaned when he caressed her most secret, feminine parts. This woman wanted him. This woman wanted to give herself to him.

Making love with a woman who enjoyed herself was a totally new experience for Dick Creevy. He felt like some irredeemable drunkard who'd spilled his beer only to discover the face of Christ staring up at him from the puddle beneath his tankard.

With a heartfelt chuckle, he said, "I'm laughing because you've made me happy. And I haven't been happy in a very long time."

Surprisingly, her gaze skittered off, and the look of confidence she'd displayed so arrogantly a moment before vanished.

A shiver rippled across Dolly's shoulders. Guilt skittered up her spine. How could she be so bold and heartless as to make love to a man she fully intended to betray? How could she manipulate a man's emotions in such a cold and callous fashion?

Averting her gaze, she drew in a deep breath.

"Have I said something to overset you?" Dick asked.

His deep, velvety voice was sufficient to overset her. Dolly closed her eyes, flashing on the memory of her husband as he set off the fateful morning of his death. Lord Boyle Baltmore wasn't one to show untoward affection. In fact, his foray into her bedchamber that chilly morn was most unprecedented. But he'd kissed her cheek as she sat brushing her long blond curls. He told her he was going to attend the boxing matches later that evening, and she shouldn't wait up for him. Then, as he paused on the threshold, he'd told her to always remember that he loved her.

Had he had a presentiment about his death?

Looking back, Dolly thought it odd that he took the time to linger over her that particular morning. Odder still that he had told her he loved her. Oh, she knew that he did; she had *always* known. But Lord Baltmore was so parsimonious with his affections; as with his money, he was loath to lose control. Dolly had learned to live with her husband's unusual thrift. She knew how to stretch a budget and postpone the creditors. She knew how to create the appearance of comfort when conditions were actually quite acute.

Illusion had become reality, and reality nothing more than a series of disguises.

But now, with Dick Creevy clutching her naked hips and inviting her to spend the night with him, Dolly couldn't find in her repertoire any costume, mask, or clever line of dialogue that fit the role she was playing. Her mind spun wildly, but she didn't know how to respond. She was acting a part that she wasn't prepared for. She was lying to herself as well as to Dick.

Because the horrible truth of the matter was that she cared for Dick Creevy. Her animosity toward him had dissolved. He wasn't what she had expected; he wasn't the murderous rogue she'd pictured in her mind when she'd hatched this silly plot to impersonate a boxing student. He was a man who would rather take a physical beating than dwell on his troubled past.

And she was determined to discover and expose his dark secrets.

A tear slid down her cheek.

Dick brushed it away, then held her hands. When he

spoke after a long silence, his voice was throaty and rough. "I've disappointed you, haven't I?"

Her eyes blinked open. "Disappointed me? In what possible way?"

"What a fool I am." He swallowed hard. "I thought I was pleasing you, but in truth, I was only pleasing myself. It was over too quickly . . . just like a school-boy. You must think me the worst sort of cad."

A lump formed in Dolly's throat. Was it possible that this man actually cared whether the prostitute he'd hired for the evening *enjoyed* herself in his bed?

"On the contrary, sir, I enjoyed myself immensely."

A tentative smile turned at his lips. " 'I enjoyed it immensely,' " he repeated, his tone gently mocking. "Dear woman, you sound as if you are judging a fine cup of Indian tea. Why the sudden show of primness? A moment ago, you were positively *wanton*."

"And did my wantonness please you, sir?"

He traced his finger down her bare stomach, toyed with her curls, then pressed his thumb against the fleshy hood above her womanhood. "It pleases me to think I pleasured you."

"You did, sir."

"Really, Dolly?" His thumb moved provocatively.

The guilt pricking her conscience was quickly drowned by a flood of erotic pleasure. "Would I lie to you?"

She leaned forward, mesmerized by the sensations streaming through her body. Common sense told her to put on her clothes and flee, lest she wind up in this man's thrall, unable to resist his influence, unable to continue perpetrating a fraud upon him. But Dolly's common sense was no match for her desire. Staring into Dick's lambent gaze, she felt a need for him that frightened her.

"Don't go," he whispered, expertly massaging her most intimate part.

Her body released a wave of liquid heat. Dolly drew up her legs so that her weight was on the balls of her feet, her thighs parted, her body completely exposed. Pressing her palms against Dick's chest, she held his gaze.

The whispering sound of his thumb against her hot, moist flesh excited her. The little contractions of pleasure that had been sucking at her insides suddenly intensified. The place between her legs throbbed. Her need for physical release consumed her.

"You like?"

Unable to speak, she nodded.

"You'll stay then?"

Unable to say no, she gave in to her climax.

Nine

Dolly had never known of any man who cared a whit whether his sexual performance was pleasing to his partner. Of course, she'd only had sexual relations with one other man in her life, and that was Lord Boyle Baltmore.

The memory of her late husband's abbreviated attempts at lovemaking brought an acrid taste to the back of Dolly's throat. Guilt assailed her as she mentally criticized Lord Baltmore's sexual technique, but it couldn't be denied: the man's lack of generosity was as apparent in matters of sex as it was in his financial affairs.

She hadn't fully realized that until just now.

As her breathing returned to normal, she smiled. Words of gratitude came to her lips, but she didn't speak them. Thanking a customer for sex was out of character for a prostitute. Dolly didn't want to do anything that would raise Dick's suspicions. If all went well, she would slip out of his town house before the morning sun shone brightly on her face. Once her powder and rouge wore off, there was a dangerously strong chance he would recognize her as his acolyte, Doll Face Mohr.

But for now, he believed she was a prostitute named Dolly, a hired courtesan who bore an uncanny physical resemblance to a young boy in his tutelage. Whatever that said about Dick Creevy's mental state, sexual predilection, or moral compass, Dolly couldn't begin to fathom. She'd ponder that mystery later, after she satiated herself with his body. She'd work on unraveling Dick's motivation after she figured out her own, a task that might prove difficult, if not impossible, to accomplish.

He'd already reached his climax, and yet he was willing to continue pleasuring her. The notion was so outrageous, Dolly giggled.

"What amuses you?" His voice was sultry.

"You do, sir. I've never known of a man who endeavored so hard to pleasure his bed partner."

"More's the pity." His brow furrowed. "What would you say if I asked Mrs. Bunratty so send you here again? Would you be opposed to visiting me on a regular basis?"

"No, sir," she said, uncertain whether she was telling the truth. After all, she couldn't expect to get away with this masquerade forever. Dick would soon realize she was Dahl Mohr. And when he did, he'd be furious, perhaps murderously so. She had taken too great a chance already. No point in pushing her luck.

His eyes sparkled in the semidarkness. His smile was slow, wicked, and utterly charming. A gentle breeze rippled through the open window, fluttering white lace curtains and kissing Dolly's naked skin. She touched Dick's lips and traced his bottom lip with her thumb. Then he drew her middle finger into his mouth and tenderly suckled it.

Dolly moved instinctively, rubbing her wetness on Dick's hard, muscular belly. Her juices mingled with the smell of his skin, giving off a musky perfume. Hungry for him, she raised up on her haunches, then lowered herself, impaling her golden thatch on his shaft.

Her inner muscles clutched him. He pushed himself upward, touching that secret spot deep inside her. Some long-suppressed need, an almost animalistic desire, uncoiled within her.

With Lord Baltmore, Dolly would have bit her lower lip and calmed herself. She would have swallowed the urge that drove her so relentlessly now. She would have behaved more like a lady, and less like the crazed wanton she was with Dick Creevy.

But Dick Creevy was nothing like Lord Baltmore. And Dolly the prostitute was nothing like Lady Dolly Baltmore. The old rules no longer applied. Sex with this man was like nothing Dolly had ever experienced, or even read about. She wondered if other women felt this much pleasure in bed. She wondered if she'd discovered something no one else knew. She wondered if something was wrong with her. She didn't care.

"Does this make you happy, Dolly?"

She realized she was smiling. She and Lord Baltmore had never talked in bed. Vaguely, for the problems of her marriage bed were not as interesting or as troubling to her as they had been five minutes earlier, Dolly wondered if she and her husband had ever talked at all.

"Yes, this makes me very happy," she replied.

Dick's hoarse whisperings thrilled her. "Don't hold back, love."

Her hips slid back and forth. Unabashedly, she ground her body against his. Her strong legs worked like mechanical springs, lifting and lowering her weight. Her bottom slapped hard and noisily against Dick's pelvis. There was no timidity or delicacy to their joining.

Clasping her hands, Dick held Dolly's gaze. His sweet, intimate words were encouraging and soothing. And arousing.

She wished to tell him how she felt, but she was too embarrassed to verbalize her feelings. She wanted to tell him that the sensation of his penis inside her was both wicked and wonderful. His hardness filled her, yet tantalized her. Greedy, she wanted more. She wanted harder. She wanted faster. She wanted to reach another climax.

He seemed to know what she wanted, even though she couldn't say it. "Do you want to come, dear?"

The intensity of her pleasure was almost painful, the throbbing between her legs torturous. "Yes," she managed to say.

The lines bracketing his mouth creased; his smile gave her permission. Relying on his kindness, his generosity, and his desire to please her, Dolly gave vent to her frustrations and her needs. The moan she heard sounded as if it were ripped from her soul. She'd never made a sound like that before in her life. But inhibitions meant nothing to her now. Throwing back her head, she came furiously and wetly and very, very loudly.

Exhausted, she rolled to his side and snuggled beneath his arm.

He kissed the top of her head and held her tightly.

Dolly waited patiently. Only when Dick's gentle snores turned to deep, somnolent rumbles, did she gingerly extract herself from his embrace, gather her clothes, and tiptoe to the door. In the darkened corridor, she hastily dressed.

Not a creature stirred as she sneaked down the steps and out the front door. The hackney cab she'd hired earlier had, by previous arrangement, materialized at the corner. Grabbing her skirts, Dolly ran like the devil was after her. Leaping into the carriage, her chest aching, she dared not look over her shoulder. The guilt she felt at leaving Dick Creevy's bed was a vise around her heart.

Dolly's shoulders sagged as she turned her key in the lock at Fontjoy Square. Once she was safe in her bed, she cried until her eyes were dry and grainy. When the morning sun washed a film of light over the furnishings of her ghostly room, Dolly prayed for forgiveness. Staring at her surroundings; she sought counsel from another presence, too. What would the previous occupant of this room have thought of her behavior? Would the same woman who loved Lord Byron's poetry condemn Dolly's deceitful masquerade?

Unable to find the answers, Dolly threw herself out of bed and grabbed her jumping rope. As her feet pounded the wooden floor, she clenched her jaw and promised herself that she would never again commit such a foolish act. She'd been insane to think she could share Dick Creevy's bed without losing her heart to him. She'd betrayed her own cause by making love to that man. She'd shamed the memory of her late husband and disgraced herself. She'd compromised her virtues; she'd acted like a trollop.

She'd never experienced so much pleasure in her life.

But she hadn't hatched this plot for the purpose of finding pleasure with Dick Creevy. She had set out to insinuate herself into Creevy's life so that she could discover how and why he'd killed Lord Boyle Baltmore. Only then would she be able to wreak her revenge. Only then would she know how best to destroy the man who had destroyed her very existence.

Dolly's scheme, however, had taken an unexpected turn when she'd realized her attraction to Dick Creevy. The knowledge that he was attracted to her—or to Doll

Face Mohr—turned her plans into an utter debacle. The ridiculous notion of sleeping with him in the guise of a prostitute . . . Well, even Dolly couldn't explain that to herself. She'd acted on impulse and she'd acted unwisely. She couldn't justify her outrageous behavior. She could only hope Dick Creevy never discovered how badly she'd duped him.

Suddenly, she loathed herself, hated the weakness of her flesh. With punishing ferocity, she jumped rope until the braided hemp burned abrasions on her fingertips, and the soles of her feet felt raw.

She'd set out to betray the man who had killed her husband and ruined her life. But now Dick Creevy held her in his thrall, and so it was he who had the ultimate power over her.

There was only one thing she could do. She had to stay away from Dick Creevy and his pugilist academy.

Her plan had failed.

The rope slipped from her fingers, and her knees buckled. Lady Dolly Baltmore, also known as Dolly the prostitute and Doll Face Mohr, the fledgling boxer, fell to the floor in a puddle, exhausted, confused, and completely without hope.

The ladies stood on the edge of the garden, their expressions grim.

"Whose idea was it to clear this patch of jungle and plant a garden?" piped Miss Millicent Hyde.

Exchanging worried glances, the ladies shrugged their shoulders in unison.

"It certainly wasn't mine," replied Dolly, at length. "Wasn't it your idea, Claire?"

In truth, it was Lady Claire Kilgarren who had first

voiced the notion of working together to clear the garden around which Fontjoy Square was erected. But if she hadn't, Dolly would have suggested the same thing. After all, her mysterious benefactor had made it a condition of her living in her fine house.

Dolly experienced a twinge of guilt. Unlike the other ladies, she wasn't taking up gardening because she wanted to. A hundred things, including needlepoint and playing the pianoforte, interested her more than weeding gardens and planting flowers. No, she was only there on that bright spring morning because she had to be.

Lady Kilgarren offered a thin smile. "I do believe my dear departed uncle who bequeathed me my home would have wanted the garden in the square to be tended."

Mrs. Rose Sinclair smoothed the front of her black skirts. "Yes, and my late husband Mr. Lyndon Sinclair would have encouraged me to stay active. It's so tempting to wither on the vine when one has lost a loved one."

Miss Millicent Hyde sniffed. "I can't say whether Daddy wants me to stick my hands in the dirt or not. At home we have servants to do this sort of thing. But if Mrs. Sinclair is going to participate, then so am I."

Lady Claire Kilgarren turned a scouring look on the younger woman. "Dear lassie, if your father is so overprotective, then what are you doing living alone in a rundown house in Fontjoy Square?"

Tension rippled through the gathering. Gasping, Miss Hyde reached for Mrs. Sinclair's arm. "I beg your pardon!"

Suppressing a groan, Dolly said, "Oh, let's not have a row. We all decided we wanted to work together to bring this garden back to its former glory. Let's not permit our petty differences to spoil things!"

Lady Claire Kilgarren opened her mouth, but clamped it shut when Dolly patted her on the arm.

Mrs. Sinclair wrapped a protective arm around Miss Hyde. "I agree with Lady Dolly. We're neighbors now, and as I've said before, we have no men to look after us. We've got to look after one another, then, don't we? 'Twould be so much more pleasant if we were all friends."

"I'm all for that," Dolly said, nudging Claire with her elbow. "Aren't you, Claire?"

"I just want to fix this garden," replied Lady Kilgarren, through her teeth.

"And we shall." Dolly looked again at the tangle of vines running up a ramshackle pergola. "It just didn't look so daunting a task from over there."

After a cursory walk around the small plot of land, the ladies again stood at the edge of the street. At least having surveyed the garden, they now knew the extent of the challenge that lay ahead. First the land would have to be cleared. That would take days. Then the flower seeds and bulbs would have to be planted. Vines would have to be hung, shrubbery trimmed. At last, the pergola, trellises, and gazebo would have to be rebuilt. In all, the ladies figured it would take a full year before the garden achieved its full potential.

But as they stood beneath the late-morning sun and discussed the tasks ahead, they grew more animated and excited about the project.

"A row of dogwoods over there would be pretty," Mrs. Sinclair said.

"I like tulips," inserted Miss Hyde. "Can we plant

some red and yellow ones, a whole bed of them, over there?"

"That would be lovely," replied Lady Kilgarren. "And I should like to have a fountain in the center of the square, with a small granite bench and trellises overhead, studded with the most exotic roses."

Dolly smiled, despite the sadness pressing down on her. Just getting out of bed that morning had been difficult. She'd still be huddled beneath the covers, her face stained with tears, if Ferghus hadn't knocked on her door and announced that Lady Claire was in the drawing room.

"It's settled then. We'll begin tomorrow." Surprised at her own enthusiasm, Dolly propped her hands on her hips and gave the garden another long, scrutinizing look. She wished she owned a camera and could take a picture of the neglected plot of land before she and her neighbors started working it. Even in her state of depression, she silently predicted the garden would one day be beautiful.

She'd initially approached this task with dread, but Dolly now began to feel excited about it. The sun on her skin felt good. The company of the other ladies was comforting, even when Lady Kilgarren and Miss Hyde were bickering. The good, hard, sweaty work that lay in store for Dolly would keep her mind off Dick Creevy.

Turning toward her house, she nearly laughed out loud. That was a lie! Nothing would keep her mind off Dick Creevy. She couldn't comb her hair without remembering the way he ran his fingers through her curls. She couldn't lace her shoes without reliving the moment when he'd pulled them off her and she'd straddled his hips. She couldn't look at her face in the mirror without wondering whether the real Lady Dolly Baltmore would be as alluring to him as Dolly the prostitute.

The ladies parted company, Miss Hyde and Mrs. Sinclair crossing the street arm in arm.

"They're an odd pair, don't you think?" Claire asked, eyeing the other two women as if she were judging a beauty contest. "Old Lady Sinclair in her widow's weeds, babbling on endlessly about her dear old Lyndon. She makes him sound as if he were a paragon of virtue."

"How boring for her," Dolly said dully.

"And that prissy Miss Millicent Hyde. Half crazed for a man, and talks about her papa as if he dotes on her. Well, if I were her papa, I'd be keeping a much closer watch on that one, I can assure you."

"Oh, they're a little eccentric, the both of them. But they seem rather innocuous, don't you think? And they've agreed to help us clear that monstrous jungle and plant a decent garden, haven't they? Having a common ground that isn't an eyesore can only improve our property values and enhance our quality of life in Fontjoy Square. Do you not agree, Claire? Claire?"

Frowning, Lady Kilgarren shook her head. "I do apologize, Dolly. Sometimes I can't help myself from falling into the doldrums. I don't know how you do it, really."

"Do what, dear? By the way, would you like to come inside for some tea?" Dolly put her arm around her friend's waist and the two women headed toward Number Two Fontjoy Square.

"I don't know how you manage to be so cheerful," Lady Kilgarren said. "You're hardly out of mourning, you've uprooted yourself, and you've got a house and garden to refurbish. Yet, you selflessly tend to a sick relative every day without fail. I see you leaving the house and walking to the corner to hail a cab. Don't you ever want to stay in bed and cry all day? Don't you ever feel the least bit of pity for yourself? Or am I just a weak and sniveling woman who is too self-absorbed to be happy?"

Stunned, Dolly guided Lady Kilgarren through the front door, up the steps, and into the sitting parlor. If she had convinced her neighbor that she wasn't bitter about her past, then Dolly truly was a world-class actress. Better than Sarah Bernhardt, even. Pulling a bell cord, she motioned for Dolly to sit. Then she settled on the sofa beside her friend, tucking her feet beneath her.

"You're not a weak and sniveling woman," Dolly finally said. "In point of fact, I envy you."

"Good heavens, why?"

Because you're so honest about your feelings, Dolly wanted to say. Instead, she said, "Because you're pretty and young and you've got your entire life ahead of you. You say you don't want a man, but one will come along some day. . . ."

"No." Lady Kilgarren's jaw set firmly. "No, I do not want a man. Never. Don't ask me why, but I do not trust men. I believe I would rather rot in hell than marry one."

The vehemence with which the duke's daughter spoke raised many questions in Dolly's mind. Clearly, there was a story behind Claire's feelings. But if Claire wanted to discuss the genesis of her antipathy toward men, she was quite capable of doing so. As far as Dolly could see, the woman who lived next door to her was not afraid of speaking her mind. It was Dolly who lived a double life, full of half truths and outright lies, not Claire.

"Don't say that to Miss Millicent Hyde," Dolly replied, attempting to insert some humor into the conversation. "She seems quite adamant about wanting a man."

"Rabid, I should say."

"She is young, isn't she?"

"Young and silly."

Dolly watched with bemusement as Ferghus entered the room, placed the tea tray on a low table, then backed out clumsily. Reaching for the pot, she said, "I'm afraid my manservant has been conscripted into woman's work. I must say, he has learned to brew a serviceable pot of tea."

Lady Kilgarren took the proffered cup and saucer. "When is the rest of your staff arriving?"

Dolly hesitated no longer than a blink. "Yes, I'm afraid there has been a bit of a problem there. It seems an epidemic of the pox has broken out on my country estate. Until everyone is well, I don't want them traveling to the city. Why bring such a dread disease to Dublin? Better to let them all get well, and then send for everybody at once, don't you think?"

Her heart skipped a beat, but she managed to meet Lady Kilgarren's frankly disbelieving gaze.

"Yes, if you say so." Lady Kilgarren focused on the remnant of a cookie she held pinched between her fingers. She nibbled and chewed, her expression one of thoughtful skepticism.

Dolly held her breath. Only the other woman's kindness would smooth over this awkward situation, for it was patently obvious that there *was* no household staff standing ready to travel to Dublin. Dolly had lived at Number Two for weeks. If a phalanx of maids, servants, and butlers was going to arrive, it would have done so by now.

"And your couple? How are they getting along?" Dolly asked.

Lady Kilgarren shrugged and glanced heavenward. "They threaten to leave me every day, but every morning, they're still here. I'm beginning to wonder if they are fugitives escaped from justice."

"Don't you know anything about their backgrounds?"

"Precious little. I retained them just before I moved here. I wasn't in a position to offer them much more than a roof over their heads and hot food."

"You've got the luck of the Irish, that's for certain."

"I amuse myself by imagining who they might be. Perhaps they were run out of the United States for their participation in some underground slave railroad. If the American government finds them, they're as good as dead."

"That's absurd, Claire." But Dolly couldn't resist chuckling.

"Why else would they be willing to work for free?"

Dolly had often wondered the same of Ferghus. "Because they are loyal to you?"

"I'm hardly the sort to engender loyalty, dear."

"I don't believe that." Dolly's troubles suddenly seemed less pressing and her future less grim. Smiling, she attributed the alteration of her mood to her neighbor's pleasant company. The pretty blond woman who'd been forced into genteel poverty—for reasons yet unknown to Dolly—seemed to accept her fate with good humor and elegance. There was dignity in the shiny elbows of Claire's ubiquitous blue suit. There was civility in her persistent kindness. Most importantly, there was refinement in the lady's lack of pretense.

"Oh, Claire." Dolly clutched her half-emptied cup of tea. The urge to tell all was nearly overwhelming. "I've got myself in a spot of trouble."

"Oh, dear. You're not with ch—"

"Good God, no!"

Fanning her face with her fingers, Claire gave a dramatic sigh. "Thank goodness. Anything other than that can be solved, Dolly. Tell me, what is it?"

"I-I lied about my staff of servants. They aren't coming after all."

"Just as I thought." Claire reached over and squeezed Dolly's hand. "It's nothing to be ashamed of."

Dolly cringed. Shame was precisely what she felt. As quickly as the urge to confess everything swept over her, it disappeared. Wondering what had come over her, she pushed back on the sofa, lifted her chin, and met Claire's sympathetic gaze.

It was the sympathy she couldn't tolerate. "What I mean to say is, they've taken a vote, all of them. They've made a collective decision to stay where they are. The new owners have promised them better living conditions, better food, shorter hours."

An elongated moment of silence passed between the women. Claire blinked, visibly confused. "I thought you said—"

"I haven't been myself of late. I'm physically exhausted, for one thing. Taking care of Uncle Hester has nearly worn me out."

"I though you said—"

"You can see I've lost weight."

"Yes," Claire said, lowering her eyes. "And you look a trifle pale."

"I suppose I will have no choice but to hire an entirely new staff of servants."

"Yes. 'Tis a pity. You must be heartbroken."

"Oh, I am." Dolly forced a brave look to her face. "That is why I admire you so much, dear. No matter what hardship befalls you, you take it in stride. While I seem to let every one of life's little troubles overset me."

"You mustn't take it so hard. There are plenty of hardworking men and women in Dublin who need a job. You'll staff your home soon enough. We'll get the garden in shape, and it will be lovely, and then . . . Well, you'll see. Everything will be so much better, then, dear."

Dolly's guilt ballooned. Now the very lies she'd concocted to impress Lady Claire Kilgarren, perhaps the only woman Dolly could legitimately call a friend, had made her uncomfortable. The duke's daughter smelled a fraud, that was obvious. But as a true, highborn lady, she was too polite and civilized to make mention of it. Instead, she looked at Dolly with sadness and compassion. The pity in her eyes nearly provoked Dolly to tears.

"Thank you, Claire, for being such an understanding friend."

"I'm just next door, Dolly, anytime you need me."

After a beat, Dolly said, "And I'm going to need you. Very soon, as a matter of fact." Desperate to change the subject, she said, "Isn't Mr. Avondale's party this Saturday?"

"Don't tell me you're not attending!"

"On the contrary, I intend to be there with bells on my toes. The only problem is, I have no idea what sort of gown I'm going to wear."

Relief washed over Lady Kilgarren's expression. "The fact that you have a choice makes me green with envy. Shall we take a look at your wardrobe?"

The two women scurried up the steps and into Dolly's bedroom. While Dolly opened her armoire and searched through the row of gowns hanging there, Lady Kilgarren wandered about the bedchamber. When Dolly, a pale gray taffeta ball gown draped over one arm and a bright green one slung over the other, whirled to face her friend, she gasped.

Lady Kilgarren stood beside Dolly's chaise longue, staring down at a puddle of dirty clothing.

It seemed like hours that Claire stood staring down at the leather trainers, jersey pants, sleeveless cotton top, and linen chest binders. When she finally looked up, her eyes were round and questioning, her cheeks a shade duskier than before.

" 'Tis none of my business," the lady said, her voice small.

The clothing, especially the linen strips with which Dolly bound her breasts, was damning evidence of Dolly's other life. But she owed no explanation to Lady Claire Kilgarren. And after nearly confessing her duplicity below stairs, only to think better of it and contrive another thinly veiled but irrefutable lie, she was even more determined to maintain her charade.

"I've been exercising, of late. You know that."

"I've seen you jumping rope."

Dolly laughed nervously. "I'm afraid I've become somewhat addicted to it. Gets your heart rate up, you see. Clears the head. Really, Claire, you should try it sometime."

"You aren't going to visit a sick relative every day, are you?"

"Don't be ridiculous. Uncle Hester depends on me!"

"You said before it was your Aunt Esther who was

in failing health. I don't believe you have a sick relative at all!"

Dolly tossed the gowns she'd been holding on the bed. "Esther sounds very much the same as Hester. I'm afraid you just misunderstood."

"Where *do* you go every day, dear?"

"I've told you." Dolly's tone had more tartness in it than she'd intended. She hated hurting Claire's feelings. But it couldn't be helped. In order to protect the web of deceit she'd woven, she had to end this interrogation *now.*

Dolly's gaze flickered to the linen bands, then back to Dolly. "It really isn't any of my concern—"

"No, it really isn't."

The pretty duke's daughter, the ever-irrepressible aristocrat who'd been forced to live far beneath her station, looked for all the world as if she were going to cry.

Oddly, her sadness fueled Dolly's anger.

"Don't worry about helping me choose a dress for Mr. Avondale's party." Rudely, she gestured toward the door. "I have plenty of dresses to choose from."

"How fortunate for you."

"Would you care to borrow one? I have noticed that you have only two dresses. In truth, that is why I invited you up here."

Claire's chin lifted. "How generous of you. Thank you, but no."

"Well, then," Dolly said, after a long, prickly moment. "I will thank you to leave me to my duties. I have a lot of letters to write."

"I suppose you do. What with your servants electing to stay in the country, and all."

"Precisely."

"Good day, then, Lady Dolly."

"Good day, Lady Kilgarren."

Dolly went over to the window and watched through the curtains as her neighbor went out of the house and crossed the street. Her stomach twisted at the thought that she'd wounded a woman who had reached out to her and tried to befriend her.

But revealing her true self to Lady Claire Kilgarren was risky. Nearly as risky as exposing her real identity to Dick Creevy. Rejection, Dolly had learned from experience, was worse than loneliness.

Bitterness poured through her veins. Dolly turned and stood beside her bed, fingering the fine gray taffeta of a dress purchased two years earlier. Her mind's eye flashed on the image of Lord Baltmore storming into the house, red-faced and grinning like a fool.

He had announced a sudden upturn of their financial situation and encouraged Dolly to commission an extravagant Paris gown.

The gown arrived and Dolly wore it once, on the last occasion she had ever attended the opera. Because by the time the mantua maker demanded payment for the dress, Lord Baltmore had already suffered a reversal of fortune. He stormed into the house again, yelling that his misfortune was the result of unscrupulous horse traders and dishonest bookies. Shortly thereafter, he descended into a black mood from which he never recovered.

Dolly's embarrassment had been acute. Madame Racine had sent a letter by post, angrily charging her with fraud and warning her never to come near her establishment again.

The gray taffeta gown was never worn again.

Until now.

Holding it to her shoulders, Dolly stood before the

looking glass. The gown was low necked, with a white satin sash at the waist and a small bustle in the rear. Black ribbons tied in tiny bows accented the hem. Cap sleeves would show Dolly's sculpted arms to perfection. Her slender figure would take on womanly curves with the help of crinoline petticoats and a hoop slip. Yes, she thought, half turning to gaze at her reflection. She would wear the gown to Mr. Avondale's party on Saturday.

And no one would know her life was in tatters.

Ten

Devon Avondale stood beneath the arched opening that led from the entrance hall to the grand ballroom. In his black tuxedo, shiny black slippers, and elegant white shirtfront, he felt a trifle awkward, as if he were dressed in someone else's clothes. After all, it was nearly five years since the last time he had donned formal evening attire. Without Mary to force him to parties and dinners and theater, he had very little use for fine clothes. He had grown quite accustomed to the woolen trousers and boots he wore while puttering in his garden.

Greeting his guests, he kept an eye peeled for his neighbors, Mrs. Rose Sinclair, Miss Millicent Hyde, and the Ladies Claire Kilgarren and Dolly Baltmore. Though he'd invited nearly two hundred people to this soiree, the event had largely been staged for them. He could think of no other way to get them into his house all at once—no other way that would not arouse undue suspicion, that is.

A steady stream of party goers streamed through the door. A few were old friends whom Devon hadn't seen since Mary's funeral. They paused, shook his hand, murmured vague words of consolation, then skittered off toward the punch table. To Devon's chagrin, they seemed uncomfortable in his presence, as if he'd done something for which he should be ashamed, instead of having nearly lost his mind to grief and tried to kill himself with drink.

Many of the guests were but passing acquaintances of his. Friends of Mary's, they included actors and actresses, politicians, writers, even controversial radicals who routinely espoused the overthrow of government. Having lived largely on the periphery of his deceased wife's social circle, Devon could only smile tightly and nod in their direction. Those who knew him as Mary's husband returned the smile. A few took the time to inquire as to his health, and commiserate with him over the loss of his beautiful, beloved wife. But as with his own close friends, even Mary's old coterie was quick to dash off for a drink.

He was a pariah, wearing his bereavement like a coat of nettles, in need of human comfort, but unable to receive it.

An elderly woman wearing white elbow-length gloves and scads of precious gems held out her hand. "Mr. Avondale. How are you, my dear?"

Devon recognized the woman as the widow of a high-ranking government official. When Mary was alive, the two women had entertained themselves at salons and tea parties and suffragist rallies. Despite the difference in their ages, they'd been fast friends and political allies. Seeing the older woman's obviously vigorous health brought a surge of bitterness to Devon's throat.

But it wasn't this lady's fault that she'd survived into her dotage while Mary lay rotting in the ground.

Devon pasted a smile on his lips. "Lady Beresford, how good of you to come tonight."

"I wouldn't have missed it for the world, my boy. Everyone has been talking about you, you know. After everything that happened, it was widely rumored you'd become a hermit of sorts. Then out of the blue, you host the grandest ball of the season. Why don't you tell this old tabby what is going on, dear?"

"You never were one to mince your words, were you?"

She smiled. "If I recall correctly, you once admired a woman who had a little steel in her backbone."

"A great deal of it, if you're referring to Mary."

Stepping an inch nearer, the woman gave Devon's hand a maternal pat. "I do hope you are over your mourning period, Devon. She never meant for you to throw yourself onto her funeral pyre, you know. This isn't India, for God's sake."

A lump formed in his throat. "I nearly died from the grief of losing her, Beatrice."

"I know, dear. But you didn't."

"No." He met the woman's pale blue gaze. In her expression was the same determination and strength that had so often glowed in Mary's eyes. Remembering Mary's admonition that *We mustn't slop over, dear,* he suppressed the impulse to throw himself into Lady Beresford's arms. If Mary could die with courage and grace, then couldn't he at least carry on his life with a modicum of dignity?

"No," he repeated. "I didn't kill myself. Tried, but somehow I simply couldn't manage it."

The silver-haired woman chuckled. "What doesn't kill us makes us stronger, my boy."

"Does it?" He shook his head. "I don't know, Beatrice. I miss her every day, sometimes so much that I fear I am losing my sanity. She was my best friend, you know. She was the kindest, most decent person I ever met. She was my life."

"She had many dear friends, Devon. 'Twas kind of you to bring them all together here. But I fear you have done so, not to honor Mary's memory, but to satisfy some sort of unhealthy obsession of your own. Am I correct?"

He couldn't answer. The lady's powers of intuition were too frighteningly accurate.

She tapped his shirtfront and clucked her tongue. "I thought as much. Look, Devon, you must go on with your life. You must cease invoking the memory of Mary each moment of every passing day. You might just as well conduct a séance and summon her ghost to live you! Oh, God, I shouldn't have put that notion into your head, should I?"

It was his turn to laugh. "Don't worry, Beatrice. I'm too afraid of ghosts to try to summon one. Besides, there are plenty of pleasant memories surrounding this place. I've no need to hire a medium in order to channel Mary's spirit. I fear it has never left me."

She gave his hands a powerful, admonitory squeeze. "Put the past behind you, Devon. That's what she would have wanted."

Rankling, Devon withdrew his hands. He didn't like being told to forget about Mary, for that was how he interpreted Lady Beresford's advice. How could he forget about the only woman he'd ever loved? Wasn't it as much a betrayal to her memory as loving another woman would be?

Lady Beresford moved on, and was replaced by a

handsome gentleman with thinning brown hair, a prominent nose, and a cleft chin.

"I'm Dick Creevy, Mr. Avondale." The man's grip was like a bear's. "We've met, but it was many years ago."

"You were a friend of Mary's."

"Indeed. Tragic, her death." Creevy's brown eyes held a hint of sadness. "She was so young and beautiful. How have you been faring these last few years?"

"It's going on five years, now. I can hardly believe it. I still wake up each morning, expecting to see her face on the pillow beside mine. Each time I finish a book, I think whether I would recommend it to her. Every time I taste a fine wine, I wonder if she would care for it. Every time I see a pretty woman, I compare her to Mary. I'm afraid the comparisons are never favorable to the young ladies I see."

Creevy laid a hand on Avondale's shoulder. "I am sorry for you. I lost someone I loved very much, too. Many years ago. She was killed in a carriage accident along with my baby daughter and her infant son."

Avondale wondered why Creevy distinguished between *his* baby daughter and *her* infant son, but he was too sensitive to the other man's suffering to ask nosy questions. "I am sorry for you, too, then. Did Mary know of your tragedy?"

"Mary was a great comfort to me," Creevy said, appearing slightly startled. "I'm surprised she didn't mention it to you."

"I am finding that Mary had a great many friends and confidants I knew nothing about. I traveled so much, you see, and she was frequently left to her own devices. She was an independent sort, but I'm sure you knew that. She had her own friends and her own life, quite apart from me. Of course, she was everything to me. The sun rose and set with Mary Avondale, as far as I was concerned."

A faraway look came into Creevy's eyes. "I understand."

"So, you're the famous boxer," Avondale said, after an awkward silence. "Mary never told me she fancied the sport."

Creevy's brows shot up. "Didn't she? Well, she only attended once, actually. I met her at Lady Beresford's and the two of them decided it would be quite a lark if they attended the boxing matches one evening. You must have been out of town."

"In Edinburgh, no doubt. I was in the whiskey business, you know."

"Yes, I recall Mary mentioning that. And now?"

"Now, I work in my garden. And miss Mary. And wonder why I allowed my work to take me away from her so often while we were together."

"You mustn't let your regrets overshadow your happy memories, Mr. Avondale."

"Don't say it: *she wouldn't have wanted that.*"

"All right, then, I won't. You already know it."

The two men shook hands again; then Creevy moved into the ball room and disappeared among the clusters of elegantly clad party goers.

A short time later, Mr. Avondale spied Mrs. Rose Sinclair and Miss Millicent Hyde coming through the door. The faintest hint of recognition sparkled in Mrs. Sinclair's eyes as she met Devon's gaze. Of course, he couldn't expect her to identify him; indeed, he hoped she wouldn't. He'd only spoken to her once, when he'd knocked on the door of her previous dwelling, a rather shabby town house on the wrong side of the Liffey—and, then, he'd been wearing a black mask.

"Allow me to introduce myself." He stepped forward, extending his hand to the raven-haired woman he knew to be Mrs. Rose Sinclair.

She smiled pleasantly, shook his hand, and introduced him to Miss Millicent Hyde.

The younger woman's large brown eyes widened impossibly. Her lashes flickered on her cheeks and her pretty, bow-shaped lips split in a tooth-baring smile. Instantly charmed, Devon Avondale bowed low over her hand, then tenderly kissed her knuckles.

This show of chivalry nearly sent the young girl into a swoon. Giggling, she blushed even darker and nervously batted the air with an ivory fan attached to her wrist by a satin cord.

Mrs. Sinclair linked her arm through Millicent's. "I had no idea this was to be such a grand affair," she said, somewhat apologetically. "We've just moved in, and we're hardly unpacked. Please forgive us if we're a trifle . . . *underprepared* . . . for your generosity."

Devon suspected Mrs. Sinclair was embarrassed by the plainness of her gown. He gave her a frankly admiring look. "You wouldn't be out of place, Mrs. Sinclair, if you were being presented to the court of Saint James. Besides, I am more interested in meeting my new neighbors than seeing their wardrobes. I would have been sorely disappointed had you not attended this evening."

The woman's smile was warm enough to be called maternal. "Have you met the other ladies? Lady Claire Kilgarren and Lady Dolly Baltmore?"

"Now he has," inserted a feminine voice at Devon's elbow.

Turning, he stared into the most incredible pair of blue eyes he'd ever seen. Taken off his guard, he was speechless for a moment, unprepared for the jolt of physical awareness that Lady Claire Kilgarren's nearness generated.

She slipped her tiny hand in his. "Mr. Avondale, I presume."

He'd met her once. Handed her a letter, even. But he hadn't experienced the sort of jaw-numbing attraction he felt now. Had the mask somehow obscured his vision?

His chest squeezed as he aligned his features into military array. It wouldn't do to slop over, as Mary would have said. He was a grown man, a veteran of the Crimean War, at that. If he couldn't control his emotions, he should become a hermit, as Lady Beresford had suggested.

"Thank you for coming, Lady Kilgarren." He brushed his lips along her satin-encased hand. Then he turned to the freckle-faced blond standing beside her. "And you must be Lady Dolly Baltmore. So pleased to meet you."

"How did you know my name?" the elfin woman asked.

"I've seen all of you in the neighborhood at various times." Surrounded by the four women, Devon chose his words carefully. One slip of the tongue could mean complete exposure. The hawkish scrutiny of four very intelligent ladies was formidable. The instincts of women could never be discounted. And they were sure to compare notes when they gathered in their sitting parlors, sipping tea, getting to know one another, sharing their own personal histories.

How long could Avondale expect them to refrain

from revealing to one another the manner in which they acquired their homes?

It would only take one of them to breach her promise and divulge the terms of the agreement she had made with the mysterious benefactor. Eyeing them, he wagered Miss Millicent Hyde would be the first to crack. Then the remaining three ladies would join the confession.

Pieces of the puzzle would be fit together. Details of their respective childhoods would be compared. Eventually, the four ladies would realize they'd all been friends—at one time or another—with Mary Avondale, previously known as the Mary O'Roarke. When they discovered that Mary O'Roarke was also Mrs. Mary Avondale, Devon's plot would be destroyed.

His mind had wandered. The ladies were staring at him as if he were daft.

"Are you all right?" Mrs. Sinclair asked.

"Yes." He pinched the bridge of his nose. "These hothouse crushes can be suffocating. First party I've had in years. To be honest, I don't know what I was thinking!"

The ladies laughed politely. All except Miss Millicent Hyde, whose gaze was riveted to the couples dancing in the room adjacent to the entrance hall.

Lady Dolly Baltmore and Lady Kilgarren looked at the young girl, then exchanged knowing glances.

Mrs. Sinclair wrapped her arm a bit more tightly around Millicent's waist. "I think we'll make our way to the punch table now, if everyone will please excuse us."

Devon bowed and thanked them again for coming.

Lady Kilgarren and Lady Dolly started to move away when a tall man with a thick mustache, curled in the current mode, blocked their path. Smiling at the ladies, the gentleman introduced himself as Rafe O'Shea.

A friend of Mary's? But, Devon couldn't remember the man's name on the invitation list.

As if he could read minds, Mr. O'Shea grasped Devon's hand and explained, "I've been to dinner with one of your guests. He promised you wouldn't be angry if he brought me along. Do forgive my rudeness."

"The more the merrier," Devon replied. "You are welcome in my home, Mr. O'Shea."

But the man's interest was clearly on the ladies. "Baltmore, did you say? I believe I know your husband."

"I'm a widow, Mr. O'Shea. My husband was killed in a boxing accident about a year ago."

"How terrible! And now I've compounded my rudeness by reminding you of your misfortune. Might I be allowed to make it up to you, Lady Dolly, by escorting you to the punch table?"

Dolly didn't think that a glass of lukewarm punch would lessen her bereavement. A protest was on the tip of her tongue.

Lady Kilgarren interjected. "Do go, Dolly. I'd like to have a private word with Mr. Avondale."

Mr. O'Shea touched her arm and gently guided her across the room. Skirting the dance floor, Dolly's mood lightened. A small orchestra played baroque chamber music in a futile effort to transcend the din of laughter and conversation. Women waltzed as gracefully as possible, hindered by hoop skirts and bustles. Gentlemen with pomade-slicked hair and waxed mustaches sipped Scotch whiskey from sliver flasks.

The overall ambience of the ball reminded Dolly of how long it had been since she'd enjoyed a carefree evening. Long before Lord Baltmore announced his financial ruin, they'd stopped socializing with their peers and family. Arriving at the punch table, she realized Mr. O'Shea was staring at her intently.

"Is there something the matter, Mr. O'Shea?"

"No, no!" His cheeks darkened. "I do apologize. It's just that . . . Well, my lady, you are a very attractive woman. I hope you won't think me too bold for saying so."

She took the glass of punch he handed her. With her emotions in turmoil, she wasn't certain whether she should be offended or flattered. "I-I've been out of circulation rather a long time, Mr. O'Shea. I'm not accustomed to such blandishments. Forgive me if I sound rude, but I am hardly out of mourning—"

"I offended you!" He looked mortified. "My humblest apologies."

Something about his affect appealed to Dolly. He looked her straight in the eye, and a spark of awareness passed between them. He wasn't an unattractive man, Dolly mentally remarked, even though he lacked the physical presence, charm, or rugged good looks that Dick Creevy possessed. Still, there was something *manly* about him—something slightly *dangerous,* even—in the way he slowly smiled while he stared so studiously at every feature of her face.

"No need to apologize," she murmured.

He led to her a quiet spot at the edge of the dance floor. Standing beside a magnificent potted palm, Dolly focused on the couples waltzing past.

Mr. O'Shea's admiring stares unnerved her.

"Where is your friend?" she asked to break the silence. In response to his bewildered look, Dolly added, "The gentleman you dined with earlier, I mean. Didn't

I overhear that you are a gate crasher at Mr. Avondale's party?"

He chuckled. "Quite right. Last I saw my friend, he was whirling a pretty young woman around the dance floor. He seems to have disappeared now. Do you suppose he has persuaded the innocent thing to take some fresh air with him?"

"I wouldn't know." Dolly warmed to Mr. O'Shea. Despite her melancholy, she shared a joke with him. "I don't know your friend. Is he usually such a rake?"

"A rake, and a fast one, at that. I'll be taking myself home in a rented carriage, if I know him at all."

"That's scandalous," Dolly said. "Do young women really behave so loosely nowadays?"

"Oh, my lady, you have been out of circulation too long!" Rafe's sparkling eyes hinted at mischief, but his smile was earnest. "Do you know that there are those among the fairer sex who believe they have a right to vote? And wear trousers? And do everything that only men can do?"

"Such as?" Dolly's own mischievous spirit kindled. Mr. O'Shea would be surprised if he knew what sort of traditionally masculine things she'd been doing these past few weeks.

Like wearing short pants. Frequenting a gymnasium. Talking to men while they stood about a dressing room wearing nothing but towels wrapped around their waists, and sometimes not even that. Exercising. Sparring.

"Why, I've even heard tell of a woman who wants to be a lawyer. And one who thinks she could navigate a flying machine."

"I see no reason why a woman could not be a lawyer or operate a flying machine. Anything a man can do, a woman can, also. At least, she should be permitted to try."

"You are shockingly modern in your views!" Mr. O'Shea stared at her over the rim of his punch glass. "I like that, Lady Dolly. Really, I do."

"Do you? Well, Mr. O'Shea, I've been known to wear trousers myself. And I've taken up exercise lately. Would it shock you to know that I enjoy the sport of boxing, both as a participant as well as a spectator?"

His eyes rounded. "Lady Dolly, while I support a woman's right to do as she pleases, I cannot endorse your climbing into a boxing ring with a man!"

"Why not? If a woman trains properly and schools herself in the art of boxing, why shouldn't she spar with a man?"

"Any man who would dare take a punch at that lovely face of yours would be committing a criminal act! You aren't big enough to fight a man, even in the featherweight category! You aren't strong enough!"

"Mr. O'Shea, you are somewhat of a hypocrite. You say you believe in a woman's right to do as she pleases, but you do not believe I should be allowed to box."

"Forgive me." He drained his glass, then placed it on the tray of a passing servant. "I have no right to tell you what to do. I don't even know you. But I should like to know you better."

Heat fanned through Dolly's body as Mr. O'Shea stepped an inch closer. She smelled his spicy cologne and saw the tiny dots of perspiration that lined his upper lip. His eyes burned brightly and his jaw clenched. He had the look of a hunter staring down the barrel of his rifle, finger on the trigger guard. She felt herself moving slowly into the crosshairs of his gun sights.

"Lady Dolly, would you permit me to call upon you?"

Her throat closed. Blinking in astonishment, Dolly stammered, "Oh, I don't think it would be proper. I am hardly out of mourning—"

"You said it has been a year. That's long enough, my dear."

There was no arguing that. One year of grieving and nursing a grudge against Dick Creevy was long enough. "Well—"

"We could visit in your parlor, or take a carriage ride, or have dinner at the Shelbourne Hotel. Have you dined there?"

"No." She'd only been there once, for tea, and then she'd wrapped a half-dozen watercress sandwiches in a napkin and slipped them in her purse before she left. Thinking back, she'd taken a fistful of sugar cubes as well.

"Well, then?"

Her pulse quickened. Rafe O'Shea was a total stranger to her. Yet his conversation was stimulating, and he was interested in learning more about her. He was flirting, something no man had done with her in years.

And that included Dick Creevy. Creevy had had sex with her, and pleasured her physically beyond any measure of decency, but he'd hardly attempted to engage Dolly in any meaningful conversation or witty banter. Their brief interlude centered around one thing, and that was Creevy's bizarre sexual fantasy. She'd been a fool to participate in it. She was lucky she hadn't already been exposed as the fraud she was.

A wave of anger toward Dick Creevy washed over her. Objectively, she had no reason to be angry at the man. *She* had duped *him;* if anyone had cause for outrage, it was he. But she couldn't be objective where Creevy was concerned. She set out to betray him, but her double cross had turned around on her. She wanted to hate him, but she couldn't. She wanted to flirt with Dick Creevy, not Rafe O'Shea. But it was O'Shea standing beside her, not Creevy.

Half smiling, she met Mr. O'Shea's hopeful gaze. Illogically, she felt she was getting even with Dick Creevy by encouraging Mr. O'Shea's suit. Her rationale was severely flawed; her motivation highly suspect. She knew all that. But on impulse, she agreed that Mr. O'Shea should take her to dinner one evening the next week.

His face lit like a schoolboy's. "Thank you." He bent low over her hand.

When he straightened, his gaze flew over her shoulder.

His smile vanished. His entire body tensed. For a moment, he froze, his eyes black, his lips set in a grim, straight line.

Looking over her shoulder, Dolly scanned the crowd for the source of Mr. O'Shea's sudden change of mood. But she saw only throngs of people, drinking, laughing, and dancing. Before she could single out anyone, Mr. O'Shea touched her elbow.

She turned back to him.

"I fear I must take my leave now, Lady Dolly."

"So soon? It isn't even ten o'clock!"

"My friend is eager to leave. I just spotted him on the other side of the room."

Dolly started to turn again, but Mr. O'Shea held her arm. His intensity alarmed her.

"Is anything the matter?" she asked.

"No." He looked embarrassed. "I fear my friend is deep in his cups again. I can hear him laughing clear across the room! If I do not assist him in getting home soon, he will embarrass himself completely. And after Mr. Avondale has been so kind to allow me to attend his party, I must not allow that to happen."

"I understand."

"Good night, then, Lady Dolly. I will see you next week."

With that, Mr. O'Shea crossed the floor quickly and vanished into the throng. She stared after him, stunned and perplexed.

"You've obtained an admirer, Dolly." Lady Kilgarren's voice drew her back to reality.

"Do you think so?" Dolly sipped her punch, perversely pleased at Lady Kilgarren's suggestion.

"Do you like him?"

"He likes me. For now, that is enough."

Lady Kilgarren's brow furrowed. "I worry about you, Dolly."

"Why is that?"

" 'Tis none of my business, but it seems to me that you are hiding something. Your unexplained absences from home . . . the boy's clothing I saw in your bedchamber . . . all that exercise. Dolly! Please tell me, dear. What is going on?"

Dolly's sadness returned. And so did her fear. Moved by Lady Kilgarren's concern and caring, she wished she could unburden herself of her troubles. She wished she could tell Lady Kilgarren what was really going on. But she could not.

Looking her friend dead in the eye, she said, "No, Claire. It is none of your business."

Claire's wounded expression was so difficult to look

at, Dolly made a pretense of searching the room for Miss Hyde and Mrs. Sinclair.

It was then, standing on her tiptoes and craning her neck, that she spotted Dick Creevy halfway across the room.

He stared back, his gaze dark and intense.

Eleven

From across the room, he'd spied her talking to a gentleman. It was the gentleman, actually, whose face first snagged Dick Creevy's attention. For an instant, he thought he was looking at his old nemesis, Rafe O'Shea. A bolt of fury surged through him as he stared harder.

Then the man dipped his head over the lady's knuckles, and Dick couldn't see his face. When he straightened, his thick, elaborately curled mustache came into view. Rafe O'Shea hadn't been sporting a mustache when Creevy last saw him . . . and Rafe wasn't as thin as that gentleman. . . .

No, it couldn't be O'Shea, Creevy concluded, releasing a heavy sigh.

But, the woman . . . The woman was very definitely Dolly, the prostitute whom Mrs. Bunratty had sent to him just a few nights before.

He skirted the edge of the dance floor, his gaze riveted on Dolly, whose back was to him. A pretty blond woman approached her, and the two women began speaking in earnest. Their conversation appeared strained. Dolly's spine stiffened. The other woman looked taken aback, rebuffed. For a long while, they stood beside each other, sipping punch and watching the dancers.

He moved closer, as stealthily as a night prowler.

No doubt Dolly's friend, clad in a well-cut but clearly well-worn gown of amber satin, was a prostitute, also. It wasn't unusual for prostitutes to dress conservatively. Dick knew that beneath Dolly's understated gray taffeta, she wore a satin bustier and lacy garters. There was no telling what the other blond wore beneath her skirts, perhaps nothing. It was that dichotomy, the contrast between Madonna and whore, that aroused him.

Glancing about the room, Dick wondered how many other working girls were interspersed among the guests. It wouldn't surprise him if Mr. Avondale stocked his party with them. After all, Queen Victoria had only been successful in sending sex underground; she would never vanquish the British Empire's taste for it.

Indeed, as somewhat of an amateur historian and social commentator, Dick thought the queen's repressive attitude was a backlash to England's licentious Regency era. Her uncle had been such a rogue, and she was determined to erase any hint of his corrupt and hedonistic influence from her court. But the Queen's puritanism had its dark side. A huge segment of the population was titillated by what it perceived as sinful and illicit. Dick thought the current prevailing attitude toward sex was unhealthy. It had resulted in a generation of women who thought something was wrong with them if they wanted sex.

Paradoxically, under Queen Victoria's tenure, prostitution had become rampant. Dick vastly preferred sex with a warm, loving woman. But since Kitty Desmond's death and betrayal, he'd been unable to form such a close bond. Therefore, he'd turned, on occasion, to prostitutes. He wasn't proud of that, but he didn't think he was on a fast track to hell because of it.

Nor did he think all prostitutes were evil creatures. He felt sorry for them. Theirs was a tough lot. He'd never met one who didn't have a tragic background. Only a girl with *nothing* would choose to sell herself.

He withdrew a flask from his breast pocket and took a swig of whiskey. If Dolly was working this party, it wouldn't do to humiliate her or cause a scene. Though he'd been bitterly disappointed when he awakened to find her gone, he realized she owed him no explanation. Even Mrs. Bunratty was baffled by Dolly's behavior. But according to the veteran madam, the young girl was a complete unknown, a new face on the streets.

"I'm sorry, Mr. Creevy," Mrs. Bunratty had calmly explained. "But you can't hold me accountable for the irresponsibility of a prostitute. If these people had manners and breeding, they wouldn't be lying on their backs all day, would they?"

But Dolly was different. Dick had sensed in her manner of speech more than a modicum of education. She was well-mannered and graceful, her movements as fluid as an athlete's. In seducing him with her brain as well as her body, she'd exhibited a high degree of intelligence and wit. She was no ordinary prostitute. And he was not about to let her slip away from him again.

A finger of ice tickled Dolly's spine. Gasping, she pivoted to face Lady Kilgarren. "We must go, Claire. Now!"

The woman's worried moue deepened to a frown. "You look as if you've seen a ghost!"

Dolly tipped her punch glass to her lips, emptied it,

then tossed it in the base of the potted palm. "Worse. Come on; let's go!"

But it was too late. Dick Creevy materialized at her elbow, a Satanic smile spreading across his handsome face.

"Hello, Dolly."

She started at the sound of her name. Then she remembered that Dick had wanted to call her Doll Face. *Dolly* was her invention. "Hello, Mr. Creevy."

Turning to Claire, he extended his hand.

"I'm Lady Kil-"

Dolly cut her off. "I'm feeling ill!" She clutched her stomach and made a little lurching motion. "Please, Claire. Take me home. Good-bye, Mr. Creevy!"

Claire wrapped an arm about Dolly's waist, and the two women hurried across the floor and out of the room.

Dick started to follow, but thought better of it. If Dolly was embarrassed to see him, there was a reason. He couldn't fathom what that reason was, but he would respect her decision . . . and her privacy.

Beneath the arch leading to the foyer, he met his host again.

"You're not leaving are you, Mr. Creevy?"

"I'm afraid so, Mr. Avondale. By the way, did you see those two prostitutes who just ran out of here?"

Avondale returned a puzzled look. "Do you mean the two blonds?"

"Precisely."

"I saw them." Avondale's expression grew wary. "The little one appeared to be sick. Hope it wasn't something she ate or drank here."

"I'm certain it wasn't. Look, I don't mean to be rude, but do you know the little one's name? Or where she can be reached?"

"I would have been glad to introduce you—"

"Oh, we've met."

"Really?"

"Indeed." Sensing the other man's suspicion, Creevy felt he had committed a grave faux pas. Was it remotely possible that Avondale didn't know the women were prostitutes? After a moment, Creevy said, "Well, it doesn't signify, does it? Sorry to have troubled you, Avondale. I'll be going now."

Avondale nodded tersely. "Be careful, Creevy."

Stepping into the night, Creevy considered his host's odd behavior. Perhaps Avondale wanted the little minx for himself. That would explain his rankling at Creevy's request for her address. Perhaps Avondale hadn't known they were prostitutes. But that seemed impossible. He had composed a guest list, after all. He would know who was invited and who wasn't.

Or—and this seemed too far-fetched to be plausible—perhaps they were *not* prostitutes.

Shaking his head, Creevy climbed into a hackney cab and headed home. His head ached from too much whiskey and emotional confusion. But Dolly's refusal to acknowledge him shouldn't be surprising. In most cases, she would be doing her client a favor by ignoring him in public. Still, *he'd* confronted *her,* and damn it, she'd acted as if she didn't know him at all.

His bitterness was like a bad penny, always turning up when he least expected it. Now, his mind flashed on Kitty Desmond's indifferent expression, the shrug of her shoulder, the arched brows. When he'd accused of her being unfaithful to him, her reaction was one of mild amusement and weary resignation, as if she were thinking, *What took you so long to figure it out, you idiot?*

Kitty's betrayal, and the ensuing debacle that resulted

in his child's death, convinced him that he was incapable of sustaining a mature, honest, loving relationship. Whatever a man needed to keep a woman happy, he lacked. Whatever powers of perception a man needed to detect a woman's duplicity, he lacked. Whatever strength of body and mind a man needed to protect and defend his family, Dick completely lacked.

When it came to love and marriage, Dick had proven himself a failure. Slamming his fist into his palm, he muttered a sanguine oath. One would think doing business with a prostitute would be a little more cut-and-dry. That was why he'd hired her, wasn't it? Because he couldn't tolerate the duplicity of women like Kitty Desmond, and he craved the raw honesty of a purely sexual relationship. How he had managed to mess things up with Dolly was a mystery.

But mess it up he had. Because now he couldn't get her off his mind. And he wasn't going to rest until he found her.

"What was that all about?" Claire huffed and puffed in a futile attempt to keep up with Dolly's pace.

Since she'd been training, Dolly's ability to trot far distances without breaking a sweat was enviable. As the two women neared Number Two Fontjoy Square, she slowed, mindful that her friend's endurance wasn't equal to hers. "Just someone I didn't want to talk to, Claire."

"That was obvious. Who was he?"

Oh, the tangled webs Dolly was weaving! "A friend of Lord Baltmore's. An old friend. A business acquaintance, actually."

"Your husband owed him money, is that it?"

"Oh, don't be silly! Boyle never owed anyone

money!" Dolly pushed open her front door and gestured for her friend to come inside.

In the parlor, they collapsed into chairs while Ferghus poured tea and passed a tray of biscuits. When he'd gone, Claire said, "If Boyle didn't owe the man money, why didn't you want to see him?"

"Not everyone has *money* problems, Claire."

"Everyone in Fontjoy Square does. They may not admit it, but I've got eyes, Dolly, and I can detect the air of destitution a mile away. Miss Hyde's precious papa hasn't so much as shown his face. Mrs. Sinclair looks as if she's on the verge of tears every time we see her. And all of us, particularly me, appear to be lacking in an extensive wardrobe. That gown of yours is lovely, darling, but it's not the latest vogue and we both know it."

"Just because I am not a slave to fashion, doesn't mean that I am broke, Claire."

"I didn't say you were broke—"

"I don't want to talk about it anymore!" Dolly practically tossed her cup and saucer on the low table in front of her. Then she clamped her hands over her ears and squeezed her eyes shut. "And I will not listen to another word of this nonsense."

A moment passed during which neither woman spoke.

At length, Dolly opened her eyes. Claire was calmly chewing a lemon biscuit. The subject was closed.

"What did you think of Mr. Avondale?" Claire asked.

"I thought he was very handsome. What did you think?"

"Oh, he's handsome enough. And a widower."

"Yes, I gathered. Are you interested in him, Claire?"

Lady Kilgarren blushed. "Hardly. Don't you remember what I said, Dolly? I don't want a man. Wouldn't have one if he *begged* me to marry him. I think men are horrible creatures, every last one of them!" She shuddered theatrically.

"I think you protest too much, to paraphrase Shakespeare."

"What about you, Dolly? That fellow . . . What was that his name? Rafe O'Shea! He seemed rather smitten with you."

"Yes, I believe he was. He wants to take me to dinner."

Lady Kilgarren sat on the edge of her seat. "Then you must go!"

"Why? Didn't you just tell me a moment ago that men are horrible creatures, without exception?"

"But you don't feel that way. I saw the way the two of you looked at each other. Go, Dolly! It's better than sitting around here doing nothing."

"I don't sit around, doing nothing."

"All right, then. It's better than piddling about in the garden with a bunch of unmarried ladies. And it's better than running off each day to stick a hot water bottle beneath the feet of your Uncle Hester, or Aunt Esther, or whomever it is you claim to be nursing."

A flush of heat fanned Dolly's cheeks. Lady Kilgarren knew she was a fraud. It was only a matter of time before she forced Dolly's hand, and demanded an explanation concerning her mysterious absences.

On the other hand, Dolly's personal life was none of Claire's concern. Just because the two were friends did not give Lady Kilgarren the right to know every little detail of Dolly's existence.

"I'm tired, Claire."

"I've offended you." Lady Kilgarren put down her tea and stood. She leaned over and squeezed Dolly's shoulder. "I was out of place, and I apologize. But before I go, Dolly, I want you to know, whatever secrets you are hiding, they cannot change the fact that we are friends."

Once Claire had left, Dolly retired to her bedchamber. The gaslamp beside her bed cast a bright honeytinted glow over the room. Agitated, she searched in her sewing basket for a pair of stockings badly in need of mending. Her darning needles clicked throughout the night as she contemplated her predicament.

By the time dawn broke, she was exhausted. But she'd made a decision. Her days of deceit were over. From now on, she was simply Lady Dolly Baltmore, a widow living in a slightly shabby town house in a fashionable section of Dublin. She had no household staff, and her budget did not include allowances for fancy ball gowns. If Lady Claire Kilgarren, the duke's daughter, could adjust to poverty and live in it gracefully, so could she.

Dolly's experience with Dick Creevy had brought her down a peg. Humbled by her failure, she vowed never to perpetrate such a heinous fraud on any other person, man or woman. Pretending to be someone she wasn't had only caused her heartache.

She pictured Rafe O'Shea's eager expression when he'd asked if he could call on her. She should be happy that a man, any man, would show an interest in her. She wasn't wealthy. And her looks, her cropped hair and boyish figure, weren't likely to appeal to the great majority of men.

She should be thrilled at the prospect of Mr. O'Shea's suit.

After all, she couldn't have Dick Creevy, or even pursue a friendship with him, because of her duplicity. The man knew her as Doll Face Mohr, a teenage boxing acolyte, and as Dolly, a prostitute. He would hate her if and when he learned the extent and nature of her hoax. He *should* hate her.

As she should hate him.

He was the man who had killed her husband, and she was no nearer to finding out why or how than she had been when she'd first shown up at his boxing academy.

Dick Creevy had been slouched over a tankard of beer since ten-thirty that morning, when it had become apparent that Dahl Mohr wasn't going to appear for his training session.

The boy hadn't been to Creevy's Pugilist Academy in over a week now. And Dick's agitation had increased with each passing day. He was miserable. A vacuum gaped where Doll Face had been; exercise and boxing simply weren't as enjoyable without someone to share them with. For the first time in years, Dick wasn't able to beat his loneliness into submission by punishing his body with jump ropes, dumbbells, and grueling sparring sessions.

He neglected his own workout regimen, sleeping more than usual, while allowing his temper to consume him over the tiniest inconveniences. Just yesterday, a young boy about Dahl's age had spilled a bucket of water on the sparring mat, and Dick had yelled so loudly, the entire gymnasium reverberated. The other men were beginning to avoid him. The dressing room fell quiet when he entered for his daily shower.

So at half past three in the afternoon, he now sat beneath an array of fishing nets and antique brass lanterns, the ubiquitous wall decorations of Dublin pubs. Dick supposed the nautical ambience was meant to whet his appetite for adventure. Instead, it depressed him—as did everything else.

O'Callahan's appearance startled him.

"Christ on a raft!" The older man plunked his body in the club chair opposite Dick. "I should have known I'd find you here. Have you gone mad, laddie? Drinkin' beer in the middle of the day when you've got a fight comin' up in less than two weeks?"

"Don't worry, Cal." Struggling not to slur his speech, Dick motioned for the tap girl to bring another pitcher. "I'll be more'n ready for Eric the Viking."

"What the hell's the matter with you, Dick?" Cal took a long draft and wiped his upper lip with his sleeve.

Pinching the bridge of his nose, Dick suppressed the hot spring of tears threatening to erupt. He didn't know how to answer Cal. "Nothing's the matter. Just tired, I guess."

"Ever hear the expression 'Don't kid a kidder?' "

There was no point in trying to fool Cal. The old man could read Dick's moods like a map.

"All right, then. I've made a mess of things."

"How so?"

"I met a woman." Dick wrapped his fingers around his beer mug. "And for the life of me, I can't quit thinking about her."

"What's so terrible about that?" Cal slapped the table and gave a great belly laugh. "Is that what you're so blue about? By the rood, boy, 'tis the best news I've heard all month! You've gone and lost your heart to some bonnie lassie, and you're as sad-eyed as a mooncalf. Pshaw! Hell, at least it proves you're human. And, by God, that you're a man!"

"Was there ever any doubt in that?" The sharpness of Dick's tone surprised both men.

Cal reared back. "Never any doubt at all, boy! Tell me, now, what's got into you? You're as prickly as a pinecone these days."

"Sorry. I didn't mean to take your head off."

Cal cooled off quickly. "Maybe you don't like to admit it, but I think you're a wee bit worried about fighting Eric the Viking."

That was the least of Dick's worries. In point of fact, the thought of taking a good, hard pounding soothed him. He deserved to get the stuffing knocked out of him. If he could do nothing else like a man, he could at least withstand the Viking's pummeling.

But he couldn't admit that to Cal. The old man would never understand the concept of trading one brand of pain for another. And he most certainly would not understand that Dick's depression stemmed not from his fear of fighting, but from his fear of loving something—or someone—he could not have.

Confused, Dick gulped down more beer than was prudent. He'd already ruined the day, he rationalized. He'd never be able to jump rope or get in the sparring ring with two pitchers of beer in his bloodstream. He might as well go all out and get completely plastered.

"I think you've had enough, laddie."

"Not nearly." Dick continued to drink.

Both men were silent for a few moments. At length, Cal said, "Doll Face didn't show today."

"Really?" As if he hadn't noticed. Dick's mug hit the table with a heavy clunk.

"Kid must be sick or somethin'. Not like him to miss a workout."

"Yes, he must be sick."

Cal drummed his fingers on the scarred tabletop. "Don't reckon he got in a fight, do you?"

A thread of fear spiraled up Dick's spine. "Fight? Why do you say that?"

"Girlish looking scamp! He's bound to draw the attention of some unsavory types. Thugs that would make a sport of picking on him; you know what I mean. And he's a feisty little thing, more so now that he thinks he can box."

"He's only taken one punch at me," Dick inserted. "A pretty healthy one, too, if I must say so."

"He's like one of them tiny lap dogs that doesn't know how itty-bitty he really is." Cal rubbed his face and chuckled. "Never seen so much fight in such a scrawny runt."

"Does he look rather girlish to you, too, then?"

"Looks more like a girl than most girls!"

"So it isn't just me who sees it?"

"Are you crazy, Dick? Put a dress on that young'un and he'd be prettier'n me own mum was when she was a green young thing!"

Dick breathed a sigh of relief. He was gratified to know that he wasn't the only man who saw a distinctly feminine aspect in Dahl Mohr's demeanor. He'd been starting to think he was a deviant. Between the intensity of his attraction toward a puny little boxing student, and his perverse desire to make love to a boyish woman with curly blond hair, he'd nearly declared himself insane. Cal's offhand comment about Dahl's girlishness restored at least a smidgen of his masculine self-image.

"If he's been in a fight . . ." Dick's voice trailed.

"Ah, I'm just talkin'," Cal said. "I wouldn't fret about it, if I were you. He'll show up tomorrow. Or the day after that. Kids these days just aren't very dependable."

"I hope you're right." Dick fell quiet again, his mind spinning. If the boy didn't show up in the next day or so, he would have to go looking for him. He couldn't tolerate Dahl Mohr's abdication any more than he could Dolly's desertion of him.

Desertion? He'd had one encounter with the woman, and already he missed her! It wasn't as if he had a history with the woman. It wasn't as if they'd share a life or a relationship. Dolly wasn't Kitty Desmond. She hadn't borne Dick's child. She hadn't told him she loved him, or that she'd wait for him forever.

It was ridiculous to compare Dolly's abandonment with Kitty's guilty flight. Yet Dick's old pain was suddenly new again. New and fierce and burning as brightly as ever.

Slamming his fist on the table, he muttered an ugly oath through gritted teeth. He was sick and tired of being abandoned.

"If the kid doesn't turn up tomorrow, Cal, do you have any idea where we can find him?"

"None." The old man shrugged. Looking puzzled, he said, "But I wouldn't worry about that too much, laddie. If I was you, I'd be more worried about that young lady you've fallen in love with. Friends are one thing; lovers are another."

"Are they?" Dick gripped his beer, wondering if Cal was right. After all, his past experiences with both friends and lovers was equally disastrous. Whenever he'd needed either, they'd abandoned him. In the case of Kitty Desmond, his former lover, and Rafe O'Shea, his former best friend, they'd abandoned him simultaneously, and in favor of each other.

As a result, he'd lived alone for years, refusing to form attachments with other human beings. He knew that falling in love would only lead to a broken heart. He'd learned his lesson. He'd never do that again.

"I'm a fool, Cal." Dick had foolishly grown attached to Doll Face Mohr. The young man had insinuated himself into Dick's life. Dick had grown dependent on the kid's company, silly chatter, dogged perseverence, friendly companionship. Then the boy disappeared without an explanation. Apparently, Doll Face didn't feel he owed Dick anything. He'd simply jettisoned their friendship as if it were excess baggage.

Dahl Mohr was as much a friend to him as Rafe O'Shea had been.

And Dolly the prostitute loved him just as dearly as Kitty Desmond had.

"Is there something about me that makes people want to hurt me?" Dick growled.

Cal was clearly puzzled by this remark. "You're too hard on yerself," he replied gruffly.

"Perhaps." Dick threaded his fingers through the thinning hair at his temples. "On the other hand, perhaps I am not hard enough."

Another pitcher of beer was placed on the table. After draining half a glass, Cal boldly changed the subject. "Look, boy, the reason I came over here is to talk to you about Eric the Viking. You've got to call off this fight! You're in no shape—"

"It's too late, now, Cal, even if I wanted to. The fight's been scheduled and well advertised. Tickets have been sold. Wagers have been made. If I refuse to fight, a lot of men will be out a lot of money."

"What are you gonna do, then? Sit here and mope about this mysterious lady friend you told me about?

While Eric is across town, training like a gorilla and promising everyone who'll listen that he intends to beat your sorry mug into a bloody pulp?"

"Is that what he's saying?"

"The odds are in his favor."

Dick's head snapped up. He hadn't been the underdog in years. "Are you serious? Eric Duffy is nothing but an overgrown infant! He's clumsy and slow, for God's sake. I can box circles around that clown any day of the week!"

"You can, Dick, and you could. If you was in top shape. But rumor has it you've gone soft. That's why the players are betting against you."

"What the hell does that mean?"

"Men talk; you ought to know that—especially those in the boxing world. They see you spending all your time with this young boy, a student! And they think you've lost interest in the sport. Got yer mind on other things."

"Are you telling me that people think I am a—"

"No one has said as much, Dick. Not in my presence, anyway. Well, they wouldn't dare, would they? But with all the interest you've shown in teaching some new lad how to box, it appears you aren't interested in your own career. The men see you laughing and smiling when you're with the kid. They think you've lost your edge, your hunger, your drive to win. They think you're going to get yourself killed in that ring with Eric the Viking."

"I don't care what everyone thinks. And to tell you the truth, Cal, I don't much care if I do get killed."

"All the more reason you should call off the fight. Something is wrong with you, Dick, and you need a doctor. Or maybe you just need a strong dose of lovin' from that woman you've taken up with. But whichever it is, you aren't going to be better in time to fight the Viking. Let me call Eric's manager and agent, Dick. Let's do it today, before this thing get any further out of control."

"No!"

"Even the newspapers are predicting you'll be defeated!"

"The press can't tell you when it is going to rain, Cal. What makes you think those rumormongers can say with any accuracy who is going to win this fight?"

"I don't want to see you get hurt, Dick, that's all."

Bitterness, anger, and embarrassment swamped Dick's emotions. He most likely *would* get killed in that ring if he didn't continue his training, increase the intensity of his workouts, and begin focusing on winning. He needed to lay off the beer and start eating differently. He needed to think about Eric's likely moves, and plan his method of attack. He needed to pull himself out of his melancholy, self-pitying mood and get ready for the most challenging fight of his career.

But he didn't know if he could do it. He missed Doll Face, and he wanted Dolly. His regrets haunted him, and the pain of past mistakes threatened to consume him. His body ached for physical release, through pain *or* erotic pleasure. His thoughts ran so quickly through his mind, he couldn't relax.

He thought he was going insane.

With his hands pressed to the sides of his head, Dick squeezed his eyes shut. The pressure between his ears seemed unbearable. He wondered if he could even get up from the table and into his own bed without breaking down. He had no idea how he was going to fight the Viking.

When the pounding in his head was a deafening roar, he opened his eyes. Lurching to his feet, he pointed a finger at O'Callahan. "Don't you dare call off this fight, do you hear me? I'm going to give that son of a bitch a beating he'll never forget."

Cal stared at him through narrowed eyes. The man's silence was pregnant with recriminations and doubt.

Dick turned away, humiliated. He had no confidence whatsoever that he could beat the Viking. But he could not look into O'Callahan's accusing eyes another second.

An hour later, as he lay in his bed, Dick's stomach roiled from too much beer and angry emotion. Doll Face and Dolly were now his twin obsessions. But try as he might, he saw no hope of reconciling his desires with his momentous failures. When Dick cared about someone, male or female, that person historically took flight or betrayed him. He'd be wise to accept his shortcomings and resign himself to being alone.

As a troubled sleep overtook him, he renewed his determination to beat Eric the Viking. He'd neglected his training, and he was in serious danger of being knocked out in the first round. But he had two more weeks in which to train. And as soon as this hangover wore off, he was heading back to the gym.

He wasn't the sort of man to wallow in self-pity for too long. Weakness hadn't earned him the title of the best boxer in Dublin and Ireland, and perhaps, the entire British Empire.

Dick Creevy was a man accustomed to punishment and pain. In his sport and his profession, he'd been unrelenting in his pursuit of excellence. He was a perfectionist of sorts, a man who couldn't easily forget a detail, a man who remembered nearly everything another person said.

His body jerked convulsively, yanking him from the edge of sleep. Dick's eyes flew open and his mind flashed on Dolly's face as she sat astride him looking down.

She had said, "I have recently discovered the benefits of exercise."

Hadn't he felt calluses on her fingertips?

And what about her enigmatic remark, "I am precisely who you want. What's more, I am precisely who you think I am. But you don't know me, Mr. Creevy, because you can't see me. You only see what you want to see."

His heart thumped furiously.

Had she got those calluses from jumping rope?

Has he been so blind and so enraptured by his own needs and desires, that he failed to see what was right in front of him?

Had he been duped yet again?

Twelve

Mr. O'Shea dropped around at Fontjoy Square the day after Mr. Avondale's party. After knocking on the door, he politely presented his calling card to Ferghus and suggested that Lady Dolly send word of a more convenient time for him to pay his respects.

The vellum card, beautifully engraved, looked rather pathetic, all alone in the silver salver on the French commode that stood in the foyer. But its singularity imbued it with a compelling importance, according to Lady Claire Kilgarren.

"You simply must allow him to visit, dear. No one else is calling. No one that I can detect, anyway."

After Dolly had balked and remonstrated for an hour, Claire convinced her that the visit would go more smoothly if she were there. "Along with Mr. Avondale, that is. I believe it only proper that we invite another gentleman."

When Dolly raised her brows, Claire explained, "So that we won't appear to be so alone in the world, dear, so defenseless and vulnerable."

"But we hardly know Mr. Avondale. We can't expect him to be our *protector.*"

"Dear, we hardly know Mr. O'Shea. We can't expect him to be a gentleman."

"There's no reason to suppose he won't be, Claire."

"Just so. And there's no reason to suppose Mr. Avondale is anything less than gallant."

A week later, Claire's deeply flawed logic having won out over Dolly's protests, the party convened in the drawing room of Number Two Fontjoy Square. Dolly sat on one end of the sofa, Claire on the other. Mr. O'Shea occupied a wingback chair opposite the ladies while Mr. Avondale stood at the mantel. Ferghus, having performed his multiple duties as butler, valet, and serving girl, hurriedly backed out of the room.

"An odd little man," Mr. O'Shea commented. "I thought he was going to break every cup on the tray when he tripped into the room. Don't you have a girl who can serve tea?"

"I like the way Ferghus serves tea," Dolly replied. She resented it a bit that Mr. O'Shea would question the sufficiency of her household staff. Avoiding Lady Kilgarren's gaze, she added, "Besides, my other servants have not yet arrived from the country, and are not expected for quite some time."

"Well, when they do arrive, I'm certain you'll have someone less clumsy to serve the tea."

"Ferghus has made himself quite handy in the garden, I have noticed," inserted Mr. Avondale.

"Yes, it is coming along nicely!" Lady Kilgarren's cheeks were unusually pink as she described to Mr. O'Shea the ladies' joint gardening project in the center of Fontjoy Square. "When we are finished, we will have trellises strewn with roses, a burbling fountain, and stone benches to sit on. Mr. Avondale has been most generous in volunteering his time and industry, as well."

Mr. Avondale smiled warmly, but only in Lady Kilgarren's direction. Watching the two, Dolly formed a seminal theory regarding their heightened colors. But she was unable to sustain her speculation. Mr. O'Shea seemed determined to capture all of her attention.

"Tell me, Lady Dolly, do *you* enjoy working in the garden?"

"I welcome the distraction," she answered honestly. The worries that plagued her were no one else's business, however. "And I enjoy the companionship, of course."

"Have you had much experience gardening?" he pressed.

"Of course not." *What does he think I am, a country bumpkin?* "Ordinarily, I would leave that sort of work to the servants."

"I didn't mean to suggest—"

Mr. Avondale interjected. "One need only to look at Lady Dolly's complexion to see that she hasn't spent a great deal of time in the sun. Her fair skin is a testament to years of staying indoors."

"But her freckles aren't," Claire blurt out.

Had the men not covered the awkward moment with polite laughter, Dolly might have throttled her friend. She had, in fact, soaked up a fair amount of sun running back and forth to Creevy's Pugilist Academy. Her freckles had darkened and her hair now glowed a brilliant burnished copper. She wore a look of health she hadn't possessed in years.

"I do believe gardening is a healthy activity," she remarked. "The sun has had a salutary effect on my respiration as well as my skeleton and muscles, too.

Really, Mr. O'Shea, you should get outside more often yourself."

"I heartily agree. My passions, I'm afraid, keep me indoors."

"And what *are* your passions?" Dolly asked, rather coolly and in a slightly bored tone of voice.

"Horseflesh, racing, cards." He met Dolly's gaze. "And boxing, of course."

An explosive shock rattled Dolly's bones. "Boxing," she managed to repeat. A sudden dryness in her throat compelled her to sip her tea. "That is quite a coincidence, Mr. O'Shea."

"How is that so?" His mustache shifted strangely as he smiled.

"My husband was a boxing afficionado. He died in the boxing ring, as a matter of fact."

"Good heavens!" Claire touched her throat, genuinely surprised. "You've never told me that, Dolly. How did it happen?"

"I-I don't know all the details. He attended an exhibition match in which famous boxers participated."

"Who, for example?" asked Mr. O'Shea.

"Dick Creevy."

"Creevy?" Mr. Avondale inclined his head. "He was a guest at my party last week. Perhaps you saw him. Can't say that I know him very well, though. He was a friend of my wife's. My deceased wife, that is. She had many friends I wasn't well acquainted with. She was unusually well liked, you see."

Noting Lady Kilgarren's mildly wounded expression, Dolly brought the conversation back to the subject of Lord Baltmore's untimely demise. "Creevy challenged the spectators to fight him. Any man in the audience who could beat him would win a handsome purse."

O'Shea folded his arms across his chest and snorted derisively. "That's rich! As if any man could best a champion fighter like Creevy."

"Why would any man try?" Lady Kilgarren asked.

"Men often overestimate their strength," Mr. Avondale said. "Particularly when they are deep in their cups."

"Oh, I'm certain Lord Baltmore wasn't drinking," Mr. O'Shea said unctuously.

"I'm sure not," Dolly lied. "But he could never resist a challenge. He and one of his cronies were in the stands that evening. For reasons I suppose I will never understand, they resolved to accept Dick Creevy's invitation."

"Both of them?" asked Mr. Avondale.

"No, just my husband. He got in the ring, and I'm told he fought handily. He wasn't a mouse, you understand. He had a modicum of training."

"But he wasn't fit to battle a champion," Lady Kilgarren remarked.

"One would think Mr. Creevy might understand that. Good heavens, he wasn't fighting to retain his title!" Despite her efforts to remain calm, Dolly's heart skittered and her voice climbed an octave. "But he fought my husband as if he were battling Goliath. Leaned into every shot, battered his body, and wore him out. In the fifth round, he landed a blow to Boyle's left ear. Boyle went down and never got up."

Lady Kilgarren gasped. "You mean he was dead?"

"As dead as can be," Dolly replied.

"Ghastly." Mr. O'Shea seemed disturbed. "Do you know the name of the man who accompanied your husband to the boxing match that night?"

"No." Dolly was hoping she would learn that from Dick Creevy. "I wish I did know. I should like to ask him what he was thinking when he encouraged my husband to accept Dick Creevy's challenge."

Mr. Avondale said, "Perhaps that gentleman's judgment was clouded by whiskey, my lady. I wouldn't dwell on such matters if I were you."

"Life goes on," Lady Kilgarren said, wistfully.

"Whether we like it or not," Mr. Avondale said.

Dolly sighed and set her teacup aside. Lord Baltmore and his friends were certainly not above drinking too much. In fact, Boyle's tendency to booze and brawl was legendary. But Dolly had never admitted, even to herself, that her husband's drinking, or the pugnaciousness that often accompanied his binges, was a major factor in their marital discontent. Come to think of it, she'd never admitted that she wasn't happily married.

Nor had she been entirely fair to Dick Creevy in her recounting of her husband's death. Blaming the unseemly incident on Lord Baltmore's recklessness or stupidity was unpalatable; it was an admission that something was wrong with her husband, and by extension, her own marriage. Dick Creevy's culpability was a crutch to Dolly; it provided a plausible reason for Lord Baltmore's ignominious death, and it allowed her to shift the blame from Boyle to some faceless amoral beast.

The problem was, Dick Creevy now had a face. And though his morality remained in question—he had, after all, commissioned a prostitute for the evening—his humanity and his compassion were well established. Dolly had insinuated herself into the man's life. She knew him now as a man, a boxer, a friend, a mentor . . . and a lover.

She knew him better than she'd ever known her own husband, better than most women ever got to know their husbands. And having seen him at his most vulnerable, when he'd confessed his self-doubt to O'Callahan, when he'd allowed himself to lose control in bed, she'd thought she loved him.

But in getting to know him, she'd deceived him. No real relationship could be built on such a shaky foundation.

The depression she'd been fighting for days rolled over her again.

"Dolly?" Lady Kilgarren's mellifluous voice gently intruded. "Are you all right? If this conversation is too unpleasant for you, dear, let's change the subject."

"It's just that talking about Boyle upsets me so."

"I know how difficult it is to lose someone you loved," Mr. Avondale said. "First you feel shock, then anger, then guilt, then a sort of relentless sadness."

She looked at the man. His eyes were so blue and kind. For an instant, she felt connected to him by a shared sense of bereavement, as if they'd lost a mutual loved one, as if they were bound together in their melancholy.

His gaze was suddenly familiar. Had she met Mr. Avondale before she moved to Fontjoy Square? Had she seen him someplace other than in the garden and at his fancy dress ball?

An eerie sensation overcame her. Dolly tore her eyes off Mr. Avondale, half certain that he could see straight through her.

Lady Kilgarren was the first to stand and make her excuses. "It's getting late," she said, though it was barely half past four in the afternoon.

"Please allow me to walk you home," offered Mr. Avondale.

In the foyer, when the others had gone, Mr. O'Shea stayed behind. He held his top hat before him, nervously edging the brim with his thumbs. "I hope you aren't overset by today's conversation, Lady Dolly."

"I hadn't expected to share such intimacies with people I barely know."

He took a step closer. " 'Tis true. We barely know each other. But I would like to know you better, Dolly. Perhaps we could go to the opera, or to dinner, or even to a boxing match. I sense that we might get along famously."

Stiffening, Dolly met Mr. O'Shea's gaze. Studying his features, she renewed her opinion that he had a handsome face. His nose was straight and keenly tipped, his mustache, thick and fashionable. His eyes glowed with intelligence. His lips, while thin, curled sensuously. He was clean and well dressed. Indeed, Dolly could find nothing unappealing about him.

Yet, she couldn't imagine kissing him. And she couldn't imagine taking off her clothes and lying beneath him, much less climbing atop him and pleasuring herself the way she did with Dick Creevy. She couldn't imagine that at all.

"You hesitate, my lady. Why? Have I offended you? I shouldn't have mentioned the boxing match, should I?"

"You've haven't offended me." On the contrary, he'd been polite, solicitous, kind.

"Give me a chance, then. Please. I should like to call on you one evening, alone." He took her hand and drew her knuckles to his lips. His mustache tickled her skin. She wondered what it would feel like if he kissed her in a certain way, in a more private place. . . .

Her eyes closed. But in her mind's eye, it was Dick Creevy who kissed her so intimately, so lovingly. . . .

Dolly shivered as a wave of guilty desire rippled across her skin. Here stood Rafe O'Shea, a good, decent man who wanted to court her. And all she could think of was Dick Creevy, the man who'd killed her husband, the man she'd deceived and defrauded, the man who knew her only as a boy and a prostitute.

"Dolly? Is it yes or no?" Rafe O'Shea's voice was not unkind, but he had every right to demand an answer to his invitation.

She opened her eyes. "Yes, Mr. O'Shea. I should like to see you again."

He smiled victoriously. Then he put on his hat and tilted it to a rakish angle. "I will pick you up tomorrow evening at eight o'clock, then." On the threshold, he paused. "Please leave Lady Kilgarren and Mr. Avondale behind this time, will you? I'm much too old for chaperones, dear."

Dolly chuckled as she closed the door behind him. She was too old for chaperones, too. But the idea of being alone with Mr. O'Shea for an entire evening made her feel uneasy.

Climbing the stairs, she attributed her apprehension to the residual effects of her disastrous encounter with Dick Creevy. Because of her own habitual duplicity, she couldn't bring herself to trust Mr. O'Shea. Like many people, she attributed her own worst qualities to others. But Mr. O'Shea had not proven himself untrustworthy. He'd been nothing but kind and straightforward. She had to force herself to forget Mr. Creevy, and the best way to do that was to get out of the house, be with other people, even entertain Mr. O'Shea's attentions, if that was what it took.

In her bedchamber, she took the jump rope that hung over her chair, and turned the rough braid over in her hands. She held the hemp to her nose, breathing in the smell of the gymnasium, perspiration, Dick Creevy. She wanted him more than she'd ever wanted anything or anyone. She wanted him to love her.

But how could he when he didn't even know Lady Dolly Baltmore existed?

"I thought you'd given up on them blasted suffragists," Ferghus said the next morning when Dolly descended the steps.

In the foyer mirror, she studied her reflection, adjusting her cap and hunching her shoulders just so, in order to hide the gentle swells of her bustline. "I thought I had, too, Ferghus, but I have agreed to attend one last meeting. Be a dear, will you, and have a bite of lunch ready for me when I get home. I expect I will be hungry."

"You always are after you come home from one of them things." The man smiled indulgently as he dusted the gilded edges of a Regency pedestal.

"Be careful not to knock old Boney off his perch." Dolly nodded at the basalt bust of Napoleon that sat atop the pedestal. Then she ran out the door and down the street to hail her hackney cab.

She'd often wondered at the choice of furnishings made by the previous owner of Number Two. Though a strong feminine influence was evident in the house, so was a decidedly progressive and diverse political attitude. Portraits of Alexander the Great hung next to those of Queen Victoria. The works of Irish revolutionaries such as Wolfe Tone and Daniel O'Connell were bookends to Byron's poetry and Trollope's social lampoons. Celtic relics lay on tabletops next to Limoges snuffboxes and Wedgwood trinket trays.

Whoever had lived at Number Two Fontjoy Square before Dolly, had been a woman of taste, wit, and forward thinking. From living among her things, Dolly concluded that she would have liked the woman.

She wasn't at all certain, however, that the woman who read *Cyrano de Bergerac* until the pages were as yellow and wrinkled as tobacco leaves would have liked her in the least.

She disembarked her carriage and walked the last few blocks to Creevy's Pugilist Academy. At the entrance, she hesitated, her heart thudding. Inside the pocket of her tweed jacket was a letter she intended to place on Creevy's desk. She had only to enter the gym, make her way across the floor, and slip inside Dick's office without notice. Her plan was not without risk. If Creevy happened to be in the gymnasium, he would undoubtedly confront her. He'd want to know why she hadn't shown up for her lessons and training sessions. He'd want to know why Dahl "Doll Face" Mohr had disappeared.

Biting her bottom lip, Dolly steeled her nerves. It was half past eight o'clock in the morning, much too early for Dick Creevy to be working out or sparring. He had never arrived before nine-thirty, not in the entire time Dolly had known him. Of course, Doll Face's sessions began at ten. And as long as Dick and Doll Face were training together, there was no need for Dick to arrive any earlier.

She pushed her way inside, determined to get in and out as quickly as possible.

In the entrance area, she practically collided with Sean Conway, the gentleman whose private parts she met eye to eye the first day she'd attended Creevy's Pugilist Academy.

Conway's handsome face split into a grin the instant he saw her. "Doll Face! Well, where on God's green earth have you been hidin' yerself, laddie? We was beginnin' to get worried about you!"

"Had a touch of the ague," Dolly said, coughing weakly into her fist.

The man gingerly patted her shoulder. "Take care of yerself, ye little leprechaun. Creevy's been a monster since ye gave up the training! Glad to see you back!"

Ducking her head, Dolly hurried across the floor of the gymnasium. The place was empty but for one man jumping rope in the far corner, and another who, with breathtaking speed and coordination, pummeled a suspended leather bag stuffed with feathers.

She darted down the hallway that led to Dick's office. The door was closed, but a strip of light glowed beneath it. Dolly paused, wondering whether Dick was inside, working at his ledgers or reading correspondence. Perhaps he'd been unable to sleep and he'd come to the gymnasium early to read the morning papers. Maybe, in light of the big fight coming up in less than a week, he'd changed his exercise routine.

Her leg muscles felt like tapioca and her knees wobbled. An hour's worth of jumping rope wouldn't have taxed her endurance as much as two minutes standing outside Dick Creevy's office door.

Holding her breath, she slid the letter from her pocket. Written on a plain sheet of onionskin, the note was a good-bye of sorts, an apology from Dahl Mohr for his disappearance from the pugilist academy. Dolly had written nearly thirty versions of it before she settled on the final edit. The letter said:

Dear Mr. Creevy,
I wish to thank you for everything you've taught
me. In the past few weeks, I have learned much

*about boxing, and more about myself. I am forever
grateful to you for believing in me. My failure is
not a reflection of the quality of your tutelage, but
of the weakness of my character. However, to the
extent I was exposed to your kindness, strength,
and compassion, I consider myself improved.
Thank you.*

Yours very truly,
Doll Face

She fingered the thick red wax that sealed the letter.
She wished she had written that she loved him, not
because she wanted him to love her back—oh, she did,
but she couldn't expect that!—but because she wanted
him to know that he was loved. He deserved that much.

But in her dishonesty, Dolly was unable to give Dick
that gift. Dick Creevy did not want to be told he was
loved by Doll Face Mohr. The very thought would
sicken and disgust him, as it would any man. If she
meant to stay in character and play the role she'd created, Dolly could only thank the man for teaching her
to box.

Tamping back a flood of tears, Dolly bent and
slipped the letter beneath the door.

Then she turned and fled Creevy's Pugilist Academy
as fast as she could.

Inside his office, Dick watched the shadows playing
at his threshold. Lying on his sofa, hands laced behind
his head, he remained perfectly still. Mentally, he wasn't
prepared to face O'Callahan. Physically, he wasn't
ready to confront his sparring partner, an enthusiastic
amateur half his age who hopped around the ring like

a bouncing ball and landed more wallops to Dick's jaw and ears than seemed strictly necessary.

So he held his breath and hoped whoever was on the other side of his door would go away.

The long white envelope that slid across his floor surprised him. The retreating footsteps, beating a wild tattoo down the corridor, confused him. The realization of Doll Face's visitation propelled him off the sofa.

He swiped up the letter and flung open the door in one fluid motion. Galloping across the gymnasium floor, he saw Doll Face's departing back, and a glimpse of the blond curls sticking out from beneath a woolen cap. He chased the lad out of the building and halfway down the street. Then Doll Face leaped into a cab and took off.

Frantic, the unread letter still clutched in his hand, Dick quickly hailed another cab. "Follow that carriage," he yelled, pointing at the black cab trundling in the opposite direction.

"Hey, ain't you Dick Creevy?" the driver asked.

Dick jumped into the driver's perch. "No time for talk. Just follow that cab and don't lose it. I'll make it worth your while, old man. Now, go!"

"Whatever ye say!" And with that, the old man snapped his whip on the flank of his lead horse.

The cab took off with a jolt, heading southeast toward a familiar section of Dublin. Dick had attended a dinner party in that quarter of the city just a week ago.

And his suspicions regarding the identity of Dolly the prostitute grew as each passing block took him closer to Fontjoy Square.

Thirteen

Devon Avondale thrust his spade into the soft black earth. With a groan, he clutched his lower back and straightened. He'd been working in the garden for half the morning, and his muscles ached. Clearing the tangled greenery off this neglected little patch of land was even more of a challenge than he'd anticipated.

Mrs. Sinclair and Miss Millicent had joined him earlier, but when it became apparent they weren't cut out for hacking underbrush and yanking weeds, he'd sent them home. His purpose in instructing the ladies to tend the garden in the center of Fontjoy Square was to bring them together, to give them a joint project and a common goal. He wanted them to befriend one another, not kill themselves sweating beneath an uncommonly warm spring sun.

He thought of walking over to Lady Kilgarren's house and asking for a cup of morning tea. But it would have been a ruse, really, a thinly veiled excuse to see her, Claire, the one woman among the four whom he couldn't quit thinking about. Thinking better of such an imprudent impulse, he turned and trudged in the opposite direction, toward his own lonely villa.

As always, when he passed Number Two, he looked

in that direction, half expecting to see his wife standing in the doorway, waving to him, or peeking from an upstairs window. She said she liked to watch him, to see his strong hands packing dirt around a flower bulb, his back bowed over a shovel, his hair wet and curly from perspiration. Often, when Devon would work in the garden, he would feel the warmth of her gaze on his neck, and he would turn and find her watching him. Knowing she was there, always, watching and waiting, had been such a comforting feeling.

But that was years ago, before Mary died of a disease in her lungs.

Now, when he passed Number Two, he saw nothing but a house, bordering on shabby, but coming back to life now that Lady Dolly Baltmore lived there. His Mary wasn't there to welcome him home or fret over the hours he spent in the sun. His Mary wasn't inside that house, reading her newspapers and books, or planning her next literary or political salon. Mary would never greet him at that door again with open arms and a ready kiss.

Which was why he couldn't bear living in Number Two. That was where he and Mary had lived. After she died, Devon had moved into that monstrous villa at the north end of the square, leaving behind Mary's books and furniture and paintings for someone else to enjoy. He hoped Lady Dolly appreciated Mary's things. He wondered what she would think if she knew she was living in the home of her childhood friend, Mary O'Roarke.

She'd figure it out eventually. She and the other ladies would piece it together someday. Though they'd all been sworn to secrecy regarding the manner in which they'd acquired their new homes, someday they would confide in one another.

They'd realize they'd all been offered a home in exchange for nothing more than tending a garden. Then they'd compare notes about their backgrounds. It might take months, but eventually they would recognize one striking similarity in their past lives: they had all, at one time or another, befriended a pretty brunette named Mary O'Roarke.

"Mary O'Roarke Avondale." He said her name aloud as if by invoking her memory he could bring her back to life. His chest squeezed painfully. He missed her so much he felt hollow inside. Rubbing the back of his neck, he thought again about knocking on Lady Kilgarren's door and asking her for tea. Or for anything. A kind word, even a sympathetic smile, would do. He hungered for a woman's touch, a kiss, a warm embrace. He was starving to love someone and to be loved in return.

But it wasn't fair to take from Lady Kilgarren what he really wanted from Mary O'Roarke Avondale.

So with a sigh, he forced himself to quit thinking about the pretty blonde at the south end of Fontjoy Square, and he tore his gaze off Number Two.

But only for a second. Because just as Devon stepped out of the garden and into the street, a dusty carriage roared around the corner and clattered to a halt in front of Lady Dolly Baltmore's house.

Dolly jumped out of the cab, threw a couple of coins at the driver, and ran into her house. She bolted up the steps, two at a time. Ferghus, a stack of towels in his arms, stood at the landing and gaped.

"I'm not here, Ferghus." She brushed past him.

"You ain't, m'lady?"

She paused on the top step and looked down at Ferghus. "If anyone knocks on that door, I want you to open it and explain that the boy who just ran into this house is a servant. No, a servant's son. And . . . and . . . the kid is on the lam because he brutally attacked someone in Ulster. And he ran out the back door and down the alley, and you don't know where he went, but he'll never be back because Lord Balt—no, no, don't say Lord Baltmore's name. Make up a name! Say that Mr. Greenwick doesn't want him here anymore and so—"

A thunderous fusillade of knocks hit the front door.

Dolly inhaled deeply. Her throat burned and her chest ached from the exertion of attempting to escape Dick Creevy. The minute she'd slipped that letter under his door, she knew she had made a mistake. When she heard him rouse, she beat it out of the gymnasium as fast as she could. But she wasn't fast enough. Dick Creevy had given chase, and he'd followed her all the way home.

He knocked again, this time louder, if that were possible.

"Who is that trying to knock down our door, ma'am?" Ferghus dropped his towels and held out his hands in a helpless gesture. "Tell me, and I'll get rid of him! I ain't gonna let no bill collector harass my mistress. No, sir!"

"He's not a bill collector, Ferghus." Dolly's calm voice belied her stormy emotions.

"Who is he, then?"

"He is Dick Creevy, the famous boxer."

Ferghus's face registered shock. Then his gaze took

in Dolly's boyish garb and her close-cropped curls. His expression changed to one of limited understanding. He didn't comprehend everything about Dolly's charade, but he realized she'd been posing as a boy, and that now the gig was up.

A renewed round of knocking rattled the chandelier in the foyer. From outside, Dick's voice boomed, "Open up, Doll Face. I swear, I will not leave these steps until I talk to you!"

"Get out of sight, lady. I'll tell the man you aren't here."

"Tell him—" Dolly thought of another story to tell, another lie to be woven into the web she had created. But the words caught in her throat.

"Tell him what, ma'am?"

She hesitated. Her world spun around her, and in a moment of brilliant clarity, she saw what she had done. She'd lied to everyone, including herself. She had been lying for years. As a child, she'd lied about her father. As an adult, she'd lied about her marriage and her husband. She hid the truth from herself as effectively as she did from others. She pretended to be someone she wasn't, someone whose life was picture-perfect.

Then Boyle had died, and instead of facing up to the truth, instead of admitting that she was poor, she had invented more lies. She'd lied to her creditors and her acquaintances. She'd lived a lifestyle she couldn't afford. She'd maintained appearances because her foolish pride wouldn't allow her to ask for help.

She had focused her attentions on Dick Creevy, the man who had killed her husband, because blaming him for her hardships was easier than admitting she'd been victimized by a scoundrel of a husband.

But then she *met* Dick Creevy and insinuated herself

into his life. She'd gotten to know the man, and she liked him. And she'd deceived him twice, first as a friend, then as a lover.

Now he stood at her front door, demanding to be let in, demanding an explanation for her behavior. And she owed him that much. She just wasn't certain she could tell the truth.

"Well, ma'am, what do you want me to do? Better tell me quick before his fist comes through the door!"

She released a breath she hadn't realized she was holding. "Open the door, Ferghus, and invite Mr. Creevy into the drawing room. Offer him some tea, if you would, and tell him to wait there. I'll be in shortly."

"Are you sure, my lady?"

She turned and headed toward her bedchamber. "Yes, Ferghus, I'm certain. For once in my life, I am going to tell the truth about who and what I am. Mr. Creevy will hate me for it, but that can't be helped now. I cannot stand this double life a moment longer."

Dick Creevy could wait, though. Dolly had no intention of meeting him on her own turf dressed as a boy.

He stood at the mantel, his back to the door. His breathing had returned to normal, but anger continued to course through his blood, heating his skin and burning his stomach. How dare that little waif run away from him! How dare that kid snub him after all Dick had done for him! Didn't their friendship mean anything?

The door clicked behind him. Dick whirled. A dizzying sense of unreality washed over him as a beautiful woman with golden curls and slender, boyish hips walked confidently into the room.

She wore a plain dark blue gown with a high neck

and long sleeves. The bustle at the small of her back lent definition to her waist, but could not conceal the straight lines of her figure or the leanness of her legs. Her bosom was compact and tantalizing. The sprinkle of freckles across her retroussé nose invited a kiss.

But the realization of who she was and what she had done to him, infuriated Dick. The delicious lick of arousal that accompanied his recognition of Dolly the prostitute, quickly turned to cold, hard anger.

"Who are you?" He couldn't soften the edge he heard in his own voice. "And what the hell sort of game are you playing?"

"My name is Lady Dolly."

"Lady?" His fists clenched at his sides. "Well, my lady, how do you manage to imitate a prostitute at night while you live your life as an aristocrat during the day? Or is it the aristocrat you are pretending to be?"

His question wrapped around her like barbed wire. Wounded, Dolly stood in the center of the floor, her hands clasped in front of her. "I suppose I deserved that."

"I don't know what you deserve, Lady Dolly. I don't know anything about you, as it turns out." He slammed his fist into his open palm. "Damn! How could I have been so foolish? You don't look anything like a boy! You don't look anything like a prostitute, for that matter!"

She might as well tell Dick Creevy everything now. She'd lost him anyway. "Would you like to sit down?"

"No, thank you. I don't think I'll be staying very long."

Despite her shaky knees, Dolly concluded it was wiser if she remained standing, too. "I'm sorry that I deceived you."

"Why did you?"

"I wanted to get even with you. But I didn't know how. I wanted to get to know you, your weaknesses, your vulnerabilities—so that I could hurt you the way you hurt me."

"What the devil did I ever do to you?" Dick growled.

"You killed my husband."

"What?" His eyes narrowed and his cheeks darkened.

"Lord Boyle Baltmore. You killed him."

"I did not—"

"You killed him just as surely as if you'd put a bullet in his back."

"The man volunteered—"

"He was an amateur, an out-of-shape, middle-aged, drunken rakehell who never worked a full day in his life. He spent his days playing cards and his nights attending boxing matches and cockfights. He was goaded into stepping into the ring with you by your reckless taunts and challenges."

"You've got it all wrong, Lady Dolly."

"No!" Hurt and outrage bubbled to Dolly's lips. She had deceived Dick Creevy, that was true. But it wasn't fair that her remorse should eclipse her anger. After all, her motivation for this charade was the murder of her husband. She hadn't set out to hurt anyone; she'd intended to avenge Lord Baltmore's death. Why was she apologizing to Dick Creevy now? "I haven't got it wrong! Boyle went to that match to watch you fight. He should never have set foot in that ring."

"It was an exhibition match! It took place in a pub, for God's sake! I never meant to injure your husband!"

"You killed him!"

"I barely touched him."

"He fell like a bolt of lightning had struck him. That's what I heard. That's what I was told!"

"Something was wrong with him before he got in that ring. There must have been!"

"There was nothing wrong with him. He had too much to drink, that's all."

"Perhaps he was sick!"

"No, he wasn't!"

Dick's eyes were suddenly wild, his voice strained by emotion. "Do you think I haven't asked myself a thousand times what went wrong that night? Do you think I haven't lain awake at night wondering why I invited any one of those drunken spectators into the ring? If I could do it over again, I would! I'm sorry for what happened to Lord Baltmore! I hardly hit him. I danced around him like I would a child. I took his punches. Good God, I've given you more harsh treatment in the gymnasium than I gave that man!"

Dolly's breathing came in short, painful pants. Confusion clawed at her. Dick looked genuinely anguished by Lord Baltmore's death. And she couldn't forget the self-loathing she'd heard in his voice when she overheard him talking about the incident with O'Callahan.

"Are you saying you didn't hit him with all your strength?"

"Of course not! I practically mollycoddled the man! The few punches I threw at him wouldn't have flattened a flea!"

"The fact remains, Mr. Creevy, my husband is dead. And you are not."

He sighed. "I've often wished I could take his place, Dolly. You have no idea how miserable I have been."

Tears stung her eyes. "Oh, I think I do, Mr. Creevy. I have been miserable, too, wondering how I was going to survive alone, without a husband, without an income, without anyone at all to share my life with."

Dick's gaze scanned the walls. "It appears to me you are prospering. I see no signs of poverty here."

She ignored that observation. It was certainly none of Dick Creevy's business how she came to acquire Number Two Fontjoy Square. Explaining her recent conduct to him was difficult enough; if she told him this house was donated to her in exchange for tending a garden, he'd think her daft. If he didn't already.

"Well, now you know everything, Mr. Creevy. I suggest you leave before this conversation turns any uglier."

"I understand *nothing!*" He took a step closer to her, his features drawn, his teeth flashing. "You haven't explained a thing to me, Dolly."

"What else do you need to know?"

"Why did you deceive me? If you wanted to know what happened in the ring that night, why didn't you just come and ask me?"

"I didn't think a murderer likely to tell the truth."

"So you concocted this scheme to dress up like a boy and pose as a boxing student?"

She dashed away a tear and lifted her chin. " 'Twas a bright idea. Or so I thought. If I got close to you, I could know what sort of man you were. I could find out what happened to my husband that night in the pub. I could wreak my revenge on you, then."

"That is the most foolish idea I've ever heard of. Beside the fact that you made a fool of me, you could have got yourself killed!"

"I was willing to take the risk."

"Ho, that is grand! Did it occur to you that I might not want to take that risk?"

"To be honest, I wasn't very concerned with your feelings, Mr. Creevy. Not in the beginning, at least."

Pinching the bridge of his nose, Dick fell silent a moment. When he looked at Dolly again, his brown gaze sparkled with emotion. "And why, pray tell, did you find it necessary to dress up like a prostitute and seduce me?"

"*I* seduced *you?*" Dolly chuckled. "Why, dear man, that is hardly what a prostitute does, is it? Wasn't it you who asked Mrs. Bunratty to furnish you with a boyish looking woman with short curly blond hair?"

"You must have enjoyed that," he snarled. "What a hilarious joke, and at my expense. How it must have amused you to impersonate the woman of my fantasies!"

Dolly's breath caught in her throat. She hated the dirty trick she'd played on Dick. And yet, the lovemaking she'd shared with him had been the most emotional and fulfilling sex of her life. Not, she reflected grimly, that she had much to compare him to. But intuitively, she knew that what she and Dick Creevy experienced in his bed that night was rare and special. He'd allowed himself to be vulnerable, to lose control. For a man like him, that wasn't an easy thing to do.

"You're quite an actress, Dolly." His voice was menacingly quiet.

"I wasn't acting that night, Dick." Her cheeks burned. Telling the truth was painfully embarrassing. "When I overheard you telling Mrs. Bunratty what sort of woman you wanted to make love to—"

"You saw another chance to *get to know me*. You saw another opportunity to humiliate me. Well, you can be proud of yourself, Dolly. You did."

"No, you don't understand. By then, I-I realized I

had made an awful mistake. I still didn't know why Boyle was killed in that boxing ring, but I knew that you, Dick Creevy, were a kind and thoughtful man. You befriended a skinny kid named Doll Face. You took pity on a puny little lad who just wanted to defend his sister. You took me under your wing. You were kind to me."

"And you repaid that kindness by lying to me."

Dolly closed her eyes and summoned all the courage she had in her body and soul. "I wanted you, Dick. I wanted you so badly I couldn't stand it. And I knew that when you discovered my silly scheme, you would hate me."

"You got that right."

She looked at him. Admitting her need for Dick created a flicker of desire in the pit of Dolly's stomach. She still needed him. She still wanted him.

And even though he might hate her, she detected a flicker of desire in his gaze, too.

Dick's stare brought patches of heat to her cheeks, her nose, her lips. He looked at Dolly hungrily, unconsciously moistening his own parched lips with his tongue. He wanted her, too. Dolly could see the conflict of hate and desire that played across his features.

She knew he would never love her, but perhaps there was a chance he would make love to her, once more. She was willing to risk her dignity, her integrity, everything, just to feel his arms around her again.

"You do despise me, don't you?"

"You've done little to endear yourself to me, Dolly— or whoever you are."

"You liked me as Doll Face, didn't you?"

Dick said nothing.

"You enjoyed making love to me, didn't you, Dick?"

A muscle flinched in his jaw.

Stepping forward, Dolly held his gaze. Tension radiated from his body, repelling her, warning her to keep a safe distance. When she stood at arm's length, she dropped her hands to her sides.

"We have more reasons to hate each other than any two people I have ever known," she said, at length. "Yet, I cannot hate you any longer."

His eyes searched hers. His Adam's apple bobbed convulsively. He looked as if he was about to speak, but instead he squeezed his eyes shut and shook his head.

"Look at me." She closed the distance between them and stood so close her tiny breasts touched his chest. "Look at me," she whispered.

His eyes opened. "Why are you doing this to me?" His voice was a ragged breath, torn deep from within. "I feel like a puppet on a string!"

"I didn't mean to hurt you, Dick."

Dropping his head in his hand, he covered his eyes. "You lied to me. You deceived me. Worst of all, you abandoned me."

"I didn't abandon you. I wanted to be close to you." Dolly gently drew Dick's hand into her own, and forced him to meet her gaze.

"I thought I was going insane," he said through gritted teeth. "I thought I was attracted to—"

"*I* was Doll Face. It was *me* you were attracted to."

Suddenly, he clasped her upper arms and drew her next to him. He gave her a little shake, and something wild, something feral, gleamed in his gaze. If she hadn't trusted him, Dolly would have been afraid.

"You're a good man, Dick." There was scant possibility he would never trust *her,* but perhaps she could make him understand that his attraction to her was a good thing.

"A moment ago, you called me a murderer."

"That's what I used to think. That's what I wanted to think. But I know you now."

"I thought something was wrong with me—"

"There is nothing wrong with you." Her hand slid down his flat stomach, to the front of his trousers.

Dick's body tensed, and his penis hardened beneath Dolly's fingers.

"Make love to me, Dick. Please." She wrapped her fingers around him, stroking him.

His fingers cuffed her upper arms, pressing into her flesh, pulling her closer to him. His breath was hot and sweet on her neck. A guttural sound escaped his throat and his eyes took on a dazed, hypnotic look.

He dipped his head and whispered, "Who are you now, Lady Dolly? A prostitute? An innocent boy?"

She wrapped her arms around his neck. "Who do you want me to be, Dick?"

"I want you to be yourself, nothing more."

She drew in a quick breath. He had no idea how difficult it was for her to fulfill his request. For as long as she could remember, Dolly had pretended to be someone else because she didn't like who she was.

"I am afraid," she answered finally. She trembled as his arms moved around her waist.

"I won't hurt you; you know that."

"That's not what I mean. I'm afraid that if you see the real Dolly, you won't like her."

He drew back and studied her. "Perhaps not." His tone was very matter of fact, not cruel. "But how will we know unless you are willing to shed the masks you have been wearing? You cannot pretend forever, Dolly."

"No," she murmured as his lips covered hers. Dick Creevy was right. If she was ever going to let the real Dolly Baltmore out, now was the time.

Fourteen

Dolly crossed the floor and locked the drawing-room doors. When she returned to Dick, he was standing near the sideboard, pouring himself a drink.

Silently, as he watched, Dolly undressed herself. Her gown, bustle, and crinoline underskirts fell in a heap to the floor. She unlaced her half-boots and kicked them off. Then she stripped off her corset and her pantaloons.

Staring him straight in the eye, standing naked in front of him, Dolly had never felt so vulnerable. She wasn't Doll Face now. Nor was she the expert woman of the night who knew how to pleasure a man. She was just herself, wearing no pretensions, wielding no artifice. She'd never been more frightened—or excited—in her life.

"You're beautiful." His rasping whisper sent tremors of need through her body.

"What do you like about my body?"

His eyes scanned her figure from head to toe. "I like your slender ankles, your muscular calves. All that exercise has made your thighs and hips lean. Yet you still have the loveliest feminine curves I have ever seen. I must have been a fool to ever have thought you were a boy."

Dolly's hands moved on her own body, outlining the shape of her hips, the indentation of her waist.

Dick's gaze lit on the triangle of golden curls between her legs. The man didn't even have to touch her to arouse her. Sipping his whiskey, he stared at her hungrily, lighting tiny explosions of warmth wherever he looked.

"And, yes, I like *that.*"

Self-consciously, she touched herself *there.* Then she quickly moved her hands away. Good heavens, she rarely touched herself like that when she was alone. The guilty pleasure of it embarrassed her.

Smiling gently, he placed his glass on the sideboard. "Don't forget, Dolly, that I know you both as a friend and a lover. You can be anything you want with me. Anything at all."

She wanted to ask whether she would ever see him again, after she had shown herself in full to him, but she didn't want to break the spell. It was incredible to believe that she could behave like a wanton without forfeiting this man's respect. On the other hand, she told herself, she already had lost his respect. So why shouldn't she accede to his sweet commands? Why shouldn't she do as Dick said . . . and please herself in the bargain?

"I have nothing to lose. Do I?"

His expression was wistful. "Nor do I, Doll Face. I believe we have shown every part of ourselves to each other. There is no sense in acting shyly now."

She raked her fingers through her coarse curls. Then she widened her legs, and spread her womanhood completely.

Dick's reaction was immediate. He groaned and ripped his tie from his neck. Violently, he ripped open his shirtfront and cuffs, popping off a spray of buttons. Then he reached for her. "God, woman! What are you doing to me?"

His hand cupped the back of her neck, and their mouths met in a clash of passion. Their tongues explored each other's teeth and lips. Dick rubbed his stubbled jaw along Dolly's neck and she gasped, startled by the excitement created by the abrasion of his skin against hers.

Musk and Dolly's wet desire perfumed the air. Dick gulped in her smell as if he were suffocating.

When his hand slid from her neck to her shoulders, goose bumps stippled her skin. On a sigh, Dolly told him how good that felt, how much she needed that.

"You like?" he whispered.

She clung to him, barely able to speak. A shiver racked her shoulders, and she gave a throaty chuckle. "Yes, yes, I like." How could she be chilled and burning in the same places? How could she feel so much need and contentment at the same time?

He stroked her neck, her bare arms, the throbbing pulse point in her throat. He squeezed her tiny breasts and tweaked her nipples, more sensitive now than they had ever been. Lowering his head, he suckled, and the sweet sounds of his nursing nearly drove Dolly insane.

Her knees felt weak. Ripples of yearning turned into waves of uncontrollable emotion. Try as she might, Dolly couldn't separate her affection for Dick from the pure lust that raged through her body. Kissing the side of his head, stroking his thinning hair, she breathed in the scent of him. She wanted everything—his smell, his body, his power, everything. She wanted all of him inside her.

In one swift movement, Dick swept her off her feet

and carried her across the room. He settled on the sofa with Dolly in his lap. Then he arranged her legs around his waist, and stared into her eyes.

She clutched his shoulders and drew up her legs. Her thighs hugged Dick's ribs; her knees nudged his underarms. Her body was totally exposed to him.

He placed his hand between her legs, and with his thumb, tenderly massaged that tiny nub of flesh. Dolly's head lolled and her eyelashes flickered. Her chest ached from the labor of breathing. She felt as if a Lucifer match had been struck inside her loins; a flood of heat gushed from her body and slicked Dick's fingers.

Shifting her weight, Dolly balanced on Dick's thighs. Her new athleticism served her well. She lifted herself to allow his fingers greater access to the swollen folds of flesh between her legs.

"Ah, Dolly, you are beautiful. So responsive. So wet." He craned his neck to kiss her mouth. "Don't hold back, darling. I want you to be happy."

The realization that she was stark naked, sitting on the lap of a fully clothed man, and allowing him to pleasure her in such a straightforward manner, passed through Dolly's mind, and might have dampened her zeal, had she been concerned about the propriety of such behavior. But Dick had given her license to do as she pleased, to be whoever she pleased, and today, this very minute, she was just a woman who needed a man, and she was not going to let anything, be it convention, tradition, manners, mores, or inhibitions, prevent her from getting what she needed.

And what she wanted.

She cried out as her need built to a crescendo.

"I thought this was what you wanted," he whispered,

slipping his finger inside her. "You asked me to make love to you, didn't you?"

"Yes." But she wanted more. "Please, Dick," she whispered. "I want you inside me, now!"

Lifting her easily, Dick stood. Dolly's legs wrapped around his waist as he crossed the carpet. Moving aside a tray laden with decanters and glasses, her placed her gently on the edge of the sideboard.

Her bottom was halfway off the table, her womanhood flush against Dick's trouser-opening, her legs spread wide apart.

He unbuttoned his clothes and released his erect penis. Dolly gasped as she felt the velvety tip of it nudging against her body. She ground her hips downward in a primeval need to join with him, to feel his manhood inside her. Her womb ached so exquisitely now that nothing mattered except having Dick inside her.

He reached down, grasped himself, and rubbed his erection against the inside of her leg. Dolly looked down; a gossamer thread ran the length of her inner thigh. She pushed her hips forward again, starving for Dick's body.

"Wait, wait," he whispered.

They cradled each other's faces, kissed deeply and passionately. They clung to each other, their uneven breathing filling the room. Heat—body heat, wet and thick—surrounded them, clung to their skin, plastered Dick's shirt to his back.

Then he tore his lips from hers and pressed his mouth to her neck. He bit her lightly on the tender, sensitive expanse of skin that ran from her earlobe to the tip of her shoulder. Dolly shuddered, sucking air through her teeth, exhaling in a hiss of arousal.

"Let it out, Dolly. Let it go."

And in an instant, she came undone like a spool of thread.

"Dick . . . please . . . I want you to make love to me *now.*"

He wanted her, too, and he told her so, but Dick used another, more elemental word, one that sent shock waves of excitement up Dolly's spine.

It seemed they'd both shed every ounce of civilization and refinement they'd ever possessed. But still, Dick managed to tip her chin and lift her gaze to his. "Are you sure?"

Dolly nodded, unable to speak over the lump in her throat.

His hands went to his penis. Dolly looked down to see his nakedness. He was huge, and she wanted him more than she'd ever thought possible.

With one hard thrust, Dick slid inside her.

Dolly cried out in pleasure and in pain. Her back arched, and her arms wrapped around Dick's shoulders as he moved inside her, slowly, patiently.

At first she was glad he didn't look at her, but rather nestled his head in the crook of her shoulder. Dolly thought she would be embarrassed if Dick saw the contortions of her face as she lost control of her herself.

But then he lifted his head and looked into her eyes. And the emotion Dolly saw there only fueled her desperation. Abandoning all her inhibitions, she held his gaze and told him everything that she was thinking, that his body felt good inside hers, that she needed him, that she was getting close to her release. . . .

Reaching beneath her, Dick cupped her buttocks and dove deeper into her body. "I need you too, Dolly."

With a low moan that Dolly could hardly believe was

her own, she lifted her legs and hooked them over Dick's shoulders.

Now he had complete and total access to her body. Dolly watched the joining of their bodies with unabashed amazement. Rocking back and forth, she accepted every thrust, clenching and clutching at every inch of Dick's rock-hard manhood. She reached down and wrapped her fingers around the base of his shaft. She loved the wet, slippery feel of his body. Gasping, she threw her head back while Dick pressed his lips to the side of her neck.

Their motions grew more frenzied, more rapid. Dick wrapped one arm around Dolly's waist; with his other hand, he revisited the tiny bud of flesh nestled between her legs. As before, his gentle rubbing sent waves of wildness quaking through Dolly. A kind of insanity overtook her. She begged Dick to do things to her that she'd never thought of, much less considered verbalizing.

Their bodies slapped together, slick skin against hot wet skin. Sounds that would have embarrassed Dolly before thrilled her now.

"Come to me," Dick urged her. "Come on, Dolly; come to me!"

"Oh, Dick, I think I am—"

"Come on, I've got you!"

The spasms rocking her body wound tighter and tighter. All her senses sharpened, focusing on that deep, aching throb between her legs. It was a need so great she couldn't imagine how she'd ever lived without it. It was a pain so exquisite, she cried out loud for blessed release.

At last, her desire exploded. Dolly's body stretched and arched, her nerves tingled from head to toe. Her womb throbbed around Dick's penis. Then little waves of pleasure followed the big explosion, like aftershocks.

"Dolly . . ." Dick's movements quickened.

She leaned back and urged him to his release.

He came inside her with a violent shudder and a groan.

After a moment, Dolly lowered her legs. She wrapped her arms around Dick's neck, and for a long time, they were silent, holding each other while their breathing returned to normal.

At last, Dick slowly withdrew and buttoned his pants.

Dolly slid off the table and gathered her clothes. In the silence that ensued, she quickly stepped into her pantaloons, slips, and shoes. Then she threw on her gown and reached behind herself to button the impossible row of buttons that traced her spine.

"Let me."

She felt his fingers move nimbly up her back. When she was dressed, she faced him.

"Well, that was . . ." Her voice faded.

"That was wonderful, Dolly." Dick's face was still flushed from sex. He clasped her shoulders and kissed her lips. "*You* are wonderful."

But the frown on his face gave a lie to his blandishments. Dick's discontent was palpable, and it stood between them like a brick wall.

"I was right, wasn't I? I'll never see you again after today, will I?"

He looked away.

"You don't have to be embarrassed, Dick." She half turned from him. It was easier not to see his handsome face while she lied. "I understand completely. I lied to you. I tricked you into sleeping with me the first time."

"I wasn't coerced, Dolly. In point of fact, it was my

idea. I'm the one who made the arrangements through Mrs. Bunratty."

"Yes, but I'm the one who intercepted your communication with her. I popped up on her doorstep, knowing that she would send me directly to you."

He looked at the sideboard, as if he were contemplating fixing himself another drink; then he shook his head. "It's no use, Dolly. It doesn't matter whose fault it is. I don't know who you are, so how can I trust you?"

"What we just did—"

"It was just sex."

"I don't believe it!" It hurt her pride to argue with him, but Dolly couldn't help it. "It wasn't *just* sex. Doll Face wasn't *just* a boxing student. We were friends. We were lovers."

"We shouldn't have done this. I shouldn't have come here." He rubbed his face. "I'm sorry."

Dolly reached out, but Dick moved away, avoiding her touch. At the door, he paused. Turning the brass handle, Dick looked over his shoulder. Tears shimmered in his eyes.

Then he opened the door, and was gone.

Dolly went to bed that afternoon, surrounded by another woman's books and paintings and furniture. Sadness weighted her heart. Her stomach felt queasy. She couldn't even summon the energy to jump rope or run laps around the square. When Ferghus knocked on her door and announced Lady Kilgarren was below stairs, she instructed him to send her away.

"Tell her I have a bad case of the megrims." The lie tripped off her tongue so glibly, Dolly didn't realize what she'd done until hours later. Pretending everything was all right had become such a habit, she did it automatically.

Everything was not all right.

Restless, she got up and stood before the bookshelves. Running her finger along the spines of the books, she wondered about the previous occupant's life. Was she married? Did she have children in this house? Why did she leave it?

And why did the mysterious benefactor choose Dolly to live there?

A certain book caught her attention. It was a thick red leather-bound book with a familiar title. Withdrawing the book from the shelf, Dolly opened Caesar's *Gallic Wars,* knowing before she saw it that the Latin version on the left-hand page was mirrored by an English translation on the right.

Smiling, she remembered how clever she and Mary O'Roarke had felt when they'd discovered this little jewel in a secondhand bookstore in Geneva. They'd laughed all the way back to the elite girl's academy they attended. Mrs. Quattlebaum would never know, they had gloated, that they'd unearthed a translation of their Latin lessons.

But, as fate would have it, the translation was flawed. Mrs. Quattlebaum found it highly suspicious that Dolly and Mary, seated beside each other, made identical errors in translating a passage from Caesar's original Latin. She swiftly accused both girls of cheating.

Standing before Mrs. Quattlebaum's desk, Dolly's knees quivered. Poor Mary, *she thought.* Her parents will be furious.

"It was I who cheated . . . not Mary," *she blurted.*

Mary gaped in shock and wonderment as Dolly confessed to copying off her neighbor's examination paper.

"Well, then, Miss O'Roarke, it is you who will be punished. Not only have you flunked Latin, but there are to be no more visits to town until you've translated a page from Cicero, as well. That should take you all of the Michaelmas holidays." The old lady sniffed. "If you are still here by then."

If you are still here. *Well, that was the rub, wasn't it? Dolly's enrollment at boarding school was always subject to her father's ability or willingness to pay. Which was why she felt it far less an inconvenience to her if she got kicked out. Mary O'Roarke was meant to graduate from St. Elizabeth's. Dolly Quinn would be lucky if she survived next term's tuition bill.*

"Oh, Mary." Dolly held the little red book to her nose and breathed in its smell, still familiar and heartwarming after all these years.

She missed Mary. At age fifteen, the girl had been her best friend, as dear to her as a sister. They shared a room at boarding school. They studied together. They commiserated over starting their menstrual periods; they shared their most intimate hopes and dreams. Mary wanted to write books or be a politician, a nearly impossible goal for a woman. Dolly just wanted to be married and loved.

Then, Dolly's father suffered a reversal of his fortunes. . . .

Dolly slammed the book shut and shoved it back in its slot. That wasn't what happened. Her father's fortunes had never been static. He'd been a gambler and a drinker his entire life, right up until the day he broke his neck in a phaeton race near London. Dolly's mother, in her grief, had told everyone her husband died of the fever while visiting his sugar plantation in the islands. But Dolly knew the truth. And she hated her father for it.

And hated herself for lying to her friends.

Days after Dolly's father's death, the news came in a letter from her mother. Boarding school was no longer in the widow's budget. There had never really been enough money for Dolly to attend such an exclusive girl's academy. So it was no surprise to Dolly that she was going home, but rather a terrible embarrassment, a humiliation for which she compensated by lying.

"Mother is so distraught; I must return home immediately," she told everyone. *"I'll be attending school in Paris, most likely, from now on. Mother has relatives there, you know."*

She packed her bags while Mary sat on the edge of the bed, staring at her.

"You don't have to lie to me, Dolly." Mary's pale, porcelain complexion was unblemished by the freckles that plagued Dolly. But her hair was as light and unruly as Dolly's. Clutching one of the history books she always seemed to be reading, Mary stared balefully at her friend.

"I'm not lying, Mary." Dolly rolled her knee-length stockings into a ball and tucked them in her portmanteau. "Father's death has devastated Mother. She'll be moving to Paris before long, I'm certain."

"Will I ever see you again?"

"Why wouldn't you? I'll meet you in Vienna this spring! We'll attend the opera—"

"That's what you said last spring, Dolly."

"But, then, Father changed his plans and took the family to Egypt."

"I don't believe you."

"Why would I lie about something like that, Mary?"

"You didn't know where the Nile began and ended when we studied it last fall."

"So, I'm not a cartographer! That doesn't mean—"

"You've lied for me, Dolly! Please don't lie to me!"

"Take it back, Mary. You're being exceedingly cruel. My father just died."

"How do I know whether he died?" Mary stood beside the bed, her cheeks mottled, her arms rigid at her sides. "I thought I was your best friend! But you've never told me the truth about anything. So how do I know whether your father died or not?"

Dolly had replied very quietly. "He died, Mary. In a phaeton accident, while racing some wealthy ne'er-do-well outside London. Chances are, he was foxed out of his mind at the time. There! Are you satisfied? Is that what you wanted to hear? My father's been on the edge of bankruptcy for years, ever since I can remember."

"You don't have to—"

"Yes, I do! Somehow, he always managed to pay the bills, to keep his family in the style to which we have become accustomed. We've learned to scrimp and save on necessities while spending just enough on the trappings of luxury to convince ourselves and others that we're doing well. My clothes are as fine as yours. I go to an exclusive boarding school! Never mind that the administrators are always threatening to boot me out! No one would know my family's true circumstances unless I told them."

"Oh, Dolly!" Mary skirted the bed and threw her

arms around her friend. "Why didn't you tell me this before?"

"Because if you knew, you wouldn't have felt the same about me. You might have shunned me. Or worse—you would have felt sorry for me. I couldn't stand that, Mary. I just couldn't stand it!"

Mary hugged her tightly. "I wouldn't have felt a bit different, Dolly. You're my best friend. No one's ever stuck up for me the way you have. You're brave and kind and . . . Oh, Dolly, let's be friends always. Promise!"

But Dolly heard the sympathy in Mary's voice. And even though she craved the warmth of Mary's friendship, she recoiled from the other girl's pity. Gently pushing her away, she sniffed. It wouldn't do to show her tears to Mary. It wouldn't do to slop over or look weak. She'd rather Mary think her mean and unfeeling than to think her needy.

"I don't need your friendship, Mary. And you don't need mine. I wouldn't fit in with your ilk."

"That isn't true. I do need you."

"No, you don't. You have everything you need. A loving family, money, beauty, intelligence. You can be whatever you want to be, with the exception of queen of England, I suppose. You'll go far, Mary, and you'll forget about me. You'll see. As soon as I'm out that door, you'll forget all about me."

"No, I won't, Dolly."

"Well, then, you should. Go back to Dublin, Mary, and your family's grand Georgian mansion. You've got servants to wait on you hand and foot, and mantua makers and cobblers to dress and shod you as if you were royalty. You'll never know what it's like to wonder if there'll be food on the table! You'll never know what

it's like to see your mother go hungry so that you can take piano or ballet lessons."

Mary gasped.

"Oh, it's so scandalous, isn't it? Well, you wanted to know, and there you have it. My whole life has been a lie, Mary! And I suppose my friendship with you has been, too!"

For a moment, Mary O'Roarke, with her pretty little complexion and her privileged little life, stood gaping, clearly at a loss for words.

Then Dolly turned her back, and said, "Go on, now, Mary. I want to be alone."

"Let me at least stay with you until the carriage comes."

"No! I don't want you here. Go, now. Please!"

The door clicked shut; then there was silence. Mary was gone, banished from Dolly's life.

After that, Dolly never again told the truth about her father, her background, or anything else.

Now, standing in another woman's bedchamber in Number Two Fontjoy Square, sadness closed in on her. It dawned upon Dolly how ironic her situation truly was. She'd married a man just like her father. Like her mother, she'd spent her adult life weaving absurd tales to explain her largely unsatisfactory life.

And her duplicity had culminated in disaster when she deceived and betrayed a beautiful man named Dick Creevy.

She wondered about Mary O'Roarke. Where was she? How had she fared? Where did she live? Had she achieved any of her ambitions? Had she written anything? Did she still have a burning interest in politics?

Cinching her flannel wrapper tightly about her waist, Dolly sighed. She'd been cruel to Mary O'Roarke; she saw that now.

She hoped the young girl had grown up happily. She hoped that Mary, wherever she was, was doing what she wanted to be doing.

A knock sounded at her door. "I'm sorry to disturb ye, m'lady," Ferghus called.

She opened the door and looked at her only servant. For the life of her, she couldn't imagine why he didn't attempt to obtain other employment. "What is it, Ferghus?"

"You've got a visitor, ma'am."

"Is it Lady Kilgarren again?"

"No, ma'am. " 'Tisn't. But I'll send him away, if you're still not feeling up to having company."

"Rafe O'Shea is here, is he?"

"No. It's Mr. Avondale, m'lady. And he says he's got something very important to discuss with you."

The last thing Dolly wanted to talk about was the garden, what sort of bulbs should be planted, or what kind of marble should be used in the fountain.

On the other hand, she could use a distraction. Her depression was growing wearisome, even to her. "Oh, all right, Ferghus. Tell him I'll be right down."

"That's the odd thing, ma'am. He says he wants to see you in here, in this room."

"In my bedchamber? Why, that's unheard of! Tell that man I will not, under any circumstances—"

But her protest was cut short by the sound of footsteps at the landing and the tread of boots coming down the hallway.

Mr. Avondale appeared in her doorway, his eyes shining, his lips set in a grim, straight line. "I'm sorry,

Lady Dolly, but this cannot wait." He crossed the threshold, and shut the door behind him.

Dolly retreated a step, shocked.

Ferghus pushed open the door and tried to get in, but Mr. Avondale forced him back out. Extracting a key from his pocket, he slipped it into the lock mechanism and turned it. Ferghus pounded ferociously on the door, but Mr. Avondale appeared oblivious to the other man's threats and promises. He stood in the center of the carpet, scanning the walls. Then, slowly, he walked around the room, lightly running his fingertips over the furniture, pausing to study a painting, or a porcelain figurine.

He stopped in front of the bookshelves, his gaze alighting on a particular volume. Dolly's heart dropped like a stone. He pulled the little red book down and held it lovingly in his hands.

Turning, he smiled. "Do you read Latin, Dolly?"

"Not very well," she stammered.

He chuckled. "No, I suppose you don't. Do you ever wish you and Mary had studied a little harder?"

Fifteen

The room closed in on Devon Avondale, overwhelming his senses. He gazed at Mary's beloved books, her gilded furniture and prized Japanese wallpaper. He pictured her in her chaise longue, reading a book by the gaslamp on the adjacent table. He heard her gentle laughter, her invitation to come to bed, her admonishments that he traveled too much. He smelled her perfume, the scent of her hair, the French lavender water she used to launder her undergarments.

He missed her so much, he thought the pain would kill him.

But, as always, the tightening in his chest subsided, and he breathed normally again. His dizziness passed.

"Are you all right, Mr. Avondale?"

"Would you please tell your man Ferghus that I am not going to molest you? Otherwise, I believe he will beat down the door."

She hesitated, but at length, called through the door to her servant. "It's all right, Ferghus! I'll ring the bell cord if I require your assistance."

The man's muffled voice could be heard. "I'll be at the top of the stairs, m'lady. Just holler if you need me!"

Devon turned the little red book over in his hands. Just standing in Mary's old bedchamber made him sick with nostalgia. He forced himself back to the present, and faced Lady Dolly Baltmore's startled expression.

"You must think I'm mad."

"A wee bit."

"Do you remember this book, Dolly?"

Her gaze lit on the volume of Caesar's *Gallic Wars*. Her forehead wrinkled with confusion. "I read it once, when I was a student."

"In Switzerland?"

"Yes. How did you know—"

"But you memorized the English translation, didn't you, and as a result, you flunked your Latin examination?"

Her eyes widened. "You're frightening me."

"Mary flunked it, too, but you accepted the blame entirely. 'Twas a very brave and loyal thing for you to do, Dolly."

"How do you know so much about me?"

"Can't you guess?"

"You're the one, aren't you?"

He smiled, half relieved that she had figured out who he was, half disappointed. "Can I trust you not to tell the others?"

"You mean you gave them their homes, too?"

"Didn't you think it a coincidence that four unmarried ladies suddenly *inherited* four houses in one square?"

"Miss Millicent didn't inherit her house. She said her father gave it to her."

"Have you ever seen her father? Has he ever visited her, Lady Dolly?"

"I wouldn't know."

Holding the book to his nose, Devon inhaled deeply. "Don't old books smell wonderful? You can practically relive them just by breathing in the odor of their pages."

Dolly was not to be distracted. Fists propped on hips, she stared at Devon through narrowed eyes. "Tell me, Mr. Avondale, why did you give us these houses? You must have a very good reason, beyond that of Christian charity. In my experience, people generally act in their own best interest, even when performing acts of kindness."

"Ah, you're a philosopher and an economist, as well as a boxer." He laughed. "But not, according to Mary, a scholar of dead languages."

Her mouth formed a little *O*. "You know about my boxing? You spied on me! How dare you!"

Devon's intrusion into Dolly's privacy angered her. He wasn't surprised. Of all the women residing in Fontjoy Square, she lived the most interesting of lives. "I had to trust you before I could confide in you."

"Trust cannot be built on lies, Mr. Avondale. I have learned that the hard way."

After a pause, Devon slid Caesar's chronicles back onto the shelf. "I suppose you deserve an explanation, Lady Dolly. Would you care to sit down?" When she shook her head, he leaned against the bookshelves and folded his arms across his chest. "My wife was Mary O'Roarke."

"My Mary?"

"Yes. Unfortunately, she died about five years ago."

Dolly looked as if she were going to collapse. Her eyes glazed over, and she stumbled dreamily to the chaise longue, where she sank onto the soft cushions, shaking her head and murmuring, "Poor, sweet, Mary."

"Yes, poor, sweet, Mary. Sadder still, she didn't die

quickly. She was ill for a year before she succumbed. Disease of the lungs, according to the best doctors in Dublin. Quite rare for a youthful woman of such apparent health and radiant good looks."

"I can't believe it."

"It took me a long time to believe it, Dolly. I know I'm bombarding you with a huge amount of information at once. I don't expect you to assimilate everything tonight. But hear me out. You can ask questions later, if you want to."

"I'm listening."

He inhaled deeply, steadying his nerves to tell the story. "Mary loved you dearly, Dolly. She described her friendship with you in the diary she wrote during the year before her death. That is why I sought you out. That is why you're here. Because of Mary."

Guilt cut through her like a thousand knives.

Dolly covered her mouth, aghast. Her best childhood friend Mary O'Roarke had died! The one person on earth who had accepted Dolly for what she was—and wasn't— was gone forever.

Her childhood confidante was found and lost again in an instant. It wasn't fair! She felt she'd been lured to this place by the promise of security. And now the rug was being yanked from beneath her feet. All she had left was the horrible realization that she'd deserted a friend, a friend who could no longer be consoled, a friend whose forgiveness she could no longer court.

One part of her wanted to clap her hands over her ears. Another part wanted to hear everything Devon Avondale had to say.

"I would start at the beginning, but I don't know where the beginning is." He didn't appear to be in a hurry. "When Mary and I were married, I thought we had a lifetime to spend together. Having been recently decommissioned, I threw myself into enterprise. I was in the business of manufacturing Scotch whiskey. My work kept me traveling extensively, and I was away from Dublin quite frequently."

"Mary must have hated that."

"Oh, she handled it rather well. She developed a salon, made friends I'd never heard of, created a life all her own, completely separate from me."

"Knowing Mary . . . that does not surprise me." Dolly smiled sadly.

"She was an independent woman in every way. She had her own money, her own interests."

"She wanted to be a politician."

"And she would have been a damn good one"—Devon chuckled—"if women were allowed to do such things."

"They will, in time."

"Ah, *time*. As I said, I thought we had so much of it. I worked hard and built up my business so that I could give Mary all the things she wanted."

"But she had money of her own. You said so yourself."

"I wanted to be the one who provided for us. It was beneath me to take money from Mary's father. He was wildly wealthy, as you may know. Always looked upon me as some grasping parvenu. I'm certain of it."

"Mary wasn't like that."

"No, she wasn't." Devon frowned and studied the floor as if something miraculous had materialized there.

"Would you like some tea?"

"A brandy would be nice. Or a glass of port."

Dolly had only to stick her head out the door and tell Ferghus what was needed. When Mr. Avondale had a snifter of brandy in his hands, he sat on the chair opposite Dolly and resumed his story.

"Six years ago, Mary got sick. At first I thought she would get better. It was inconceivable to me that Mary, my Mary—who'd always been the picture of health—would be so seriously ill. We made the rounds; we even went to London to discuss experimental treatments. But in the end, it was Mary's decision. She died here, in this room."

A chill ran up Dolly's spine. She'd been sleeping in Mary O'Roarke's bed, reading her books, gazing at her paintings. And all the while, Devon Avondale had been spying on her.

She wasn't the only resident of Fontjoy Square who harbored secrets.

There was something mysterious about Devon Avondale, now that Dolly studied him. His dark brown hair was a wild tumble of curls. The graying tendrils at his temples lent him the look of premature madness. His brows arched devilishly, and his mouth—so shapely it could easily be called womanly—quirked and twisted as he talked. Regret was etched so deeply in his face, his smiles often looked like grimaces.

Leaning forward, elbows on thighs, he rolled the snifter between his palms. Long, elegant fingers warmed the glass. He was a handsome man, Dolly thought, approving Mary's choice. She pictured them together, a handsome, bright couple with everything to live for. And they were so in love. They must have been the envy of their friends.

Until tragedy struck.

"I'm sorry for you," Dolly whispered, uncertain what to say.

Mr. Avondale swallowed hard and rubbed his hand across his chin. "She was very peaceful at the end." His voice held the weight of his emotion.

"For that, we can be grateful." Dolly waited.

At length, Mr. Avondale looked at her. "During her last six months, she was completely bedridden. She slept most of the time—like a cat, I used to tease her. She had little strength, except for writing. She never kept a diary before, and I thought it a rather odd time to start one. But it gave her something to do, something to make her feel productive."

The clock on the mantel ticked off a full minute. Dolly's skin rippled with apprehension. Gripping the armrests of her recliner, she held her breath.

"I'm sorry I waited so long, but I—"

"It doesn't matter, Mr. Avondale. You had your period of mourning, just like I had mine. Each of us responds to grief in our own way."

"Yes." Slowly, Mr. Avondale reached inside his coat pocket. He extracted a small, brown leather-bound diary, the sort young girls wrote in, with gold-edged pages and a rudimentary lock. "I said she had many friends, Dolly, but that was a miss-characterization. She had many *acquaintances*. She was well loved. Everyone wanted Mary in their salon and at their dinner parties."

"True friends are rare."

"You were one of her true friends. Her others are your neighbors. Here. Read this." Mr. Avondale held out the diary.

Dolly hesitated. "It wasn't meant for my eyes."

"It's the only way you'll understand."

Her heart thumped wildly as she reached toward Mr. Avondale. The sensation of holding Mary's journal in her hands dizzied her. She rubbed away tears with the heel of her hand. When she recognized Mary's handwriting, she pressed the diary to her heart, soaking up

its warmth. Then she quickly handed it back to Mr.
Avondale.

"No, it was her private diary."

He reached for it slowly, as if he were very weary.
Though he stared intently at the words written there,
Dolly surmised he knew them by heart.

Slowly, his frown eased, and a sparkle lit his eyes.
"She wrote about your departure from school. She described how you exonerated her from the cheating scan-
dal, even though she was as guilty as you. It's all here,
if you ever want to read it. I don't think Mary would
object to your reading that portion of her diary. Other
passages are far more . . . intimate."

"I understand." But Dolly didn't understand why Mr.
Avondale had chosen her to live in Mary O'Roarke's
house. "I thought she rather disliked me after I left
Switzerland."

"She thought you were the bravest girl she'd ever
met."

Dolly nearly laughed. "Brave? Why, I was a coward!
Afraid to let anyone know the truth about my family!
Afraid to let anyone see the real me!" She made a de-
risive sound, and waved her hand in the air dismissively.
"Why would Mary O'Roarke think I was brave?"

"She thought she was the coward. She never forgot
what you did for her. Taking the blame for cheating off
her examination paper was an act of courage in her
opinion."

"She would have done the same for me."

"But she didn't." He pointed at the diary with his
chin. "She was too afraid of her parents' censure. You,
on the other hand, remained loyal to your friend,
fiercely so. Don't be so hard on yourself, Dolly. You're

a good person. I trust my Mary's judgment of character, don't you see?"

A lump formed in Dolly's throat. "She wouldn't think me very brave, now."

Mr. Avondale arched his brows. "Strictly speaking, my lady, your personal life is none of my business. But I saw Mr. Creevy at your door."

She shuddered. "He despises me."

"Why?"

"I deceived him, too. You read Mary's diary. Surely, you can see that I am incapable of being myself."

"I saw you run down the street in your short pants and boots. Please don't be angry. I followed you at a distance, too. I saw you going into Creevy's Pugilist Academy."

"So you know—"

"It wasn't difficult to figure out. I realized you had bought yourself quite a bit of trouble when Mr. Creevy asked me your name at my party. He thought you and Lady Kilgarren were prostitutes. You needn't explain how *that* misunderstanding came about. I don't want to know. Suffice it to say, I determined that my intervention might be opportune."

"A sort of divine intervention, if we credit Mary."

"By the way, you made quite a fetching little boy."

"Don't make me laugh." Dolly met Mr. Avondale's gaze, and they both squelched a chuckle. Her masquerade had been so outlandish, there had to be some humor in it.

But Dick Creevy was not amused by Dolly's shenanigans. He felt nothing but bitterness and resentment toward her. As well he should. Her behavior had been abhorrent.

"Care to tell me why you attempted such a charade?" Mr. Avondale asked.

Considering her visitor's request, Dolly slowly stood. Then she crossed the floor and opened her bedchamber door.

Ferghus nearly fell on top of her.

"Oh, Ferghus, I'm quite safe, I assure you. But I'd like a glass of whiskey." If she was going to tell Mr. Avondale her story, Dolly needed something stronger than tea coursing through her veins.

"Mr. Avondale, I agree to keep your secret if you swear that you will keep mine."

"My lips are sealed, dear lady."

Facing Mary O'Roarke's husband, Dolly squared her shoulders and steeled her nerves. A sudden clarity altered her perception. Perhaps she *could* be brave, after all.

Mary O'Roarke's diary had awakened a long-dormant bud of courage inside Dolly. She hadn't been afraid to accept the blame when she and Mary were caught cheating. She deserved Mrs. Quattlebaum's disapprobation. But she'd never considered her behavior noble. Indeed, according to Dolly's code of ethics, loyalty demanded that she protect Mary.

She wasn't a bad person; Dolly just thought people wouldn't like her if they really got to know her.

So she'd taken great pains to define her image and present to the public only that which was attractive.

Settling across from Mr. Avondale with a small tumbler of scotch in her hands, Dolly felt a great weight lift from her shoulders. She'd wasted a lot of time and energy being someone else. Dick Creevy helped her learn that she could not be anyone but herself.

Mary O'Roarke reminded her who she was.

All Dolly wanted now was forgiveness, not from

Dick Creevy and Mary O'Roarke, although the knowledge that she'd hurt them filled her with guilt. No, she wanted absolution from the only person who could truly give it to her. And that person was *herself.*

First she would have to figure out who *she* was.

Getting acquainted with the real Dolly was going to be a long, arduous journey. Or a fascinating adventure.

After his encounter with Lady Dolly Baltmore, Dick threw himself into his training. The fight with Eric the Viking was just around the corner, and he couldn't afford to slack off now. His determination to win the match was stronger than ever. Beating the Viking meant affirming his masculinity. Winning the fight of the century would prove to everyone, including himself, that he was not a gullible fool capable of being tricked and deceived by any bit of baggage that came alone.

He started off the day by running the length of Dublin's docks. Then, after a quick shower, he ate a hearty breakfast of fried eggs, soda farl, black pudding, and sausages. Afterward, he sparred with the toughest men in the gymnasium, urging them to throw their best and hardest punches. He didn't want to be spared their most brutal pounding. He wanted to be ready for anything Eric the Viking could dish out.

After his midday meal, he jumped rope and pounded punching bags until the gymnasium emptied and the sky turned dark. Then he took another lonely run along the banks of the Liffey, breathing in the acrid smells of smokey factories and coal-burning furnaces.

At night, he retired to his favorite pub, where he drank beer and ate fresh oysters or smoked salmon or Dublin coddle. He didn't believe in starving himself while training. The more bulk he put on his body, the more power he packed in his punches. Besides, Eric was a good head taller than he and considerably heavier. Dick knew he would need every ounce of strength he could muster in order to knock the man down and keep him down.

O'Callahan was his shadow, his coach, and his drill sergeant. While Dick ate or jumped rope or had his aching muscles massaged, Cal talked. He lectured incessantly about Eric's fighting strategies.

"The Viking likes to batter his opponent's body. He likes to stay close and work on your kidneys and ribs. He'll wear you down, laddie, if you're not careful. You've got to move your feet and protect your body."

And he had to stay far enough away from the Viking to be able to land a blow to the man's head. Dick's best shot at winning the fight was to knock Eric out early. If he let the fight go too many rounds, it was sure to be long and brutal and bloody. In that scenario, the younger man would fare much better.

At night, Dick sat in his parlor, drinking port and reading. And despite his best efforts not to, he thought of Lady Dolly Baltmore.

And Doll Face Mohr.

And Dolly the prostitute.

As his loneliness deepened, his anger toward Dolly intensified. He felt as if he'd been promised a great treasure, only to have it snatched away from him. But he knew that was foolish, because she'd never promised him anything. Unlike Kitty Desmond, Dolly Baltmore had never told Dick she loved him.

He wondered if she regretted her actions. He tried to figure out her motives. He imagined her hurt and bewilderment at the moment when the news of Lord

Baltmore's death reached her. He understood her anger. But he couldn't understand why she hadn't come to him and asked *him* what had happened that night.

Because murderers aren't likely to tell the truth. That was Dolly's rationale. Upon reflection, he supposed that if he had been in her shoes, he might have thought the same thing.

Night after night, Dick relived that evening in the ring. After a year, he still couldn't fathom what had happened to Lord Boyle Baltmore. The man appeared sober as a judge the night he died, though later Dick learned he was a heavy drinker. No doubt, he was goaded by his peers into accepting Dick's challenge, though no man came forward to say he was with Boyle that night. And despite Baltmore's assertion that he had taken boxing lessons, he fought like a punk when he climbed into the ring with Dick Creevy.

From the beginning, Lord Baltmore's death had been a mystery. Just recently, a detective employed by Lloyd's of London had come to Dick's office. The gentleman asked many questions regarding the circumstances of Dick's challenge and Baltmore's unfortunate demise. Dick answered as best he could, and the detective went away.

At the time, Dick supposed that Baltmore's wife or business partner had insured his life for a large sum of money. He knew now that Dolly hadn't collected any insurance. According to her, Baltmore's death left her hovering on the edge of poverty.

But something Dolly had said rang in Dick's ears.

He was an amateur, an out-of-shape, middle-aged, drunken rakehell who never worked a full day in his life. He spent his days playing cards and his nights attending boxing matches and cockfights. He was goaded into stepping into the ring with you by your reckless taunts and challenges.

Was that the sort of man whose business partner would insure his life through Lloyd's of London?

Was that the sort of man who would even *have* a business partner?

If his wife didn't insure him, and he didn't have a business partner, why was Lloyd's of London's investigating the man's death?

Dick jerked awake one night, bathed in sweat, his heart pounding ferociously. He'd dreamed he was in the ring with Eric the Viking. The crowd was going wild. Dick's sides ached after ten rounds of a relentless beating. His eyes were nearly swollen shut, but he could see a man standing beside the ropes, just behind the Viking's corner.

He couldn't make out the man's face. But, whoever he was, he was smiling demonically. . . .

Sixteen

Outside Creevy's Pugilist Academy, Lady Dolly Baltmore and Mr. Devon Avondale sat in his elegant carriage. A morning drizzle had slicked the cobbled streets, and a light mist muted the grays and browns of Dublin's ship-building district. Fishwives wearing colorful scarves and carrying huge straw baskets hurried toward the docks, occasionally bumping elbows with the men who streamed in and out of the boxing gymnasium. Dolly knew she had to get out of the cab and go inside, but fear and apprehension anchored her to the leather squabs.

"Go on, then," urged Mr. Avondale. "We haven't got all day."

She nibbled her lower lip. In the past twelve hours, her entire world had tipped upside down. She'd learned who her mysterious benefactor was, and why he had chosen her to live in Mary O'Roarke Avondale's former home.

"This is my way of repaying the kindness you showed to Mary," he'd explained the night before, long after Ferghus had given up his post as sentinel. "After she died, I didn't know what to do with myself. I read her diary over and over. I felt like I *knew* you at some point . . . as well as Mrs. Sinclair, Miss Millicent, and Lady Kilgarren. If you were Mary's friend, then you were mine, too. So I decided to find you."

"It mustn't have been easy. My maiden name was Quinn."

"It took me nearly a year to find the four of you. Then I had the bright idea of bringing you all together."

"Without telling us why." Dolly leaned forward. "You haven't explained that one, yet, Mr. Avondale."

"I wanted to get to know you *before* you realized I was Mary O'Roarke's husband. Had you known, it would have changed your perception of me entirely."

"Isn't it irritating to be identified as your spouse's mate?"

"That's not why I kept my identity a secret. If you knew I was Mary's husband, and that she had died, you'd have regarded me as a sad old widower with an unrequited obsession for his dead wife. If you knew I gave you a house, you would have been grateful to me, even deferential. I don't want your gratitude, Dolly. In fact, it is I who should be grateful to you."

"What about the other ladies?"

"They know nothing about me. And you are sworn to secrecy."

"Mr. Avondale, I do believe you are as double-faced as Doll Face Mohr." Suppressing a grin, Dolly pulled her cap lower over her forehead. "How do I look?"

"Like a beautiful woman masquerading as a boy."

"Well, I managed to fool Dick Creevy."

"That's only because he saw you first as a boy. He didn't expect to find a pretty female in his gymnasium, and so it was easier for him to suspend his disbelief. You fooled quite a few people, Dolly. But I suspect they would have eventually discovered the truth. You're not the manliest lad I've ever seen."

"I'm a lightweight, Mr. Avondale," she quipped, pushing open the carriage door. With the alacrity of a cat, she leaped from the cab and landed on the street.

"You are anything but a lightweight." Smiling, Mr. Avondale reached for the door handle. "Good luck, Doll Face."

Dick, his bare chest bathed in sweat and his heart galloping, stood beneath a red leather punching bag. His gloved fists moved in a whir, battering the little stuffed bag so methodically and violently, a casual observer would have thought that all his frustrations were centered there. The sound of leather against leather, in a tattoo as constant and unrelenting as rainfall, echoed through the gymnasium.

He didn't see the little blond slip through the door.

But O'Callahan did. "Well, well, Dick! Look who's back. And actin' mighty sheepish, if you ask me. 'Pears he's unsure whether to come over here or run back out the door."

The bag stilled. Dick's fists remained suspended in the air, while his mouth fell open and his gut twisted. Slowly, dreading what he expected to see, he looked over his shoulder.

Dressed in knickers, woolen stockings, and a tweed jacket, she crossed the gymnasium floor. Her shorn curls glowed beneath the brim of her cap. Her expression was open, vulnerable, and clearly apprehensive. Standing before him, she lifted her chin and thrust out her hand.

"Good day, Mr. Creevy." She nodded her hello to O'Callahan.

The old man wisely excused himself.

Dick said, "What the hell are you doing here?"

"I would thank you not to curse in front of a lady."

"A lady? Why, you're no—" Dick clamped his lips shut.

She plucked off her cap and shook her head. Glistening ringlets curled around her face and fell on her shirt collar. It was amazing how quickly Dolly made the transformation from boy to woman. Or had she always been that feminine? Perhaps Dick was just a fool who didn't see the obvious. Or perhaps she was a master at disguises. Either way, Dolly's trickery robbed him of control; her deception put her in control, not Dick. And for that reason alone, he never wanted to see her again.

"I think you should go." He spoke as quietly and calmly as he could.

A hint of fear widened her eyes. "It took a lot of courage for me to come here, Dick. But I wanted to tell you something."

"I don't want to hear it."

"Can we talk in your office? People are staring."

"No." Dick turned away, his fists aimed at the little leather bag above his head.

"I can't make you talk to me," she said to his back. "But I'm going into your office. Follow if you wish. If you're not there in five minutes, I'll leave and never darken your doorstep again."

Her boot steps sounded on the wooden floor. Dick pounded the bag a few times, but his heart wasn't in it. He didn't want to talk to Dolly. She'd humiliated him—made a fool out of him. He was so angry at her, he could barely stand to look at her. Yet the thought of her never darkening his doorstep filled him with terror.

He didn't know what he wanted.

But he knew he didn't want *her* to be in total control. If Dick never saw her again, that was *his* choice. *Not hers.*

Rationalizing that he was keeping his options open— not to mention grabbing the reins of control—Dick turned and followed her.

Closing the door behind him, Dick stepped inside his office. He grabbed a towel off his desk and draped it around his neck. In his boxing shorts and leather trainers, he felt naked. Odd that he should be so aware of his masculinity in the presence of a woman dressed as a boy.

Careful to avoid making physical contact with Dolly, he skirted his desk and stood behind it. She stood beside the sofa, her arms at her sides. For an elongated moment, there was nothing but silence filling the space between them.

At length, she said, "I came to apologize."

A harsh bark of laughter escaped his lips. "That is absurd! You must be joking! Apologize? Dear lady, it isn't as if you spilled a spot of tea on my jacket! I appreciate your show of good manners, but I'm afraid an apology won't do!"

But the memory of their lovemaking tempered his sarcasm. Dick's laughter abruptly ceased. Dolly's lovely upturned nose was just as kissable as it had been the night she played the part of a prostitute. Her parted lips were just as inviting as they had been the afternoon he'd barged into her house and accused her of deceiving him. Clenching his fists, Dick steeled himself against the onslaught of her charms.

"Did you really expect that I could forgive you?"

She held his gaze. "No, but perhaps I can make you understand why I behaved the way I did."

"You've already told me, Lady Dolly. You thought I was a cold-blooded murderer, that I killed your husband without the slightest compunction. You wanted a pound of flesh from me in revenge. So you concocted this implausible scheme to insinuate yourself into my life. Your ultimate plan was to hurt me, to ruin me, if you could."

"My plan was ruined the moment I laid eyes on you."

"You used me, you spied on me, and you deceived me, Dolly. And despite my attraction to you, I simply cannot tolerate that sort of disloyalty. Not from my friends and certainly not from my lovers."

"I wasn't disloyal!"

"It certainly felt that way to me."

She dashed a tear from her cheek, then drew herself up. "You're right about everything except my motivation. If you won't forgive me, I deserve that. But at least hear me out! Please, Dick! I'm begging you!"

The pain in her voice nearly drove him crazy. He'd have liked nothing better than to wrap her in his arms and kiss her tears away. Yet his impulse to toss her out of his office and tell her never to return was equally strong. Conflicting emotions warred in his chest. Breathing a sigh of weary resignation, Dick said, "Go ahead, then. I'm listening."

Her sniffles subsided as she told her story. "I grew up in Waterford, the youngest of three. My mother was a sweet woman, but she was inordinately concerned about what the neighbors thought. When I was ten years old, she told her friends that Father took us on a

Roman holiday, when, in fact, we'd been packed off to the country to visit relatives while he went to Edinburgh to play at the casinos."

"A gambler, eh?"

"The very worst sort, I'm afraid." Dolly looked down. "You'd think I would have known better than to marry someone just like him. It was as though Lord Baltmore and my dear old Dad were cast from the same mold."

Dick took in a deep breath. Dolly's story was already making him uncomfortable. The last thing he wanted was to start feeling sorry for her. "Go on."

"Boyle simply couldn't help himself! It was like a disease! The poor man would say he meant to do better, but then he'd go and gamble all his money on some knobby-kneed little pony he'd taken a fancy to. Sometimes he won, and we were plump in the pockets for a month or so. But more often, he lost and we were robbing Peter to pay Paul."

"I don't suppose old Boyle had a *vocation*."

"If you mean gainful employment, of course not." Looking up, Dolly gave a toplofty little sniff.

"Didn't mean to offend."

"You didn't—" Her cheeks colored instantly. "Well, I suppose that the old Dolly *would* have been offended by the suggestion that her titled husband *had* to *work* in order to earn a living. Aristocrats don't work, you know."

"Perhaps you haven't been keeping up with current affairs. The days of the first estate are numbered, dear."

"I may have been a lazy Latin student, Mr. Creevy, but I was wide awake when Mrs. Quattlebaum was teaching the French Revolution."

"Good for you." He gave her a grudging smile. "Proceed."

"I tried to keep up with appearances. At first, it wasn't so difficult. Boyle had a small pension left him by his father. For years we got along, and we lived well. Not extravagantly, but well enough so that Boyle's sister envied us and our neighbors regarded us as genteel."

"That's what counts."

"But the pension ran out. And Boyle's risk-taking increased. In the year before his death, putting food on the table became a challenge. I hate to admit it, Mr. Creevy, but I ate dinner at the Shelbourne Hotel once, then left without paying the bill. I did it because I was hungry, and I had too much pride to ask anyone to help me."

Dick averted his gaze. Dolly's humiliation pained him. And though he wanted to remain angry with her, he couldn't squelch the tide of sympathy rising inside him. "I am sorry."

"I don't want your pity, Dick. I just wanted you to understand why I deceived you. You see, I've always thought that people would look down on me if they knew the truth."

"I don't understand. It wasn't your fault that Lord Baltmore was a profligate gambler."

"Nor was I to blame for my father's recklessness. But like my mother, I assiduously covered up the sordid details of my marriage. I pretended everything was all right, that I was happy and well taken care of."

"How does this explain the deception you perpetrated on me?"

"I became a facile liar, Mr. Creevy. And a skillful actress. I knew you wouldn't tell Lady Dolly Baltmore what happened the night my husband died. But I thought you might eventually reveal something of that evening to Doll Face Mohr."

He studied her intently, wishing earnestly that he could see inside her heart. He wanted to believe her, yet his anger still simmered. He wanted to reach for her and taste her sweet, inviting lips, yet his better judgment warned him not to.

He wanted to forgive her, yet experience had taught Dick the folly of forgetting a woman's indiscretions. Kitty Desmond had thrown herself at his feet, begging his forgiveness and promising she would never communicate with Rafe O'Shea again. But less than a year later, Dick found the two in *delicto flagrante,* in his own bed, so caught up in their passion for each other that they hadn't even heard him pounding up the steps.

No, he could never *forgive and forget* Lady Dolly Baltmore's duplicity. No matter how badly he wanted her.

"Well?" She waited. "Do I leave now, Dick? Or can you find it within yourself to understand?"

"I don't know what I feel," he said, the raw truth of his confession jarring, even to him. "I do not know whether I can forgive you."

Sadness washed over her features. "I understand."

Dick couldn't let her go away thinking he didn't care for her. In two steps, he was around his desk and standing in front of her. He squeezed her upper arms and peered into her eyes. "Listen to me, Dolly. I'm not the right man for you. You'll find someone else, someone who will cherish you and take care of you."

"I don't want someone else."

"You will, eventually. You'll forget about all this—"

"No, I'll never forget you!"

He ran his hands up her shoulders. "I'm not the sort

of man who falls in love easily, Dolly. I'm happier living alone, with no one to depend on, and no one depending on me. You know what Sir Walter Raleigh
called his loved ones, don't you? *Impediments to fortune.* Well, that's the way I feel. I'm a professional
boxer, Dolly! I haven't got time to be in love."

She rubbed her wet cheeks with the heel of her hand.
"I understand."

Dick pulled the towel from around his neck and gingerly blotted her nose. "There now, don't cry. You haven't
lost all that much. Who wants a broken-down fighter
with a crooked nose and cauliflower ears anyway?"

"You're not broken down."

"No, but I soon will be if I don't beat Eric the Viking next week. And if I don't get back out there and
continue my exercise, he'll have a remarkable advantage
over me."

He knew he should let her go, send her home, and
banish her from his thoughts, but her hiccups and sobs
defeated him.

"I'll be all right." She looked up, eyelashes sparkling, lips parted.

If there was ever a woman he'd wanted more, Dick
couldn't remember. He could have stared at her face
forever. He could have held her in his arms for eternity.

But he didn't want to mislead her. He could never
give her the love she deserved. The mistrust that had
developed between them stirred too many bad memories. He'd given Kitty Desmond the power to break his
heart, and she did. Dick didn't intend to make the same
mistake twice. "Dolly, perhaps you should go—"

"Kiss me first." She closed her eyes and tilted back
her head.

Suddenly the temptation she presented was irresistible. Suppressing a groan, Dick inched closer to her. He'd already had sex with this woman; he knew what charms and pleasures her lips promised. And he wanted her, all of her. His need for her consumed him, eclipsing his uncertainties.

Cupping Dolly's face in his hands, he stood flush against her, his arousal straining against his trousers. Dimly—because the heaviness in his groin was so distracting he could hardly think—he questioned his own motives. Why was he unable to release Dolly? He didn't want to love her, or anyone else. He wanted his old life back, his comfortable, lonely, boring life, the one in which he couldn't get hurt because *he* was in control.

Was his need to possess Dolly wrapped up in his need to gain control over her?

Or were his physical needs simply getting the best of him?

With her palms on his bare chest, she pushed him to arm's length and gazed at him. "What do you want from me?" she whispered.

"I don't know yet."

Dick stared into eyes that were glistening with tears, but behind Dolly's gaze, he sensed a strength of character that he'd never known in a woman. There was no duplicity, no pretension in Dolly's emotions. Fear shone in her eyes, but courage blazed there, too.

Lost in her penetrating stare, he pressed his lips to hers. Her eyes fluttered and closed. Her breath caught, and her body melted into his arms.

Their breathing mingled. The warmth of Dolly's tongue on his lips and at the corners of his mouth heated Dick's blood. Her gasp of surprise sent a thrill up his spine. When she coiled her fingers in his nape, his knees nearly buckled.

He barely managed to reach over and lock his office door. Then with one hand, he dragged a straight wooden chair across the floor.

Sitting, he reached inside Dolly's jacket and put his hands around her waist. She quickly shrugged out of her boyish coat, and tossed it on the sofa behind her. Then Dick wedged his knees between her legs, and she slid onto his lap, straddling his hips.

For a long time, they kissed. Deeply and desperately.

With her arms around his neck, Dolly could almost believe Dick wasn't angry with her.

Of course, it stood to reason that he *was* still angry. The fraud she'd perpetrated on him was unforgivable. No man on earth could forget the humiliation of having been lied to, tricked, and deceived.

But he stared into her eyes as if he *wanted* to forgive her. And he'd dried her tears with genuine tenderness. The warmth Dolly felt in Dick's kisses was undeniably real. A man couldn't pretend this sort of passion, could he? A man couldn't fake this sort of desperation. . . . *Would he?*

Who was she lying to now?

Leaping off Dick's lap, Dolly stood before him. Her heart thundered as she stared into his stunned expression. Propping her fists on her hips, she tried to regain some measure, or at the very least, a semblance of her self-control.

"I said, kiss me, not ravish me!"

A slow smile spread across his face. "You're free to go."

"Just like that?" She snapped her fingers. "You would dismiss me, as if I were some errant schoolboy?"

"You're the one wearing knickers, Doll Face."

Fury and desire clashed within her. Her body throbbed and ached for Dick's touch, but her rational mind cautioned her.

"You're trifling with me," she accused him. "You tell me that you don't want to be in love—"

"I don't."

"Yet you want to make love to me!"

"Sex is not love."

She was grateful that he didn't make any gratuitous remarks about her imitation of a prostitute. She knew sex was not love. But she also knew that love made sex better. And sex with Dick was the best she'd ever had. 'Twas only logical to conclude that something more than animal lust existed between them.

"I promise you nothing, my lady." But his voice was warm and velvety, confusing Dolly. His eyes were pools of liquid brown, capturing her. His mouth was full and luscious, possessing her imagination.

"I want you, Dick, not merely to satisfy my sexual desires, but because I like you and I think you are a fine, decent, and honorable man."

"My feelings toward you right now, dear, are not entirely honorable."

A glance at the thickening beneath his trousers confirmed that. Dolly's pulse skittered. "I ought to leave."

"If you expect me to love you or, God forbid, marry you, you should."

"But I want to stay."

"Do as you please, Dolly."

"Your attitude is very frustrating, Mr. Creevy."

Again, that slow liquid smile, almost arrogant in its sureness, appeared on his lips. He turned up his hands, palms to ceiling. "My lady, I have nothing to offer you but myself. If you choose to enjoy an afternoon with me, I invite you to stay. What transpires between us is no one's business, save ours. And I see nothing wrong or immoral in two consenting adults giving each other a few hours' worth of pleasure."

Tilting her head, she considered her answer. "Did you like me when you thought I was Doll Face Mohr?"

"Yes. You were feisty and funny and full of life. You were strong and relentless. You embraced challenge as if it were a lover. You were an inspiration, Dolly. You renewed my zeal for pugilism."

Dolly's inhibitions began to thaw. "And did you like me when you thought I was Dolly the prostitute?"

"You were the third prostitute I have ever slept with, and—I promise you this—there will be no more. Yes, I liked you. More than liked—I was obsessed with you."

"Who did you like best, Dick? Doll Face or Dolly the prostitute?"

He chuckled. "Ah, now that is a tricky question! The *real* Dolly is a tomboy dressed in boy's clothing, a dignified lady with fine manners and the courage to apologize, a spunky widow who refuses to be taken advantage of. . . ."

"Do you like the *real* me?"

"Yes, my lady."

"Then, why—"

"I've already answered that, Dolly. I do not want to fall in love. I will not." He held out his hand. "Now, do you want to stay, or do you want to go? I will harbor no ill feelings toward you, no matter your decision."

She wanted to stay. More than anything else, she wanted to feel Dick's arms around her, and taste the salty sweetness of his skin. She wanted to press her bare chest to his and soak up his warmth. And she wanted to feel his body moving inside her, urging her to ever increasing heights of pleasure.

She shed her clothes and stood naked before him.

Then she bent over him, and framing his face in her hands, kissed his mouth. How could anything this comforting, this pleasurable, be wrong?

With a groan, he drew her onto his lap. Dolly sat astride him, her hands laced behind his neck. Their lips joined and their flesh met. Dick nuzzled her neck, and she arched her back as little candle bursts of pure ecstasy traveled down her throat and across her shoulders.

He kissed her collarbone, her shoulders, her arms. His breathing grew more labored. Through the thin cotton of his boxing pants, Dolly felt his penis nudging her naked body.

Dolly's need accelerated.

Cradling his head, she buried her nose in his fragrant hair, breathing in the scent of him, reveling in the feel of his bristly jaw against her bare skin. Pure instinct compelled her; she'd lost her ability to reason. As a wanton, she succumbed completely to her desires. Lifting one small breast, she directed Dick's lips to her nipple.

He looked up at her, his eyes drugged with desire. "Dolly, I don't want to hurt you. . . ."

She understood what he meant. Their passion was not counterfeit, but Dick promised nothing in the way of a permanent relationship. When she left him today, Dolly might never see him again. But he was here now, and this moment was hers. She did not intend to renounce the only true happiness she'd ever felt.

Guiding his mouth to her breast, she smiled wistfully. Then Dick greedily suckled the nipple in his mouth and her back bowed as she cried out. She clung to Dick's shoulders as wave after wave of pleasure rocked her body. Sensation pooled between her legs. A throbbing need clawed at her, and she ground her hips onto the hardness beneath Dick's pants.

Shifting his weight, Dick reached beneath her. Expertly, he explored the hot, swollen flesh between her legs. Dolly's pleasure turned to exquisite pain, a need that had her squirming on Dick's lap.

Then he slipped one finger inside her.

Shocked by the unbearable pleasure Dick gave her, Dolly shuddered. Her muscles contracted, gripping Dick's finger, drawing it deeper inside her.

Inserting another finger, he stroked her intimately. Slowly at first, then deeper and more vigorously. Dolly's hips bucked and gyrated against the heel of his hand. She needed Dick inside her. . . . Her hunger for him was agonizing.

Spasms quaked through her body and built to a climax. Pleasure and pain merged, ignited, then finally exploded. Dick's fingers slipped from inside her and moved to the drawstring opening of his boxing shorts. With a sigh, he freed his arousal. Dolly lifted her hips, then hunkered over him, her drenched flesh aching for the fulfillment that his penis promised.

"Are you sure?" The tip of his erection touched her body.

"Quite." But the only thing Dolly was sure of was how much she needed Dick inside her at that moment.

His hands bracketed her hips, guiding her down onto him.

Her thigh muscles tensed as she lowered herself.

Slowly, the length of him slid inside her. Dolly was

slick and hot and wet. Crazy with desire, she rocked up and down on Dick's lap without inhibition.

They reached their climax together.

Afterward, they held each other for a long time, until their breathing normalized and the sweat from their bodies evaporated.

"I love you, Dick," she whispered in his ear.

And immediately felt his body stiffen.

What a fool she was! He'd told her he didn't love her, and wouldn't love her, and he'd warned her that she should go. Yet she'd stayed, knowing full well that sex with Dick Creevy was simply that. She had no right to tell the man she loved him. Now Dick's memory of her would be tainted by guilt—as well as by the knowledge that she'd lied to him!

Little was said while Dolly dressed. Dolly glanced at Dick as she laced her boots and buttoned her knickers, but his gaze never met hers. He busied himself with papers on his desk and frowned. Only when she stood at the door did he look up.

"I'm sorry, Dolly. Truly. I wish I could—"

She held up her hand. "You owe me no apology."

"You owe me none, either," he replied.

"Are we even then?" she said lightly, slightly gratified to see Dick's wounded expression, and to know that her flippancy distressed him. "In boxing terms, would this be judged a tie?"

He nodded.

"Well, then, I will go now, and as I promised before, Dick, I will never darken your doorstep again."

He watched her slip through the door, his heart breaking. If this were a boxing match, he told himself, he would demand a rematch. Because Dolly had taken him completely off guard. Dick hadn't been prepared for the challenge of deflecting her charms.

But he definitely was not down for the count.

Seventeen

"Lady Dolly, this has been a perfectly agreeable afternoon, don't you agree?" Rafe O'Shea balanced a cup and saucer in one hand, while languidly stroking his mustache with the other.

Perched on the chair opposite him, Dolly wished fervently that she had invited Lady Kilgarren for tea this afternoon. She didn't much like being alone with Rafe O'Shea, though she couldn't say precisely why. There was nothing in his demeanor that offended, and little in his appearance she found unattractive, save that infernally elaborate mustache. But something about his presence unnerved her.

Nibbling a lemon cookie, she told herself there was nothing wrong with Mr. O'Shea. He was good and kind and highly recommended by Mr. Avondale.

Or was he?

Dolly frowned. Come to think of it, Dolly knew nothing about Mr. O'Shea, except that he was a friend of Devon Avondale's. Or a friend of a friend of Devon Avondale's. Was that sufficient to recommend him? Silently, she reminded herself to inquire into Mr. O'Shea's background the next time she saw Mr. Avondale.

Despite her recent vow of truthfulness, Dolly would have avoided Mr. O'Shea's call if he'd given her any advance warning. But when he'd emerged from his carriage to find her weeding a corner of the garden in the center of the square, she'd had no ready excuse to defend against his visit. He'd practically invited himself inside, claiming to have reserved this afternoon for them.

"I thought you understood I was coming today. Is it too late for lunch at the Shelbourne? Would you like to go there anyway?"

"Another time," she murmured, as bitter memories of a previous meal taken at that hotel resurfaced.

An hour after Mr. O'Shea had arrived, the two sat in Dolly's parlor. Conversation had long since fizzled out. The silence between them was punctuated by the sound of Mr. O'Shea's clattering teacup and the satisfied sighs he made as he curled his mustache around his long, lanky fingers. He seemed content to sit with Dolly in utter silence.

The boredom of his company nearly drove her insane.

"There is something I've been meaning to ask you, Dolly." His voice, while pleasant enough, raised gooseflesh on her arms.

"What is it, Mr. O'Shea?"

"I would like to know . . . if you would grant me the pleasure of your company next Saturday night."

Dolly's breath snagged in her throat. This was what she'd been dreading, and yet how could she say no? Mr. O'Shea had been nothing but courteous toward her, and if she turned him down . . . Well, if she sat at home, she would do nothing but sit and knit and think of Dick. If she intended to get on with her new life—

her new life as the *real* Dolly—she had to rid herself of her obsessive thoughts.

And she was obsessed with Dick Creevy. There wasn't a minute of the day when the man didn't cross her mind. She thought about how much she'd despised him before she met him, and how she'd instantly been attracted to him when she did finally meet him. She thought of the hours they's spent jumping rope, exercising, and talking about boxing. She thought of the friendship they'd shared.

And the passion.

Making love to Dick Creevy had given Dolly the most exciting, fulfilling moments of her life. She had no regrets in that regard.

Her stomach twisted at the thought that she'd never see him again. She missed him so much, she was nearly ill with grief.

Which was why she accepted Mr. O'Shea's invitation.

"Delightful!" He ceased stroking his mustache in favor of rubbing his hands together. "I shall arrive Saturday at six o'clock in the evening, my lady. Oh, we'll have a wonderful time. You wouldn't object to attending a boxing match, would you?"

"A boxing match?" Her heart fell like a boulder.

Mr. O'Shea's face lit gleefully. "Eric the Viking versus the famous Dick Creevy! Have you heard of Creevy? He's widely reputed as the most skillful boxer in Ireland!"

"I-I believe I have seen mention of him in the newspapers."

"He's pitted against the biggest, meanest, strongest fighter I have ever seen! The Viking is positively brutal! The match is being billed as the fight of the century.

'Tis bound to be a bloodbath. Oh, dear! Is that too sanguine for your tastes? Would you prefer to attend the opera?"

Black spots danced before Dolly's eyes. The thought of Dick battling a brute like the Viking made her head swim. "Oh, I like boxing."

" 'Tis all the rage! Even ladies attend the matches nowadays. Tickets to the Creevy versus Viking fight are being sold for twice what they normally are. I was damn well lucky to get two!"

Dolly would hardly have noticed O'Shea's profanity had he not been so contrite afterward.

His face darkened and his Adam's apple bobbed convulsively. "I do apologize, Lady Dolly. Please forgive me! To speak so callously in the presence of a lady is simply uncalled for. And you are a *lady.*"

There was something odd about O'Shea. He seemed to alternate between fawning patronization and crude roughness. Having listened for years to Lord Baltmore's blustering expostulations about fights he'd wagered on and cards he'd been dealt, she recognized O'Shea's male bravado for what it was worth, which was precious little. But she could not understand his oily and ingratiating tone, the urgency with which he seemed to be courting her. Indeed, his enthusiasm for her company was tiresome.

"Has my faux pas condemned me to your disfavor?"

She shook her head. "I will be happy to accompany you to the boxing match, Mr. O'Shea." She wouldn't have missed it for the world, in fact.

Standing, he breathed a sigh of relief. Then he bent low over Dolly's hand and kissed her knuckles. "Saturday night it is, then."

As he left the room, she stared sickly at the smudge

of wax left by his mustache on her skin. The man's touch left her cold as ice. But she'd have allowed him to take her to the North Pole if that's where Dick Creevy was.

Ship's masts and fluttering sails flew past in a blur. Dick set a pace, running at the edge of the river, dodging stevedores and pallets, wooden casks and spools of rope. His heart worked diligently as his arms pumped at his sides. His thighs burned and his knees ached. He'd run seven miles already, and would run three more before he quit.

Preparing for his fight with the Viking meant pushing his body to the limits of his endurance and beyond. But it also gave Dick an outlet for his frustration. And with thoughts of Dolly constantly intruding on his mind, he was grateful for the distraction that physical pain allowed.

He couldn't cease thinking about her. He missed her company, her easy laughter, her feisty determination to excel. His exercise regimen was tedious now. Working out wasn't nearly as satisfying without Doll Face; the gymnasium seemed a bleak, dreary place without her. The faces of the other men in the sparring ring depressed him. He wanted to see Dolly's freckled upturned nose. He wanted to see her smile. He wanted to be with her.

He missed the *other* Dolly, too—the woman who seduced him, and the one who told him she loved him. His body hardened at the memory of their lovemaking. He knew that he would never want another woman as much as he wanted Dolly. He'd meant what he said when he told her he would never patronize another prostitute. Dolly had embodied everything he wanted in a woman. Sex solely for the sake of physical release no longer held any appeal. Dolly's way of making love had stimulated his mind as well as his body.

Dolly was alternatingly sweet and saucy. Her capacity for duplicity disturbed him, but he had to admit that he was intrigued by the many facets of her personality. She was a complex woman who had exercised faulty judgment and was profoundly remorseful for her wrongdoing. He just wasn't sure whether he could forgive her.

As night fell, the air turned colder, searing his nose and lungs. His chest tightened as his feet pounded the cobbled stones bordering the Liffey. Dolly wasn't perfect. But Dick recognized that he wasn't perfect, either. And the pain in his chest reminded him he wasn't getting any younger. He was alone, without family, without anyone to love him. He didn't relish growing old in solitude. If he could find it in himself to forgive Dolly, perhaps he could share the remaining years of his life with someone he loved.

It was easy to blame Dolly for his unhappiness. But gazing at the black river water, he reflected that no one was without fault, without sin. Dolly's mistakes made her human. Dick's ability to forgive her would be the measure of his character.

Turning for home, he thought of Kitty Desmond and the child she'd given him. He'd thought she loved him, once, too. But the joy he'd shared with her was only equal to the pain he endured when she left him. Her death, and the death of their child—for which he held himself responsible—had nearly put him in his own grave. He swore he would never love another woman again. The risk of being hurt was far too great.

But perhaps loving—and forgiving—Dolly was worth the risk.

At home, he sank into a bath of steaming water. His muscles relaxed beneath the heat; soon, the knots in his back and shoulders eased. With his arms resting on the sides of the claw-footed tub and his head pillowed on a thick towel, his anger toward Dolly began to dissipate. A new perspective entered his thinking. He was a fighter, and fighters sometimes got hurt. But the tough ones got up again and kept fighting.

If a man was afraid to step into the ring, he would never win the prize.

He slipped beneath the water and held his breath until his chest hurt. At last, he pushed himself to a sitting position. Water sloshed over the side as he stepped from the tub and wrapped a towel around his waist.

In his study, he sat at his writing desk arranging paper, pen, and ink before him. A drop of water from his forehead blurred the words *Dear Dolly,* but he kept writing.

Dick wanted Lady Dolly Baltmore more than anything else in the world. He hadn't earned his reputation as a champion boxer by refusing to fight.

The four widows of Fontjoy Square stood beneath a threatening sky. Bent from the waist, her apron stained with black dirt, Mrs. Sinclair gazed at the black clouds.

"I've been feeling it in my bones for days. We're going to have a terrific thunderstorm."

Miss Millicent, whose chore for the day had been to weed a small patch of ground at the edge of the garden, stood up and propped her fists on her hips. "I don't know whose idea this was, but I for one do not fancy this sort of work."

Lady Kilgarren and Dolly exchanged knowing glances.

Mrs. Sinclair said calmly, "Millicent, dear, you cast your vote with the rest of us. We all thought having a pretty garden in the center of the square would be a good idea. If we make a joint effort, the work will go faster. Now, be a good girl, and get on with your digging."

A streak of lightning, followed closely by a clap of thunder, split the sky. Miss Millicent shrieked. All four women stood, tossing spades and pruning shears to the ground. Hurriedly, they crossed the street, their soiled clothing dappled with rain. Not more than an instant after they found shelter beneath the overhang of Dolly's front porch, water poured from the sky as if from buckets.

Ferghus brought his ubiquitous tea tray to the drawing room. Before he departed, he made a small fire in the hearth. While rain battered the rooftops and windows, the women sipped hot tea and ate cookies and scones. A generous serving of smoked salmon and chopped eggs was presented. Since Dolly's budget no longer included boxing lessons, she could afford such small luxuries. The small stipend that her benefactor gave her was generous compared to what she was accustomed to living on.

Glancing around, Dolly realized that Mr. Avondale

must be paying monthly stipends to each of her neighbors, as well. His desire to help four women, related to one another through friendship to his wife, continued to intrigue her. His insistence that she protect his secret was stranger still. Why didn't he just tell the women that he wished to repay the kindnesses they'd shown to his wife? Why didn't he want them to know what truly linked them? What sort of experiment was Devon Avondale conducting?

Though she now knew the identity of her benefactor, his motivation was more mysterious than ever. According to him, he revealed himself to Dolly because he recognized her crisis and the need for his intervention. But was he being totally honest? Did he have an ulterior motive in taking such a protective attitude toward her? And when did he plan on telling Mrs. Sinclair, Lady Kilgarren, and Miss Millicent that he was their fairy godfather, and not just the lonely widow down the street who wished to help them in their garden?

Meeting Lady Kilgarren's gaze, Dolly couldn't resist wondering where *she* had met Mary O'Roarke.

"Penny for your thoughts," the duke's daughter said, eyeing Dolly over the rim of her tea cup.

"I was just thinking how much work we have ahead of us. Another year at least."

"Four seasons of this drudgery!" Miss Millicent pressed the back of her hand to her forehead. "Dear Lord, I don't think I can do it! My fingernails are already ruined. And my skin is turning . . . *brown!* In a year, I'll look as if my hide has been tanned."

Lady Kilgarren giggled. "Miss Millicent Hyde, whose hide has been tanned. I rather like that."

"Once the plot is cleared, the work will be less difficult." Mrs. Sinclair could always be counted on for a word of kindly encouragement. "If we're lucky, we'll get some bulbs and seeds planted before it's too hot. Come summer, we'll have a riot of color in the garden."

"In the winter, we won't have to do anything," Millicent said. "It will be too cold, and surely no one expects—"

"You'll do your part," Mrs. Sinclair said firmly.

Dolly stifled her chuckle. The handsome woman with jet hair and violet eyes was patient to a fault. Still clad in widow's weeds, Mrs. Sinclair chastened Millicent with a schoolmarmish look and a pursing of her lips. Raising the histrionic younger woman seemed to be Mrs. Sinclair's new lot in life.

"The rain has abated. I think we'd best take our leave." As Mrs. Sinclair stood, Millicent did also.

When they'd gone, Lady Kilgarren burst out laughing. "Did you hear that silly girl? I vow, Dolly, she does complain about everything!"

"And Mrs. Sinclair complains about *nothing.*"

"Is that the basis of their friendship? They appear to be as attached to each other as mother and child."

"I believe you answered your own question, Claire. Miss Millicent is far too young to be living on her own. That is painfully obvious. For whatever reason, which we may never know, Mrs. Sinclair has taken it upon herself to guide and instruct the child."

Lady Kilgarren shrugged. After a pause, she said, "I saw Mr. O'Shea at your door yesterday."

"My, this is a cozy neighborhood," Dolly murmured. For a woman with so many secrets, she was constantly under observation. She only hoped Lady Kilgarren wasn't as nosy as Devon Avondale. One spy in Fontjoy

Square was sufficient. "Mr. O'Shea has invited me to a boxing match on Saturday evening."

"Oooh, that is so exciting. You are going, aren't you?"

"I'm going."

"You don't look very excited, Dolly."

"I *am* excited." Dolly bared her teeth in a smile.

"No, you're not. That is a fake smile."

"Is it?" Dolly attempted to improve upon her facial mask, but Claire's level gaze was full of skepticism. "So, you're right," she finally admitted, allowing her lips and cheek muscles to relax. "It is a fake smile."

"I've told you before, Dolly, you don't have to keep secrets from me."

No, she didn't. And she was sick of pretending to be happy and cheerful all the time.

If Dolly seriously intended to drop her pretensions, now was the time to do it.

But after years of hiding her emotions and making up stories to suit the occasion, Dolly found it nearly impossible to speak candidly to Lady Kilgarren. Her pulse quickened as she drained her tea. Her saucer rattled as she placed it on the tray. Her nerves were suddenly stretched to the limit. Just beating back the impulse to bolt from the room took all the energy she had.

"Will you promise to tell no one?"

Lady Kilgarren crossed her hand over her heart.

"I have no servants in the country, Claire. Ferghus is my only employee. I haven't the funds to pay a valet, a butler, and a cook. Boyle left me with nothing. I was very nearly destitute when—"

Dolly stopped short of admitting how she had acquired her house. Mr. Avondale had sworn her to secrecy, and her newfound honesty did not require her to breach a confidence.

"When what?"

"When Boyle died, he left me nothing save this house. Luckily, there was the house. But I have nothing else."

"You put on a good show, old girl."

"Thank you, but I'm tired of putting on a show."

A tear glistened in Lady Kilgarren's eyes. "Thank you for telling me, Dolly. I won't mention a word to anyone else. We needn't bare our souls to everyone. Isn't that what Mrs. Sinclair said to Millicent?"

The ladies enjoyed a chuckle before Lady Kilgarren picked up the thread of their former conversation. "But you never told me, dear. Why aren't you pleased at Mr. O'Shea's invitation?"

"I don't like him very much."

"Then why are you going to the boxing match with him?"

"Because of Dick Creevy."

"Who? The famous boxer, is that who you mean? Didn't I see him at Mr. Avondale's party?"

"You did, indeed."

Dolly settled back in a deep wingback chair, pulling her feet beneath her. Across the room, the fire crackled, dispelling the chill and tinting the air with a homey, smokey smell. It felt good to have a friend to talk to, and Dolly needed desperately to confide in another woman.

Oh, Mr. Avondale was sweet and kind and inordinately helpful. He'd coaxed her to be honest with Dick Creevy, and he'd even driven her to the gymnasium. His support and encouragement could not be underestimated. But only a woman could truly understand what another woman felt.

Claire's blue eyes held the promise of trustworthiness. Inhaling deeply, Dolly took the plunge . . . and told her everything about Boyle's death and the ensuing deception she'd perpetrated on Dick Creevy.

At the north end of the square, a small commotion was taking place. It seemed a tall, thin gentleman wearing a nondescript suit and gleaming top hat had been caught skulking around Avondale's villa. Avondale's driver and self-appointed bodyguard tackled the man behind a row of shrubbery, then dragged him by the scruff of his neck to the front door.

In short order, Mr. Avondale himself threw open the door and emerged, his white lawn shirt open at the throat, sleeves rolled to his elbow. He clenched his fists at his sides, and growled, "What brand of scoundrel have you brought me this time, Farraday?"

"Caught him hiding in the bushes, Mr. A. Thought you might want to see him before I toss him in the river."

Avondale's gray hair curled wildly in the humid hair, and his blue eyes flashed. The interior house lights outlined his broad shoulders and slender hips, lending him an otherworldly, devilish look. Clearly, he was displeased by the manifestation of an uninvited visitor. The faint odor of tobacco on his clothes suggested he'd been roused from a relaxing moment.

As he stood beneath his porte cochere, his agitation grew. He didn't like being disturbed once he'd sequestered himself inside his house. The walls of his villa protected him. The isolation of his existence insulated

him from other humans and the almost certain pain that
came from forming attachments with them.

Despite himself, Devon glanced southward and to-
ward the lights flickering in the windows at Number
Three Fontjoy Square. He wondered what Lady Claire
Kilgarren was doing now.

And the realization that he cared made him even an-
grier.

The man at his feet, collared by the chubby hand of
Farraday, a pock-faced, gin-reeking, barrel-chested
tough guy, whimpered for mercy. "I did nothing wrong!
I came here merely to ask Mr. Avondale a few questions!"

"Release him," Avondale said quietly.

Farraday obeyed.

The skinny man scrambled to his feet, indignantly
dusting the crown of his hat, now dented and dirty.
"There was no need for violence, Mr. Avondale." He
sniffed. "I assure you, I am a peaceful man."

"Who are you?"

"Name's Alvin Corrigan." For an instant, he looked
as if he might stick out his hand. But meeting Avondale's narrowed gaze, Corrigan apparently thought better of such folly.

"Corrigan." Avondale rolled the name on his tongue.
"Do I know you?"

After a brief hesitation, during which the man appeared to take a deep breath and garner his fortitude, he
replied, "No, you do not. I am a detective, Mr. Avondale.
Hired by Lloyd's of London. I'd like to ask you a few
questions, if I may." He threw a sullen glance over his
shoulder.

Farraday snarled.

Flinching, Corrigan gripped the brim of his hat.

"Why would a detective from Lloyd's be wanting to talk with me?"

"I'm investigating the death of one Lord Boyle Baltmore, sir. And I have reason to believe that you might shed some light on the matter."

Eighteen

Saturday night arrived alarmingly quickly. In her bed-chamber, Dolly stood before her full-length looking glass awaiting Mr. O'Shea's arrival. Her handsome pin-striped suit, with a ruffled collar and cameo broach at the neck, fit a bit too loosely through the bodice. Weeks of exercising with Dick Creevy had resulted in a thinner frame and tauter muscles. Smoothing the pleats of her skirt, Dolly appreciated the flatness of her belly. She'd enjoyed the physical exertion of training in the gymnasium. Regardless of the failure of her relationship with Creevy, she intended to continue her regime of jumping rope and running.

She wondered if she could buy a punching bag. With a wry smile, Dolly imagined Claire walking into the drawing room, only to find a little red punching bag hanging above the mantel. The pretty blond would roll her gaze to the ceiling and shake her head. The notion amused Dolly. She made a mental note to tell Claire that she intended to purchase a set of dumbbells, as well.

She finger combed her hair, still damp from her bath. Dolly's sense of relief after confiding in Claire was im-mense. A huge weight of guilt and tension had fallen from her shoulders. Dropping her mask freed her to make a friend. She'd done what Mary O'Roarke had encouraged her to do so many years ago. Odd that a child Mary's age could have been so prescient. Dolly only wished she could have trusted Mary the way she trusted Claire. Her insecurities cost her years of Mary's friendship.

But apparently, not her love. Devon Avondale was adamant that Mary treasured her memories of Dolly Quinn. His belief in Mary's love for Dolly was strong, so strong that he had committed himself to helping Dolly get on her feet. He had helped her. He helped her financially, and that was a blessing. But more importantly, he'd reminded her that she was a person worthy of love and friendship. Her masquerade was unnecessary. For that, Dolly would be forever grateful to Devon . . . and Mary.

She still couldn't believe how drastically her life had changed in the short time since she moved to Fontjoy Square. Dolly's attitude was completely rehabilitated. Now she found the strength and courage to face her troubles, rather than glossing over them or pretending they didn't exist. She was content and hopeful, not nervous and angry. Her obsession over Boyle's death had faded. She had her friends, her house, and her garden to worry about. She no longer fretted over what the neighbors thought, or whether she'd have to sell the silver in order to keep the bill collectors at bay.

The only remaining sorrow in her life was her missed opportunity to make a friend of Dick Creevy. That endeavor she'd botched completely. She accepted her failure and resolved never to attempt such a duplicitous, conniving scheme again. Her bright idea was snuffed like a doused taper. She hoped never again to wear a pair of knickers or bind her breasts. She hoped never again to see the look of anguish on a man's face when he discovered she had betrayed him. She hoped never again to feel the guilt and pain of hurting a friend.

The sound of a knock below stairs startled Dolly from her reverie. Butterflies swarmed her stomach as she descended the steps. At the landing, she met Mr. O'Shea's gaze and smiled. He was a nice man, she told herself. Lady Kilgarren endorsed him as a fit suitor. Dolly's doubts about him were unfounded; her feelings for Dick had invariably muddled her thinking and obscured her judgment. If she had any sense at all, she would erase her apprehension and enjoy the evening.

Placing her hand in Mr. O'Shea's glove, she emerged into the cool evening air.

Once inside the carriage, she searched for words to fill the awkward silence that always befell them. "I'm looking forward to the boxing match. In point of fact, I've been thinking of nothing else for days."

She had never been more honest. A royal decree couldn't have banished Dick Creevy from her mind.

"That's lovely." Mr. O'Shea's mustache shifted in a manner that made Dolly believe he was smiling. "Please, Dolly, call me Rafe. By the end of this evening, I hope that we will be fast friends."

"One can never have too many friends." Dolly drew her cape more tightly about her shoulders. It really wasn't that cold in Mr. O'Shea's rented cab, but a shiver rippled across her skin as they clattered through the streets of Dublin.

There was just something about Rafe O'Shea that unsettled her nerves.

* * *

Devon Avondale pounded his fist on Lady Dolly Baltmore's door. "God almighty, open the door, Ferghus!" If he had to, he'd tear it down with his bare hands.

The door swung open to reveal Ferghus's bewildered face.

Crossing the threshold, Devon shouldered the smaller man aside. "Where is she?" He cupped his hands around his mouth and called up the steps, "Lady Dolly! Come here at once!"

"I'm afraid she isn't here," Ferghus offered, wringing his hands.

"Where is she?"

"Well, sir, I don't know if that's any of your bus—"

"Damn it!" Devon stood toe to toe with the man and bellowed, "Her very life could be in danger if you don't tell me where she is!"

Ferghus blanched. "Gone out, Mr. Avondale. With Mr. O'Shea."

At the open door, Alvin Corrigan took a sharp inhale. "Just as I suspected. They've gone to the fight, Mr. Avondale."

Devon nearly knocked Mr. Corrigan down as he recrossed the threshold. "If anything happens to that woman, I shall hold you personally responsible, Corrigan. You knew what sort of villain O'Shea was, yet you didn't warn her!"

"I didn't know what part she played in the scheme!" The lanky man hurried down the sidewalk after Devon. "I had to find out whether she was involved in the perpetration of a fraud before I revealed O'Shea's identity."

On the street, Avondale's carriage awaited. Farraday sat in the driver's seat, whip poised, ribbons held lightly in his gloved hands.

"Head west, Farraday." Devon opened the carriage door and leaped inside. "Come on, Corrigan. We'll get out where Bridge Street meets the Quay, and walk from there!"

Corrigan got one foot inside the carriage before it took off with a lurch. Thrown inside, he landed on the floor, his legs sprawled akimbo. Avondale reached over and pulled shut the door.

"My hat is ruined," the detective mumbled, scrambling onto the leather squabs.

"If O'Shea lays a finger on Lady Dolly," Devon replied, grinning maliciously, "you won't need your hat anymore."

Corrigan gulped. He didn't need to ask why.

The line of carriages outside Creevy's Pugilist Academy stretched three city blocks long. Impatiently, Mr. O'Shea rapped on the trap door inside the darkened carriage. "How far is it?"

"You could walk from here," the man answered.

Dolly was glad for the fresh air. Especially when she stepped inside the gymnasium.

Tobacco smoke, spilled beer, and the smell of too many bodies pressed together tickled her nose. Stunned, she wavered just inside the entrance area. When Mr. O'Shea impatiently grabbed her hand, she was surprised to notice the spectacles adorning his face.

"They're for seeing at distances," he explained. "I don't want to miss a single punch, dear."

With his hand pressed to the small of her back, Mr. O'Shea guided Dolly to two empty seats in the middle tier of a wooden scaffold hastily erected for the fight. Gathering her skirts, she settled on the hard bench. All around them, gentlemen wearing elegant suits and neckties studied their betting sheets, while women wearing bustles and high-necked collars cooled themselves with ivory fans.

Though Dolly had heard the late Lord Baltmore describe professional boxing matches, she was unprepared for the circuslike atmosphere. The younger men surrounding the boxing ring below reminded her of the groundlings at Shakespeare's Globe Theater. Scruffy-looking lads in knickers tossed oranges and peanuts to customers willing to toss a halfpenny in return. A din of excited voices, laughter, and shouted wagers assaulted her ears.

Entranced, Dolly shivered with anticipation.

Beside her, Mr. O'Shea stroked his mustache, and turning his head from side to side, scanned the audience.

"Are you looking for someone?" she asked him.

"An old acquaintance of mine who invariably shows up at these sort of events."

"What does he look like? I'll watch for him."

Mr. O'Shea grinned crookedly, or at least his mustache tilted at a precarious angle. "Balding on top, black hair at the sides, beady eyes, and an infectious grin."

Dolly laughed. "Sounds like my late husband, Boyle."

"Really?" Mr. O'Shea glanced at his neighbor's betting sheet. "I see that Mr. Creevy is now favored two to one."

"You could double your money if you bet on him." Dolly felt a twinge of pride. There as no doubt in her mind as to who would be the victor.

"That's only if Mr. Creevy wins, dear."

"You haven't placed a bet on Eric the Viking, have you?"

"I wouldn't worry about it were I you." He couldn't tear his gaze off the crowd. "When this fight is over, I'll be a wealthy man. No matter who wins."

"What do you mean by that?" A chill ran up Dolly's spine. It seemed strange to her that after all his fawning and courting, Mr. O'Shea would suddenly be so disinterested in her that he couldn't look her in the eyes. It seemed stranger still that he peered at the crowd through glasses so thick they disguised his features. His comment about being wealthy after the fight, no matter who won, completely baffled her.

"I said, what do you mean by that?" she demanded, drawing a raised eyebrow from the stout, overdressed woman seated on the opposite side of Mr. O'Shea.

Facing her, Mr. O'Shea put a finger to his lips. "Dear, you'll create a scene! Do be quiet."

"I don't want to be quiet," she said through gritted teeth.

His whisper was full of malice. "Be quiet, or I shall punish you when we leave here. You'll be sorry if you refuse to do as I say."

Dolly's anger bubbled to the surface. Her instincts had been right after all. Rafe O'Shea was not a nice man.

She had a small amount of money in her purse; she could leave if she wanted, hail a hackney cab outside, and go home. Lady Kilgarren would still be awake. She'd knock at her neighbor's door and invite herself in for hot chocolate and a chat. Yes, that's exactly what she would do.

With a huff, Dolly started to rise.

But Mr. O'Shea stood with her, his right arm encircling her waist. Something hard poked Dolly's middle. Looking down, she saw that Mr. O'Shea held a tiny pistol in his left hand. A casual observer could not have seen that he nudged the tip of it in Dolly's waistline.

Gasping, she slowly sank to her seat.

Mr. O'Shea, still holding her tightly to his side, sat down also. "There, now, you don't really want to leave, do you?"

"You're mad!"

"Keep your voice down. If I get excited, the gun might go off, and there's no telling who might get shot."

Indignation and fury roiled through her. With a shudder, Dolly whispered, "Take your hands off me."

His arm slid from her back, but he moved closer to her on the bench so that the tiny gun remained pointed at her ribs. "Don't try anything foolish, Dolly. Just sit tight and watch the show. I believe you will be quite surprised by what you see."

In his dressing room, Dick Creevy sat on the edge of a massage table, his shoulders draped with a hot, damp towel. He held out his arms while Sean Conway wound tape around his hands.

"Sure you're all right?" Sean bit off a length of tape, then smoothed it over Dick's knuckle.

Dick looked up as O'Callahan entered. "Is she out there?"

"Aye, she's there." The old man sighed. "By the rood, I didna' want to tell you. But I suppose if you didn't know she was there, you'd be frettin' over her all night."

"Where is she?"

"I don't want you lookin' for her—"

"Where is she?"

"In the bleachers on the south wall, fifth row up. Seated beside a queer-looking gentleman with thick glasses and a mustache."

"I'll see her."

"Now, look, Dick, it's enough that she's here. You gotta forget about her."

Sean took a step back. "I don't know what you fellows are talking about, but I wouldn't be looking for a lady just now, if I were you, Dick. You've got enough to worry about with Eric the Viking coming at you."

O'Callahan grunted. "From your lips to God's ears. But I can't get him to stop bellyaching about this little blond filly."

Conway's thick black brows arched. "Did you say blond?"

"Remember Doll Face?" Dick said.

"Indeed, I do."

"Well, this lady is . . ."

Dick said, "Sister," at the same time O'Callahan blurted, "Cousin!"

"His cousin, that's right." Dick chuckled. "Name's Dolly Baltmore. O'Callahan's right. Can't get my mind off her."

"Well, you'd better," Cal growled. "Concentration's the most important thing now. Come on, let's get your gloves on. Referee says he's going to ring the bell in three minutes."

Three minutes. Dick drew in a deep breath and rolled his shoulders. Closing his eyes, he forcibly evicted Dolly from his thoughts. Cal was right. He couldn't afford to think about her now. A single instant of distraction could cost him the fight, or worse. He was a professional, and he knew how to focus his energy on a single goal. His goal that night was to knock out Eric the Viking as quickly as possible.

Outside, a roar erupted from the crowd. Dimly, Dick heard the announcers as they tried to shout above the noise. His heart quickened, but his focus narrowed. He filled his lungs again, breathing in strength and calmness, exhaling fear and weakness. When O'Callahan slapped his back, he slid from the table and tossed off the towel. He was ready to meet Eric the Viking. He had trained as hard as he could, and the moment of reckoning was nigh.

Pounding his gloved fists together, he jogged in place for a moment, just to get his blood flowing and his muscles warm. Then, accompanied by a coterie of trainers, water boys, and supporters, he strode down the corridor. When he stepped into the lit gymnasium, the crowd went wild.

Eric the Viking entered from the opposite side of the gymnasium, and a chorus of booing went up.

The men met in the center of the ring, touched gloves, and retired to their respective corners. Dick shuffled his feet as he scanned the crowd.

He saw her.

Their gazes locked as the bell clanged.

Dick turned to O'Callahan and said, "There's a letter on my desk. Make certain she gets it."

With a shake of his head, O'Callahan shoved him toward the center of the ring.

The instant Dick's gaze lit on her, a wave of heat suffused Dolly's face. The awareness that connected them was palpable; she was surprised everyone in the gymnasium didn't see it, and feel it, too. But in a blink,

Dick turned and whispered something to his trainer. Then the bell was rung and the fight began.

Despite her animosity toward Mr. O'Shea, Dolly listened intently to his running narration of the fight's progression. He clearly possessed an inestimable breadth of boxing knowledge.

"See, there, Dolly, the disparate styles of the two boxers. Mr. Creevy feints and dodges, ceaselessly moving his feet. While Eric swings and punches, relying on his superior strength and endurance."

"Dick's endurance is Herculean," Dolly retorted. "The Viking cannot wear him out."

But as she watched, the Viking landed a series of punches to Dick's stomach and ribs. Dick drew his gloves to his middle, protecting his body. But at the end of round one, he had not landed a single blow to Eric's jaw or head.

Round two set Dolly's nerves on edge. Eric closed in on Dick, hugging him in a bearlike embrace. Dick's fans roared their disapproval. O'Callahan could be seen in Dick's corner, shaking his fists at the heavens.

But before the round was over, Dick directed a nasty uppercut to Eric's jaw. The Viking's head lashed backward, and his eyes bulged. Stumbling back, shaking his head, flailing his arms, he looked like a wounded animal. When the bell rang, he slumped onto a stool in his corner, holding his head.

Dolly's gaze was riveted to the goings-on in Dick's corner. O'Callahan toweled the sweat off Dick's forehead. A young boy Dolly had never seen before dipped a ladle in a bucket of water. Dick poured the water down his throat, then leaped to his feet as round three commenced.

For four more rounds, the men battled like gladiators,

Dick dodging and dancing, looking for an opening for his lethal straight-left punch, while Eric simply closed, hugged, and pummeled. Both men dripped with sweat, but as the match progressed, Dick's feet moved less swiftly and his reflexes slowed. In round eight, he took a damaging blow to his kidneys, and stumbled to the ropes. If the bell hadn't saved him, Eric's lumbering advance would have finished him off.

By this time, the roar inside the gymnasium was deafening. Though she hadn't forgotten about Mr. O'Shea's gun, her attention was focused on Dick. She loved him, and nothing in the world would ever change that. To see him hurt nearly drove her insane. If she weren't being held captive, she would have run to the ringside and begged him to stop the fight.

Tears blurred Dolly's vision so that the orange vendor had to lift both arms above his head and wave to get her attention. She shook her head, declining the fruit. But he held up a white envelope indicating the letter was for her.

"Ah, someone has written you a letter." O'Shea sent a coin flying through the air, and soon he had the letter in his hands.

"Let me have that!" Dolly reached for it.

O'Shea's hand closed around her wrist like an iron cuff. He slanted her a warning look. She withdrew her hand and watched him slowly rip open the sealed envelope.

Over his shoulder, she read Dick's letter. He opened with *Dearest Doll Face.* He told her he loved her. He said he needed her and wanted her more than any other woman in the world.

He said he forgave her, and that if she would have him, he would cherish her forever, all of her, every particle of her, no matter who—or what—she chose to be.

"Isn't that sweet?" Mr. O'Shea cooed.

She rubbed her damp nose with her sleeve. "What are you up to, O'Shea? You might as well tell me now, before I start screaming bloody murder. Or fire! I'll have the whole place up in arms in a matter of seconds."

"Aren't you afraid I'll shoot you?"

"I'm not afraid of anything now."

He chuckled. "Then you are more of a fool than I had thought, Lady Baltmore. Have you noticed the gentleman standing just behind Mr. Creevy's corner. Look closely. His face is bathed in shadows, but if you squint your eyes . . . Yes, that's it. Do you see him, dear? The balding man with the easy smile? Does he look familiar to you?"

Dolly's scream was lost in the roar of the crowd. Dick Creevy threw a punch to Eric's temple, knocking the big man to his knees. Everybody in the gymnasium, including Dolly and Mr. O'Shea, leaped to their feet. But for the first time all evening, Dolly was only dimly aware of the action in the ring.

She'd just seen a ghost.

Lord Boyle Baltmore folded his arms and gazed right back at her.

Nineteen

"He isn't dead!"

"No, dear, I'm afraid not. Though I should not shed a tear if he turned up his toes tonight."

Dolly's knees buckled, and she sank back onto the wooden bench. For a brief interval, she thought she was going to faint, but somehow she managed not to. Her blood felt like icy water flowing through her veins. Her teeth chattered. Whatever dastardly plan Mr. O'Shea had concocted, it couldn't equal the shock of seeing her late husband, alive and seemingly well, gazing at her from across the gymnasium.

"What sort of evil game are you playing, O'Shea?"

An oily smile spread across his face. "I suppose it wouldn't hurt to tell you, now. You'll find out soon enough, anyway, when Baltmore is handed the ransom note."

"Ransom note?"

He jerked his head in the direction of the ring. "See the little scamp down there with the water bucket?"

She glanced at Dick's corner, nodding.

"Clever little rapscallion, as sharp as any pickpocket I've ever come across. But he's not picking pockets tonight, my lady. Tonight, he is serving libations to Mr.

Creevy, courtesy of yours truly, of course. And he's also delivering the post, if you will, to Lord Boyle Baltmore. You see, I've sent my lord a ransom letter. If he pays me one half of the loot we earned together at the time of his *supposed* death, I will allow you to live. He does still love you, you know. The fool told me as much."

The hair at Dolly's nape prickled as her husband's criminality came into focus. "Do you mean to say that Boyle *faked* his death?"

"For the insurance money. Quite a bit of it."

"But his life wasn't insured."

"Yes, it was, Dolly. In favor of his business partner."

"What business partner?"

"Me, of course."

Each piece of the puzzle hit her like a battering ram. Stunned, Dolly stared in disbelief at the shadowy figure lurking behind Dick Creevy's corner of the ring. "But I don't understand. Boyle never had a viable business—"

"We concocted one. I believe the barristers refer to such entities as sham corporations. At any rate, I was a principal in the firm of O'Shea and Baltmore. When Lord Baltmore died, Lloyd's of London endowed me with a huge sum of money."

"Then what happened?'

"That greedy bastard Baltmore stole it back from me. Walked into the Edinburgh bank one day, told the officer he was Rafe O'Shea, wrote a draft for the money, and walked out with it. Absconded to London with me in hot pursuit. What do you think of that, dear?"

"The many faces of Lord Boyle Baltmore . . ." Her voice trailed off.

"He's quite an actor, wouldn't you say? I do believe you share that talent, Dolly. I've been watching you for quite some time, you know. When you moved to Fontjoy Square, I suspected Boyle had cut you in on his ill-gotten gains. How else could you have acquired such a fine, if not slightly rundown home? But, after following you for a few weeks, I figured out the lay of the land. Boyle wasn't going to pop up, but your dalliance with Dick Creevy gave me another idea. Watch the water boy, dear. His sleight of hand really is remarkable."

"How did you know Boyle would be here?"

"Didn't I tell you? He wouldn't miss the fight of the century, even if it meant exposing his face to the authorities. Your dearly departed husband, my dear, has a gambling problem. He simply cannot stay away from gaming hells, boxing theaters, and racetracks. Surely, you don't deny that!"

She couldn't, of course. "That only leaves about a hundred other questions unanswered."

"We haven't much time, Dolly. The next round will begin soon. Watch the water boy. Are you watching?"

Shaking the fog of confusion from her head, she peered down at the ring. She saw the water boy set down his bucket, dash over to Lord Baltmore, and hand him a folded paper.

Lord Baltmore unfolded the letter, and in a moment, his hands trembled. His head shot up, and he looked from Dolly to O'Shea and back again.

Dick, meanwhile, sat slumped on his stool. His shoulders sagged and his chest heaved. Sweat sparkled on his bare skin and plastered his hair to his head. The sight of him, badly beaten, sickened Dolly. She needed to go to him. She had to find a way to get to Dick Creevy. Lord Baltmore's deception would be dealt with later. Aside from the shock of discovering he was alive, she cared nothing for him. His complicity in O'Shea's nefarious scheme to swindle Lloyd's disgusted her.

The water boy returned to his duties, scooping water from the bucket, pouring it over Dick's head and in his mouth. O'Callahan hovered over Dick, whispering in his ear and massaging his biceps.

"Are you watching the water boy, Dolly?"

"What's so damn special about that water boy?" she snapped.

Her outburst provoked O'Shea to laughter. "He's not really a water boy, dear. Don't you remember me saying I was going to be rich when I left here, no matter what happened? Well, I have a small fortune riding on the Viking."

"He can't possibly win," she hissed.

"Yes, he can. When my little pickpocket dumps a vial of liquid opium into Dick's water bucket, the Viking will have no choice but to win. He could break his leg and still win! Isn't that funny, Dolly? Don't you find my little plot amusing?"

He laughed so hard, he bent over double. Staring at him, Dolly ignored the curious looks of the neighboring spectators, half seated, half standing. She felt the poke of his gun ease from her ribs. Rafe O'Shea guffawed until tears rolled down his cheeks. Gasping for breath, he yanked a handkerchief from his pocket. Pushing his glasses up on his head, he dabbed at his red-rimmed eyes.

Dolly saw her opportunity.

She reached up and flicked her fingers at O'Shea's spectacles. They flew off and landed in a woman's lap, three rows in front of where O'Shea and Dolly sat. The lady, startled to find a pair of spectacles landing in the folds of her skirt, turned, held them up, and searched for their owner.

Instinctively, O'Shea stood and held out his hands to catch the glasses as they were tossed back to him. His pistol was in plain view. But it wasn't pointed at Dolly.

Mr. Avondale, flanked by Farraday and Corrigan the detective, crossed the street at a dead run. Entering the gymnasium, they encountered a wall of people, all of them yelling and screaming their encouragement to the fighters in the ring. Pushing through the crowd, the three men emerged ringside in time to see Eric stumble and fall to his knees.

A bell rang, and Dick Creevy returned to his corner where a gnarled old man and a young water boy huddled around him. From Eric's corner burst two burly men who lifted the Viking under his arms and dragged him to his stool. With the match between rounds, Devon had the perfect opportunity to look for Dolly and Mr. O'Shea.

Farraday saw her first. "There she is, next to that odd-looking bloke with the mustache."

Devon's gaze followed the trajectory of Farraday's pointed finger.

"And there's O'Shea!" exclaimed Corrigan.

Lady Dolly was a good fifty feet away, and clearly in danger. But as the crowd surged to its feet, she was lost from Devon's view.

Corrigan grabbed his arm. "Turn around. Look over there! It's Lord Baltmore . . . in the flesh! Good God, it's just as I suspected. The man's alive, damn it! I've proved my case. Baltmore and O'Shea defrauded Lloyd's, and I've nabbed them both."

It took a moment for Corrigan's news to sink into Avondale's head. The notion that Lord Boyle Baltmore would fake his own death was preposterous. But as the pieces fell into place, the picture puzzle faded into focus. Baltmore needed a fresh infusion of cash, so he climbed into the ring with Creevy, took a few punches, and pretended he was fatally injured. O'Shea carted Baltmore's seemingly lifeless body away, then laid claim to the insurance money.

Something went awry after that.

Mr. Corrigan excitedly furnished his hypothesis. "They must have had a falling out of some sort. Thieves often differ in opinion as to how their booty should be divvied up."

"Want me to summon the *gardaí?*" Farraday asked.

"No need." Reaching inside his jacket, Corrigan produced a pair of manacles and a small pistol. "Before I worked for Lloyd's, I was a mercenary in Africa. I know how to take a man into custody, I assure you. If he resists, a cap in his knee will calm him down."

A flash of golden curls caught Devon's eye. Pivoting, he saw Dolly dashing down the rickety steps that served the wooden bleachers. She waved frantically at Devon, then picked up her skirts, and ran toward him as fast as she could. Steps behind her was Rafe O'Shea, his mouth constricted in anger, his eyes flashing wildly. In one hand, he clutched a pair of gold-rimmed spectacles. In the other, he waved a tiny snub-nosed pistol.

Devon tensed, every nerve in his body tingling.

Just then, the bell sounded the ninth round of the fight. Devon looked up just in time to see the water boy lift one more ladle of water to Dick Creevy's parched lips.

"No!" Dolly screamed, lunging at the ropes cordoning off the boxing ring.

Dick's head snapped up as Dolly tried to scramble into the ring. His eyes narrowed and his jaw fell slack.

For an instant, a hush fell over the crowd. Then a collective shout of titillated approval reverberated through the gymnasium. No one understood why a pretty young woman had just tried to throw herself into the ring, but it was great sport, and that's all that mattered. When Rafe O'Shea grabbed her skirt and yanked her to the floor, applause and foot stomping rattled the scaffolding that held the rows of wooden benches.

Instinctively, Devon ran toward Dolly, bent over her, and reached down.

O'Shea kneeled beside her, one hand on Dolly's shoulder. With his other hand, he pulled back his coat and displayed his pistol, now tucked inside the waistband of his trousers.

"O'Shea!" Dick Creevy, apparently recognizing Dolly's captor, stood up. He took a step toward Dolly and O'Shea, then abruptly halted. "Hurt her . . . and I'll kill you!" His speech was slurred, expression confused. Rubbing his head, Dick rapidly blinked his eyes.

"He's been drugged!" Dolly cried before O'Shea clamped his hand over her mouth.

Devon glanced at the water boy and saw the lad tap a cork into a small brown vial. Creevy *had* been drugged; it was obvious. If the fight continued, he would lose . . . or get himself killed.

"Get on with the fight!" someone yelled, and the sentiment was loudly echoed by a hundred other jeering fans.

The bell clanged again. This time Eric the Viking came roaring out of his corner like a bull.

* * *

Dolly sank her teeth into O'Shea's cold flesh. Yelping, he jerked back his hand, allowing her the chance to scramble to her feet. In one easy movement, Devon Avondale pulled her to safety. Drawing her to his side, he snatched O'Shea's pistol.

"I suggest you stand here quietly until the fight is over," Avondale told the villain. "Then I will turn you over to the authorities, and your fate will be decided by a jury of your peers. Otherwise, I will have no alternative but to shoot you."

"Don't shoot, Mr. Avondale. I should like to see the outcome of the fight myself."

Dolly's relief at having been released from O'Shea's captivity was overshadowed by her horror as she watched the fight. The Viking lowered his head and advanced on Dick. Dick, his eyes glazed, his skin a sickly shade of green, raised his gloved fists and leaned forward.

Eric made a wild swing.

Dick ducked, barely escaping a blow that would have knocked him out cold.

But as he straightened, the full impact of the Viking's weight crashed into him. Dick planted his feet and didn't waver. Instead, he collared the Viking, and grasping the man's head under one arm, battered him freely with the other. It was a deadly hold made deadlier by the fact that Dick's equilibrium was quickly waning. He held on to Eric to keep himself upright. Blindly, he pumped his arm in a staccato pattern, violently pummeling Eric's nose, jaw, ear, and chin. Within a matter of seconds, the Viking's legs collapsed and his body sagged.

Dick let go and stumbled backward. Eric hit the mat with a thud and never got up.

Against the deafening roar of the crowd, O'Callahan limped across the ring and held up Dick's arm in victory.

Dolly tore herself from Devon Avondale's protective embrace, crawled through the ropes, and ran to Dick. She wrapped her arms around his body, soaking up his pain and his warmth. His cheek nestled on the top of her head as a throng of people clustered around them. She and O'Callahan supported his weight as he stood in the center of the ring, a champion.

"I love you, Dolly," he whispered thickly.

She rose on her tiptoes and pressed her lips to his. "I love you, too."

Then his eyes rolled back in his head, and he fell into the waiting arms of O'Callahan and Devon Avondale.

A crack of gunfire split the air.

The pandemonium of Creevy's victory and Eric's defeat erupted in chaos. Spectators scrambled for cover and women shrieked. People trampled one another in an attempt to get out of the gymnasium. But when the crowd cleared and the confusion abated, only one man lay on the floor, his shirtfront bloodied.

Lord Boyle Baltmore, it seemed, had died his second death, this time at the hands of his coconspirator, Rafe O'Shea.

Dolly followed Dick's entourage from the ring toward his dressing room. Standing in the corridor that led from the gymnasium to his private quarters, she turned and stared. A brace of blue-uniformed Dublin police had arrived. And there was a very tall, nervous-looking man with a battered top hat loudly complaining that he didn't know how O'Shea had taken his gun from him, but it was all an accident, and it didn't matter anyway because Lord Boyle Baltmore had already been dead a year. . . .

"He is going to have a very difficult time explaining that." Mr. Avondale took her elbow and guided her down the hallway. "I wouldn't worry about those two. They won't be darkening your doorstep ever again."

She finally released the breath she hadn't realized she was holding. Linking her arm in Mr. Avondale's, she accompanied him to Dick's dressing room. Her life had turned completely around in the last few months, and she credited him for many of the good things that had happened to her.

"I can never repay you for what you've done for me. But I hope, Mr. Avondale, that in the future, I can do something to help you. You've got a friend in me, you know. And in Dick Creevy, too."

He squeezed her hand. "You've already done more for me, Dolly, than you'll ever know. You've drawn me out of my shell a little. Mary would have liked that."

"Mary was a lucky woman to have been loved by you."

"She was also fortunate to have had you for a friend. She said you taught her the importance of loyalty. And, though you never understood it yourself—until now, that is—you also taught her the importance of being oneself. Those were lessons she never forgot, Dolly. She loved you. She wanted you to love yourself."

Emotion swelled in Dolly's chest. She squeezed shut her eyes. Mary O'Roarke. The child's sweet face hovered in her mind.

"I shall think of her as my guardian angel," she whispered.

She opened her eyes as Mr. Avondale kissed her forehead.

They were in the threshold of Dick's dressing room. Dick was flat on his back on the massage table, senseless. A surgeon drew back the boxer's eyelids and peered at his pupils.

"He'll sleep it off," the doctor said.

O'Callahan clapped his hands. "Everybody out. He's gotta get his rest, like the doc ordered!"

Slowly, the crowd of people dispersed. Mr. Avondale clasped Dolly's upper arms, and said, "Stay with him. You'll be the first person he sees when he awakens. He'll want it that way."

Smiling through her tears, she nodded. The room emptied, but she remained. Standing beside Dick, she held his hand. His strong fingers closed around hers, and he moaned.

She laid her hand on his forehead. "Don't worry, Dick. I will never leave you. Ever." She had the bright idea to love this man for as long as he drew breath. And she knew, this time, that she, Lady Dolly Baltmore—*the real Dolly*—was all the woman Dick Creevy needed.

Epilogue

Dick swam through a sea of blackness, back to consciousness. His eyes blinked open, and a scalding pain shot through his head. "Oh!" The light hurt his eyes. In fact, everything hurt—his legs, his arm, his muscles. He felt like he'd been beaten to within an inch of life by an army of titans.

But strong fingers closed around his hand. Dolly's presence filled him with happiness.

As he turned his head to look at her, a wave of queasiness swamped him. "What happened?" He sounded like he had cotton packed in his mouth.

"O'Shea bet against you; then he drugged you to make certain he would win a fortune. Unfortunately for him, you beat the Viking anyway. Fair and square." She bent over, brushing her lips on his forehead. "I love you, Dick."

"O'Shea," he croaked. "He still hates me. . . ." Later Dick would tell her the whole lurid story, how he'd discovered Kitty was having an affair with his best friend, Rafe, and how Kitty swore it would never happen again. Then Dick went to India in service to the queen's army. He returned to find Rafe and Kitty in his bed.

The memory stirred bitter feelings. But Dick resolved to put those feelings aside. Dolly wasn't to blame for Kitty's betrayal. He'd been nursing a grudge against the entire female population for years, years that he'd wasted, living alone, eating alone, loving no one but himself. Now he had a kind, warm woman to love him and share his life. And he intended to take full advantage of his good fortune. Kitty's legacy had long since been renounced.

Yet in his half stupor, his mind harkened back to the tragedy that had changed his life. To wound him further, Kitty had told Dick that their youngest child wasn't his. In his fury, Dick vowed he would take his only daughter, and legally deprive Kitty of custody. In retaliation, she and Rafe O'Shea bundled *his* family into a carriage in the dead of night, and headed north.

When a servant tipped him off, Dick gave chase. But Rafe drove like a madman, outdistancing Dick until they made it to Newgrange. There the two carriages hurtled down a rutted road, careening around corners on two wheels.

That's when the accident had happened.

Kitty and the children were killed, but Rafe had survived. And he'd been plotting his revenge against Dick Creevy ever since.

Struggling to keep his eyes open, Dick gazed into Lady Dolly Baltmore's sparkling green eyes. Her cropped curls made him smile. Her upturned nose, her freckled face, her smooth, unadorned skin . . . He could look at her forever.

"Never leave me," he managed to say just before his eyes fell shut again.

"Don't worry, darling. You couldn't get rid of me if you tried."

His lips quirked in a smile as he faded from consciousness.

If you liked A BRIGHT IDEA, be sure to look for Cindy Harris's next release in the Dublin Dreams series, WOLF AT THE DOOR, available in August 2001 wherever books are sold.

Millicent is determined to become a "modern" woman—and her *joie de vivre* intrigues Captain Alec Wolferton, the famous Sea Wolf—a reputed scoundrel! Thrilled by her own passionate attraction to this blackguard, Millicent suddenly finds herself swept up in a perilous, romantic adventure—complete with spies, scheming rivals . . . and the discovery of perfect love!

COMING IN MAY 2001 FROM
ZEBRA BALLAD ROMANCES

__MY LADY IMPOSTER: The Sword and the Ring #1

by Suzanne McMinn   0-8217-6875-1 $5.50US/$7.50CAN

Upon his return from the king's campaigns in France, Damon of Sperling found his father dead and his demesne ravaged by plague. Now he must restore order to his estate, and to the lives of his four orphaned sisters—a task that seems best accomplished by wedding Lady Lorabelle of Orrick, to whom he has long been promised.

__BEAUTY AND THE BRAIN: The Dream Maker #2

by Alice Duncan   0-8217-6879-4 $5.50US/$7.50CAN

Actress Brenda Fitzpatrick is accustomed to hiding her intelligence behind the facade of a featherheaded blonde. But not when it comes to Colin Peters, a research assistant on the new romantic movie she's starring in. Now Martin Tafft has asked Brenda to loosen Colin up. It isn't long before attraction blossoms into a love more real than any fantasy.

__ANNE'S WISH: The Wishing Well #3

by Joy Reed   0-8217-6810-7 $5.50US/$7.50CAN

Anne Barrington's hopes for escaping life in the court of Queen Charlotte are shattered when the courtier she loves jilts her for an heiress. Her devastation is witnessed by James, Lord Westland, who offers marriage as a solution to both of their dilemmas: Anne desperate to leave the Queen's service; James needs a wife to provide him with an heir.

__REILLY'S PRIDE: Irish Blessing #3

by Elizabeth Keys   0-8217-6811-5 $5.50US/$7.50CAN

Quintin Reilly had come home to run his family's shipyard. The last thing he expected was to find himself with a wife! Shannon Murray was little more than a child when he'd gone off to sea. Now she was a widow boldly proposing marriage! Quin hesitated, until "Reilly's Blessing" convinced him that this beauty was meant to be his bride.

Put a Little Romance in Your Life With
Shannon Drake

__Come The Morning	0-8217-6471-3	$6.99US/$8.50CAN
__Conquer The Night	0-8217-6639-2	$6.99US/$8.50CAN
__The King's Pleasure	0-8217-5857-8	$6.50US/$8.00CAN
__Lie Down In Roses	0-8217-4749-0	$5.99US/$6.99CAN
__Tomorrow Glory	0-7860-0021-X	$5.99US/$6.99CAN

Merlin's Legacy

A Series From
Quinn Taylor Evans

___**Daughter of Fire** $5.50US/$7.00CAN
    0-8217-6052-1

___**Daughter of the Mist** $5.50US/$7.00CAN
    0-8217-6050-5

___**Daughter of Light** $5.50US/$7.00CAN
    0-8217-6051-3

___**Dawn of Camelot** $5.50US/$7.00CAN
    0-8217-6028-9

___**Shadows of Camelot** $5.50US/$7.00CAN
    0-8217-5760-1

Call toll free **1-888-345-BOOK** to order by phone or use
this coupon to order by mail.

Name _____

Address _____

City _____ State _____ Zip _____

Please send me the books I have checked above.

I am enclosing $_____

Plus postage and handling* $_____

Sales tax (in New York and Tennessee) $_____

Total amount enclosed $_____

*Add $2.50 for the first book and $.50 for each additional book.

Send check or money order (no cash or CODs) to:

Kensington Publishing Corp., 850 Third Avenue, New York, NY 10022

Prices and Numbers subject to change without notice.

All orders subject to availability.

Check Out our website at **www.kensingtonbooks.com**

The Queen of
Romance
Cassie Edwards